"Chief Petty Officer Sam Shaymore, U.S. Navy SEALS," he whispered into her ear.

Warm breath feathered over Kelly's cheek. The delicious masculine scent of leather and sage became stronger and enveloped her like a lover's arms. She knew this scent. Knew this body…had felt it atop hers years ago.

When he'd laid her down on his bed, kissed her and then had taken her virginity.

The muscled SEAL's heavy weight shifted, allowing her to roll over. He straddled her, sitting on her hips, his hands easily pinning her down.

Indifferent, almost cruel concentration on his face turned to shock. Those penetrating hazel eyes widened and then darkened.

"Kelly," he said softly.

Books by Bonnie Vanak

Harlequin Nocturne

The Shadow Wolf #120
**The Covert Wolf* #141
**Phantom Wolf* #162

Silhouette Nocturne

The Empath #30
Enemy Lover #51
Immortal Wolf #74
Holiday with a Vampire #77
"Unwrapped"

*Phoenix Force

BONNIE VANAK

fell in love with romance novels during childhood. After years of newspaper reporting, Bonnie became a writer for a major international charity, which has taken her to destitute countries to write about issues affecting the poor. When the emotional strain of her job demanded a diversion, she turned to writing romance novels. Bonnie lives in Florida with her husband and two dogs, and happily writes books amid an ever-growing population of dust bunnies. She loves to hear from readers. Visit her website, www.bonnievanak.com, or email her at bonnievanak@aol.com.

PHANTOM WOLF

BONNIE VANAK

ISBN-13: 978-0-373-88572-5

HARLEQUIN BOOKS

PHANTOM WOLF

This edition published by arrangement with Harlequin Books S.A.

For questions and comments about the quality of this book, please contact us at CustomerService@Harlequin.com.

Printed in U.S.A.

Dear Reader,

Can a pair of star-crossed lovers with enough magick between them to level a building find forgiveness and the trust needed to love again?

That's the question I asked myself when writing *Phantom Wolf*. Samuel "Shay" Shaymore is a powerful shape-shifting Elemental Mage and navy SEAL on the elite Phoenix Force. But years before, he was a reckless young man deeply in love with Kelly Denning, a lowly Arcane Mage. Sam and Kelly cared nothing for class differences, but when her father stood accused of setting a fire that killed Sam's entire family, the two lovers parted. Afterward, to release his pent-up emotions, Sam turned into a dangerous feral wolf. He's since vowed never to lose control again.

Now Kelly is back in Shay's life and desperately needs his help to find some missing children in Honduras before they're claimed by evil forces. He knows the pretty Arcane who once claimed his heart can still cost him everything. But the problem is the sexy SEAL wants her more than ever before!

Happy reading!

Bonnie Vanak

For my dear sister-in-law, Sissy Fischer. Love yah!

This one's for you, you amazing Southern spitfire!

Prologue

Kelly Denning was in love. She barely felt the cold of a Tennessee winter as she raced across the meadow and headed for the barn where Sam always waited for her.

He knew she'd never enter the secret passageway in the barn alone. If Colton Shaymore caught her, he'd be furious. Sam's father had forbidden his Arcane Enchanter Mage servants from using the underground tunnels.

Arcane Enchanter Mages were forced to carry identification cards and worked as servants or in low-wage positions. Elemental Mages, especially blue bloods like Sam's family, held the power and the wealth. The discrimination had happened because three hundred years ago an Arcane Enchanter had embraced evil and transformed into the most powerful Mage of all—a Dark Lord. The Dark Lord had slaughtered hundreds of Elementals and stolen their powers before being killed. Now the more powerful Elementals had burned all but their most rudimentary spell books to prevent another Dark Lord uprising.

A low growl rumbled from the corner as she entered the barn.

Kelly froze, fear curdling her blood. Opening all her Arcane senses, she inhaled the air. Smelled fresh sage, sharp leather and crisp autumn leaves.

Sam.

The black-and-white timber wolf stepped out from the corner. Kelly's fear evaporated as she crouched down. The wolf playfully bumped into her as it rested its head upon her leg and rubbed against it.

Marking her with his scent, she thought with a secret rush of pleasure. Sam had already marked her two months ago by becoming her first lover.

The wolf sniffed the crisp night air. Baring its massive teeth in a growl, he loped over to the doorway to make sure no one had followed Kelly and then trotted over to her.

Fast as the beat of a hummingbird's wing, the wolf shifted and became a human male—his naked body slick with sweat, his sleek, muscled flanks tensed. His sandy-brown hair was boyishly ruffled, and an impish mix of sexual promise and mischief gleamed in his hazel eyes. Samuel Jackson Shaymore was a privileged Elemental Phantom Mage who could shift into any life-form he chose to duplicate.

Kelly didn't care if he shifted into a sea slug, as long as he turned back into her beloved Sam.

She extended her finger for him to touch. The ancient greeting among Mages was now used by Elementals to single out her people. Arcane auras sparked more crimson than the pure gold of an Elemental aura.

Sam flashed the infectious grin that had first stolen her heart, and they touched index fingers. A brilliant flare of crimson and gold colors leaped between their hands.

Breaking contact, she pointed to his muscled, bare chest. "Aren't you going to conjure some clothing?"

"Why? You always liked the view before."

The teasing remark made her cheeks heat. Sam laughed and waved his hands, clothing his body by using magick.

"Why did you shift into a wolf?"

"Couldn't take any chances that my father watched me leave. It's a good disguise." Sam tilted his head back and gave a low, mock howl. "Besides, I love hunting through the woods as a wolf. Fires my blood."

A shiver of anticipation snaked down her spine at the heated promise in his eyes. Sam stroked a single finger down her right cheek, just as he'd done the first time they'd kissed. Every time they met, he repeated the gesture. Once she'd asked what it meant.

"I'm reassuring myself that you're really here," he finally told her.

She stepped into his embrace, loving how his arms gathered her close, how he was just tall enough to make her feel sheltered but not overwhelmed. Heat smoldered in his hazel eyes as Sam looked down at her.

Taking her hand, Sam opened the trapdoor leading to the underground passageway and guided her down the stairs to his secret bunker. An enormous bed stood in the room's middle, touched by the golden light of the lamp Sam switched on.

Kelly hesitated. "Your father is so strict about Christmas tradition. If he finds out you slipped away from the caroling to be with me..."

"The hell with him. I'd rather be with you," he murmured, drawing her into his arms.

Sam kissed her hard and long, as if he'd die if he couldn't have her. Kelly wrapped her arms around his neck, kissing him back.

"What I want to give you for Christmas can't be wrapped in a box," he murmured, twirling a strand of her hair around his finger. Sam pulled, drawing her close. "And you can thank me with those sweet little screams I love to hear in bed."

Kelly placed her palms on his chest. She wanted this so

badly. She knew their affair was all wrong, and lately the tension had gotten worse. Sam's father kept scowling at her, as if he suspected. And sweet, innocent Petie, Sam's little brother, almost caught them in the barn last week.

Even her own father, a widower since her birth eighteen years ago, wouldn't approve. Cedric Denning wanted his only child to join his secret fight for equality for Arcanes.

She and Sam were on opposite sides of a great chasm. But chasms could be breeched, and love conquered all. She didn't want Sam's money, or his position. Just him.

"Your father would get his shotgun if he knew. He'd rather see you with a damn Yankee than an Arcane." Kelly rested her head against Sam's broad shoulder.

"I'd protect you. He can't tell me what to do." Sam nuzzled her neck, his warm breath tickling her ear.

"Sam, he suspects something. He's trying to set you up with Lisa. That date…"

"It was just a date, Kel. Make the old man happy and get him off my back. Nothing happened. If you want, I'll take you next time." He dropped tiny, hot kisses on the juncture of her shoulder blade.

Jealousy coiled in her stomach. Last week Sam's mother had held a tea party and invited Lisa Smith, daughter of a wealthy Elemental blue-blooded family. In childhood, Kelly and Lisa were inseparable, until the day Lisa discovered her best friend was only an Arcane servant. Lisa made new friends, and they all ridiculed her each time Kelly came into town.

It had stung her pride to serve her former friend tea, but it stung even more hearing Lisa brag about dancing with Sam at a society ball.

Sam escorted privileged Elementals like Lisa to black-tie galas.

Sam escorted lowly Arcanes like Kelly to his hidden bedroom.

She pulled out of his embrace. "Your father wants you to marry a blue-blooded Elemental like Lisa. Nothing would make him happier."

A low snort of derision. "Father can pressure all he wants. I'm crazy about you, Kel. I don't care what anyone says."

Feeling years older, and wiser, she sighed. "You'd care if we were out and I got caught without my ID. They'd toss me into prison."

"I'm not going to let anything happen to you."

Emotion clogged her throat. "You can't guarantee it, Sam. My people have little rights. Yours have all the power."

His expression lost its tender, teasing look and turned determined and ruthless. The swift change was startling, as if Colton Shaymore's twenty-one-year-old son had shown exactly what kind of man he'd become.

"No one's going to touch you, or I'll show them the business side of my fists. You're mine and what I claim, I protect. Now close your eyes."

Something delicate and cool slipped around her neck. She opened her eyes and lifted the silver pendant with its three intertwined and intricate spirals.

"It's not just a Christmas gift, Kel. The triskele is sacred among my people."

"It's lovely."

His velvet tone turned rough. "It won't make you invincible, but if you wear it around your neck, it'll act like a shield and prevent all but the darkest magick from hurting you. Plus, it will amplify your own powers. Never lose it. If I'm not around..."

Putting a finger to his mouth, she shook her head. The consequences were too terrible to bear. Life without Sam?

Kelly kissed him. His mouth was warm and he tasted like brandy and mints. His scent wrapped around her like a blanket, the promise of pleasure lingering as he licked the inside of her mouth and palmed her breasts.

Tearing off their clothing, they fell into the bed.

His lovemaking was tender and slow. After, Sam held her close for a long while, as if afraid of letting her go.

The mood was too somber for the holidays. Kelly sprang out of bed, tugged at his hand. "Let's go for a walk in the moonlight, and then you can shift into a wolf and sneak back into the house."

Sam sat up, the sheet spilling to his lean waist. Candlelight glistened on the sweat-slicked muscles of his abdomen.

"No more sneaking out. Get dressed. I'm taking you with me to the house."

The declaration shocked her, as if he'd decided to walk into the mansion stark naked.

"You can't! What about your father?"

"The hell with him. He'll adjust. I'm tired of being under his thumb. If he doesn't like it, I can make it on my own." Sam swung his long legs over the bed and pulled on his trousers.

They dressed quickly. Cold air slapped them as they ran out of the barn, laughing and talking. Kelly's pulse quickened. Despite the practical worries niggling her, she couldn't help dreaming. A home of their own, maybe the cabin he owned where they'd first made love. Far away from their families, they could make their own little world, where the Arcane and Elemental classes didn't matter.

And only their feelings did.

The dream burst apart into a shower of sparks. Kelly halted, staring in horror at the stately Shaymore mansion with its columned portico, black shutters and marbled hallways.

Orange flames licked the windows, smoke pouring out of the house in thick, black ribbons.

Now they were running across the field. Not fast enough. Every step they took, the fire grew. Oh, gods, she thought in terror, Sam's family was inside.

Her father, as well. He'd been charged with setting out the antique oil lamps and lighting them. A centuries-old tradition insisted upon by Annabelle Shaymore, who banned electricity for this special night.

Then a tall man burst out of the house by the front door. Laughing crazily, he rubbed his hands together like Lady Macbeth. White bolts of energy shot from his fingertips, crackling in the air. He turned, his face showing clearly in the moonlight.

Cedric Denning. Her father.

"You goddamn bastard, what did you do?" Sam screamed at him.

Her father ran down the driveway. Numb, she watched her lover race toward the smoke and flames pouring out into the night.

With shaking hands, Kelly tried channeling her own powers to help put out the flames, knowing it was too late. Knowing the fire consumed the mansion, Sam's family dying inside.

Knowing her world would never be the same again.

Chapter 1

"Please, don't let him take me."

Kelly Denning's heart twisted as his large blue eyes beseeched her. "I won't, Billy. I'll do my best to keep you safe."

"Promise?"

Kelly made a large *X* over her rapidly beating heart. Nothing was going to happen to Billy. "Cross my heart and hope to..."

Die. Not today. *Not on my agenda this week.*

She forced a bright smile, hoping the terrified child could see it in the dimness. "Cross my heart and hope to never lie."

"But you're an Arcane. My mommy says Arcanes lie all the time because your magick is weaker, not like us Elementals. Is she right?" His voice shook. "I don't know what to believe anymore. I just want to go home."

Not wanting his mother's prejudice to shake his faith, Kelly chose her words with care. "I promise you, I'll do everything I can to get you back to your parents."

"They won't want me anymore after this," Billy said in a

small voice. "I won't be an Elemental if they drain my powers like they keep saying they will."

Emotion clogged her throat. Billy wouldn't be alive, either. But she had no intention of scaring him further.

"Your powers are still inside you. No one can take away who you are, honey."

"Not even a Dark Lord?"

Kelly sucked in a breath. Dark Lords were rare, but they were the most powerful Mages of all, created from pure evil. Only Arcanes were known to achieve this transformation through an ancient spell, which gave Elementals a natural fear of their weaker brethren.

"Especially not a Dark Lord."

"Will anyone save us? My dad knows some navy SEALs. They rescue people." Billy's voice trembled.

The two fangers upstairs would drain a navy SEAL dry. Ordinary navy SEALs couldn't save them. They needed someone higher on the food chain.

Her thoughts drifted to Sam Shaymore. He was a powerful Elemental Phantom Mage and, her sources said, a navy SEAL. Sam would rescue Billy, but Kelly doubted he'd take her along. Because, like other Elementals, Sam Shaymore blamed her father for killing his entire family.

I'm not like my father, Sam.

"Maybe," Kelly ventured. "But if they don't, we have to save ourselves. Just stick close to me, and do as I say."

No matter what happened to her, Billy must live.

Kelly hugged her knees, winced. Not a good idea. Still hadn't healed yet. Scanning the inside of the cramped, dark room, she assessed their prison's weak points as Billy huddled close.

He was the privileged son of a powerful Elemental Phantom Mage. Someone had stolen Billy out of his bed and brought him to this island to siphon away all his ripening magick. The process would kill him.

Not as long as I'm here, Kelly thought grimly.

Kelly's organization, Sight Finders, rescued Mage children. She'd discovered the missing Billy's whereabouts through an anonymous email tip. But the words that chilled her the most had been these: *Arcanes are conspiring to create a Dark Lord. They plan to execute all Elemental Mages.*

The email warned Billy was in Florida, where he'd be transported to this tiny island in the Caribbean. She'd stolen aboard the boat in Miami and nearly succeeded in freeing him. But the fangers had caught her and imprisoned her, as well.

Kelly stood, wincing at her protesting leg muscles. She peered out the slats of a narrow window. A thin ray of sunlight speared the darkness. They'd have to make a break for it now, before the vampires awakened. She could create a diversion and…

"Someone's coming," Billy whispered.

Heavy footsteps. Her palms grew clammy. Kelly rubbed them against her dirty jeans. Oh, gods, she knew what was coming next. She slipped the silver pendant off her neck and put it around Billy's neck.

"This will keep you safe. The triskele has much power."

Billy's eyes grew huge. "No, Kelly, what about you? You need magick protection, too!"

"I'll be fine. Stay in the corner. They can't hurt you if you wear the necklace."

"Kelly." The little boy's voice came as a whisper. "You're an Arcane. My mother says Arcanes are bad people. They're different from us and can't be trusted to be anything more than servants."

Grief twisted her heart. She knelt by the little boy and gathered his hands into hers.

"Listen to me, Billy. Whatever you've been told is wrong. My people are gentle and would rather practice their craft of chanting spells. Yes, they've been subservient for generations to Elementals. But they would sooner die themselves than turn to darkness and kill another to gain more power."

Billy's eyes were solemn. "But someone among your people has."

She squeezed his hands, unable to argue that point.

The door opened, showing a shaft of sunlight. Kelly winced as someone seized her wrist. The Arcane Mage grinned, showing a row of yellowed teeth. Her stomach roiled at the thought of a fellow Arcane hurting an innocent child. She laughed, hoping to calm Billy's fears. "Time to play the game again, right boys? It's a fun game."

Out of the corner of her eye, she saw another Arcane slap a heavy stick against his fat thigh. Her knees felt weak.

"Right," said the voice thick with menace. "Time to play the game."

As he swam through the clear Caribbean water, U.S. Navy SEAL Sam "Shay" Shaymore fought the instincts of his Mage shifter magick to change into an ocean-dwelling animal. With the three other SEALs using the nav boards equipped with compasses, they moved silently in swim pairs, their Dräger rebreathers showing no telltale bubbles.

He kept his breathing even, slowed his banging heart rate. Dangerous as hell executing an op in broad daylight. But their orders were clear. Attack in the daylight, soon as possible. Ensign Grant "Sully" Sullivan had done recon on the target's mansion. Billy was being held in a first-floor room, guarded in daylight by two Arcane Mages armed with M16s and two nasty vamps at night. The heat sig from the night-vision binocs showed that he was still alive as of last night. A female, probably the nanny who'd kidnapped Billy, remained with him.

The top brass ordering this op knew nine-year-old Billy Rogers, the only son of a powerful U.S. senator, was being held captive. Keegan Byrne, the four-star admiral and Primary Elemental Mage who commanded the SEALs, knew a little more. Like the fact that Billy's dad was also a Phantom Elemental and an Elder on the stately Council of Mages.

It was an op loaded with policy-maker land mines. The worst kind for a SEAL on the elite Phoenix Force, a secret group of navy SEALs who were all paranorms. A human media explosion would ensue afterward, followed by the paranormal uproar created by the powerful Council of Mages.

Shay didn't care. The hell with afterward. Billy was all that mattered.

He and his teammates surfaced near the seawall. Blending in with the craggy rocks, they removed and stashed their gear.

Shay slicked back his hair with a hand, scanning the lush grounds for movement. Their point man, Lieutenant Matthew "Dakota" Parker, gave the signal for all clear. No one around. *Time to move in, boys.*

With a flick of his wrist, Shay cut the alarm by sending an electromagnetic current rippling into the system. The four SEALs crept up near a stand of palms, HK416 assault rifles at the ready. Silent as wraiths, they slipped away.

Shay hunkered down behind a group of palm trees, watching the other SEALs. Dakota shifted into a wolf and ran up the outside stairs. The Mages on the balcony would catch his scent and investigate, leaving the way clear for Sully and Petty Officer Third Class Ryder "Renegade" Thompson to capture the nanny and dipatch the vamps and Mages and grab Billy.

He clicked his radio twice. Answering clicks signaled as they all moved into position.

And then a woman stepped out of the house onto the patio and sank into a chaise longue by the pool.

Damn! Shay lifted his binoculars. The female daylight hugger must be the nanny. He bit back a curse and spoke into his throat mic, breaking radio silence.

"Alpha One, this is Bravo Two. I have a visual on Tango Five. Oscar Mike."

Double clicks on the radio acknowledged the transmission.

It took seconds for him to analyze the new threat. He could take her out, but brass wanted her for questioning. Instead of stealth, he opted for shifting. His magick was powerful, but the form was nonthreatening.

Inside he smiled.

Little Miss Sunshine, you're all mine.

Every bone in her body hurt. As part of the game, they'd beat her while she tried to stifle her screams to keep from terrifying Billy. Kelly refused to talk as they tried to get information on how she'd discovered their operation. As punishment, the Mages would dump her in the cell for a few minutes to assure Billy she was still alive and then put her into the sunshine.

Unlike other Arcanes, Kelly healed from exposure to direct sunlight. Probably a result of wearing the powerful triskele for so many years.

They'd bring her back into the darkness when she recovered. Just to hurt her all over again. Only this time, they'd beaten her a little harder. Billy had given her back the triskele to wear.

"Please, Kelly. It has good magick and will help you," he'd whispered.

She closed her eyes, and the ache in her muscles eased as the triskele amplified the sun's gentle strength. She heard a small, hopeful meow.

House cat. She gave a vague smile.

"Where did you come from, kitty? I thought the vamps didn't let anything smaller than a tank hunt on their turf?" Too hurt to wonder what it was, she closed her eyes. And then she heard a scream upstairs.

Billy! She started off the chaise.

Bam! Next thing she knew she was lying flat on her stomach, a heavy male weight pressed into her back.

"Chief Petty Officer Sam Shaymore, U.S. Navy SEALs," he whispered into her ear.

Warm breath feathered over her cheek. The delicious masculine scent of leather and sage became stronger and enveloped her like a lover's arms. She knew this scent. Knew this body…had felt it atop hers years ago.

When he'd laid her down on his bed, kissed her and then had taken her virginity.

The muscled SEAL's heavy weight shifted, allowing her to roll over. He straddled her, sitting on her hips, his hands easily pinning her down.

Indifferent, almost cruel concentration on his face turned to shock. Those penetrating hazel eyes widened and then darkened.

"Kelly," he said softly.

A gleam of recognition and pure sexual awareness. She felt the jolt as if Sam had branded her with a white-hot iron. Sheer desire whipsawed through her, making her tremble as he held her down. The last time they'd been in this position, Sam had been thrusting deep inside her, as she'd clung to him and moaned.

The erotic current between them fizzled as anger flushed his handsome face. "What the hell are you doing here?"

Power hummed in the air, radiating off him in waves. Sam could generate electromagnetic current strong enough to turn a building into dust. A navy SEAL and a Phantom Mage? Forget the vampire guards. They had baby teeth compared with Sam's T. rex magick.

Fear coated her mouth. Kelly wriggled, but he held her down easily. Disgusted with her weakness, she scowled into his face.

"Mind getting off me, Sam? We're not lovers anymore, and this brick is awfully hard."

Those chiseled features narrowed. He wore a black headband around his forehead, keeping his shoulder-length brown hair in place. A nasty-looking weapon hung from one broad shoulder. He was clad in some kind of green camouflage. Kelly felt a shiver snake down her spine.

"Let me go. I have to get to Billy…"

He touched an earpiece and glanced upstairs. "Billy is safe."

"But the Mages…"

"Dead." His gaze flattened. "Why did you take him, Kelly? This your new hobby, stealing innocents?"

"I didn't kidnap Billy. I was trying to free him when I got caught. My organization is Sight Finders."

Those dreamy hazel eyes widened. "Those nutjobs? The ones who steal Mage children in domestic disputes?"

"My organization rescues Mage children in trouble."

"My organization is the U.S. Navy. You're my prisoner." Sam eased back and snapped plastic ties around her wrists.

Her jaw dropped. "You can't do this!"

"Just did."

"But I'm on your side."

"Can't trust that, until the situation is secured." Then for a sheer moment, the indifferent mask dropped. Torment shadowed his face as he stroked a light finger down her cheek. His touch made her shiver, and remember.

"Sam," she began, but he slid off and pulled her upright. Even with his incandescent rage, his touch was considerate and gentle.

Always the Southern gentleman. Even when taking prisoners, she thought dully.

She struggled against the ties but failed to break them. Sam gave her an amused look. "Don't waste your energy. I laced them with magick. I'm an Elemental."

"You were," she whispered. "Now you're just a bastard. When did you become one, Sam?"

Regret flashed in his eyes, and then the hardness returned. "The day your father escaped after killing my whole family."

He walked her to a sturdy coconut palm. Before he secured

her to it, he cupped her cheek with his palm. Despite the wet, thick gloves, she felt the warmth of his touch like a brand. He studied her solemnly. "Kel," he murmured.

So close he seemed ready to kiss her. She closed her eyes, remembering those firm, warm lips nestled against hers.

When she opened her eyes, he'd vanished.

Kelly struggled against her bonds. Gunfire erupted amid loud explosions upstairs. A SEAL emerged from the house, carrying a terrified Billy. He was sobbing.

"Give him to me," she cried out.

Sheer strength and her own secret store of magick shattered her bonds. Kelly rushed forward, only to feel the cold pressure of a gun barrel pressed to her temple. "Don't move," came Sam's deep voice.

"I'm here to save Billy. I'm not his enemy!"

"Maybe not his," he said in a soft, drawling voice that rubbed against her skin like warm velvet. "But, sweetheart, you are most definitely mine."

Chapter 2

Propping his heavy boots on the table in front of him, Shay took a swig of bottled water and stared at the opposite wall of Phoenix Force's ready room. Framed photographs of SEALs who'd died in combat stared back. Shay gave them a solemn salute with the bottle.

Kelly Denning. Even now, years after they'd parted, the memories rushed back in a cascade of searing heat. But now they said she was a scumbag, worse than a pyrokinetic demon. According to the rumors swirling around the SEAL Team 21 compound, she'd used her organization as cover to steal Elemental Phantom Mage children to drain their powers. Billy was the first. Others would follow if Kelly wasn't stopped.

The door slammed behind them as Renegade and Dakota paced into the room. The two Draicon werewolves looked ready to take someone down.

Gods, he knew what they felt. They hated the mass of red tape caused by the senator whose son they'd saved. Everyone on the SEAL 21 compound was on edge. ST 21 was thought by humans to be "norms." No one in the human world knew of the existence of paranorms. If they did, they'd freak.

And now the senator had brought an entourage of humans into the compound. "Are they done with her yet?" he asked his lieutenant.

Dakota shook his head. "Humans are. FBI and brass are letting her go. No evidence she was working with the kidnappers. But as soon as they're gone, Senator Rogers wants a crack at her."

He exchanged glances with a scowling Renegade.

"The senator wants blood. He says she's lying, because all Arcane Mages lie." Renegade shook his head. "Seems we're in the middle of a damn blood feud."

"Rogers is an Elemental Elder on the Council of Mages. He doesn't trust Arcanes. This little incident fuels his reasons even more," Shay explained.

And he had the power to fry Kelly with a flick of one hand. *Not if I'm around.*

Stretching languidly, Renegade winked. "That Kelly is hot. Heard you were childhood friends and then lovers."

Shay stiffened and then crushed the bottle in one hand. "Not anymore."

"Bad parting?" Dakota took a chair, swung it around and straddled it.

You might say. Shay gave his friend and lieutenant a meaningful look. The Draicon werewolf got it and shut his trap. *Thank you.*

But Renegade, a loudmouth and player, shook the topic like a wolf with a tasty bone. "I don't get this crap about Elementals and Arcanes. You're all the same race, all Mages."

"Long history." Shay pitched the empty bottle into a waste basket.

Renegade tapped his fingers on the desk. "I bet you got into it with her father because she's an Arcane and you're a powerful Elemental. You seduced her. Classic case of the maid seduced by the nobleman."

Shay's blood pressure rose. The desk began to vibrate beneath his clenched fists. Electromagnetic currents rippled in the air, sparks crackling with magick.

"And then..." Renegade grinned. "Her father went after you with a shotgun."

"No. Her father killed my entire family."

Both SEALs stared at him. Shay felt his temples begin to pound as he recognized the troublesome look in Renegade's eyes.

"All that over a little something-something? Day-um. That Kelly she must be great in the sack. Those long legs..."

Shay's temper snapped like dry kindling. "That's it. You're going down."

He vaulted over the table, aiming for the SEAL. As Renegade shape-shifted into a wolf, Shay used his Phantom powers to shift.

Snarling, the two wolves clashed in midair, heavily muscled bodies thunking hard against each other. He raked his claws over the other's muzzle, heard an answering call of pain. Renegade's teeth closed over Shay's left shoulder, biting hard. As the burning agony hit, so did logic. Tearing free, Shay spun around, his large paws digging into the linoleum.

His Kelly? Since when? The man inside the wolf howled for reason. This was Renegade, a bastard, sure, but his teammate, a fellow SEAL who would give his life for the teams. And Shay.

Dakota stormed forward, backhanded them both. "Stand down!"

The two wolves shifted back and Renegade clothed himself by using magick. He looked badly shaken. Blood dripped from three furrows on his face. The coppery scent hung in the air.

Shay shifted back, feeling deeply ashamed. He conjured on clothing and swallowed hard, looking Renegade in the eye.

"I'm sorry, man," Shay said.

"My bad." The other SEAL looked abashed.

A vein jumped in Dakota's temple. "Are you insane? The senator's human aides are in this building! We're pooling all our efforts to make SEAL Team 21 look like just another SEAL team and hide our powers. And you two shape-shift in broad daylight?"

He turned to Renegade. "You. Fifty laps around the compound. Now. And you..."

Dakota waited until Renegade left. "Shay, dial it down. I know what it's like to lose your head over a woman, but you're not doing her any favors by pulling crap like that."

"It won't happen again."

He meant it. Because the feral rage scared the ever-living crap out of him. Gods, he hadn't shifted into a wolf since the day he'd nearly killed a rancher almost eleven years ago. If not for his uncle's high standing on the council, Shay would have been executed. They didn't kill him, because he was a privileged Elemental Mage. After, Shay joined the navy, became a SEAL. The disciplined life had saved him.

Dakota's cell rung. The Draicon glanced at caller ID, and his scowl softened to a smile. He answered. "Hey, sweetheart."

Sienna, the wolf's mate. She'd taken this man of brass and turned him into mush with a simple phone call. A hollow ache settled in Shay's chest. Glancing over his shoulder, Dakota whispered, "Go take care of yourself, Shay. You're bleeding all over the place."

He nodded. "Tell Sienna I said hello."

When he returned, Lieutenant Commander Dale "Curt" Curtis, commanding officer of ST 21, sat beside Dakota in the ready room.

"Curt? What's the deal?"

His CO snorted. "Show's about to start. And I can't do a damn thing about it. My hands are tied by all this red tape."

The door burst open. Senator Robert Rogers walked in,

accompanied by his well-groomed wife and a pretty, blonde woman with a tense look and wide, scared eyes. The woman carried a pad and pencil. In the senator's wake was a parade of dark-suited aides, two Secret Service agents, Admiral Keegan Byrne and all the SEALs on the Phoenix Force except Renegade.

It's a freaking party, Shay thought humorlessly.

Rogers gestured to the aides and agents. After some protest all the humans left, the aides casting anxious glances at their boss.

As the door closed behind them, the woman sat and flipped open her pad. Rogers escorted his wife to a chair and glared at Curt. "I assume these quarters are private so I may question the suspect as I am entitled to under Mage law?"

His CO's expression tightened. "You're entitled. But this is a military base. My unit. If you deviate from the rules, you leave."

Rogers nodded at the blonde woman. "Catherine is my personal assistant. She serves as secretary for the Council of Mages and will take notes for my report to them."

Two MPs brought Kelly in, removed her handcuffs and left. She sat on a gray folding chair near the front. As she rubbed at her wrists, her gaze caught Shay's. She'd cut her waist-length hair. The wavy locks tumbled past her shoulders, still the color of a copper penny shimmering in the sunlight. With her heart-shaped face, pert nose and full red lips, she had an alluring combination of innocence and sensuality. Shay felt another jolt of pure sexual awareness. Just like the first time they'd noticed each other on his father's estate.

She had a figure, yowza, that would knock the socks off a eunuch sworn to celibacy. Hourglass, all smooth curves that tempted a man into tracing every single luscious inch of her skin with his hands, and his tongue.

His cock went instantly hard. Shay gritted his teeth, his

breath easing out in a harsh whistle of air. Air. Man, he needed air. He could hardly breathe.

A side door opened, and Renegade strolled in and slid into the seat next to Shay. The SEAL's tongue nearly dropped down like one of those stupid cartoon wolves. "Day-um. Now I see why you were into her," he muttered.

"You're supposed to be doing laps around the compound," Shay snapped, possessive male urges cranking from mild to overdrive.

"Dakota didn't say anything about the outside of the compound, so I jogged around the courtyard." The Draicon wolf's gaze riveted to Kelly. "Besides, I needed to check if you still had a pulse. You okay?"

Shay felt a flash of gratitude. "Yup." Renegade could be a bastard, but he was cool when it came down to it.

Shay stalked toward the room's front and stood against the wall, folding his arms. He couldn't get involved, but the vulnerable shadows beneath her blue eyes punched his gut.

The heels of Rogers's polished black shoes clicked across the linoleum. In his dark gray suit, with silver edging his short hair, the senator looked urbane and handsome. But beneath the charming smile lurked something nasty, like an oil slick.

"Now, Miss Denning." Rogers took a seat behind the desk, steepling his fingers. "You kept asserting your innocence before military authorities and the FBI. Without evidence to hold you, they released you."

Rogers's smile darkened. "Under human law, you are free to go. But Mage law is not so liberal. As Chief Elder on the Council of Mages, I ask you now, who gave the orders to steal my son?"

Kelly rubbed the heel of her hand against her cheek. "I'm innocent. Sight Finders helps Mage offspring. We're the only ones protecting the children of both Elemental and Arcane Mages."

"Don't play the naive card with me, Denning. You were

not imprisoned with Billy when the SEALs rescued him. You were lounging by the pool."

"Billy will tell you—I was rescuing him."

"He's too traumatized to speak." Rogers waved a hand. "Where is the nanny who took him? Was she working for you?"

"Dead," Curt said, his gray gaze steely. "My men killed the vamps and both Mage guards on the island. When the Mages died, they assumed their original forms. One was the nanny."

"So she was working for you." Rogers turned his attention back to Kelly.

Curt and Shay exchanged glances. No words needed. Shay could read his CO's mind. The powerful Primary Mage had little tolerance for a slick politician with a hell-bent agenda.

What an asshole.

"Your organization is a front for stealing Elemental children to drain their magick and enrich your own powers. You would have killed my son had you the chance!"

"Never! I was protecting him."

"Where did you get the knowledge of siphoning Elemental magick? The dark spell books were all destroyed."

Kelly rolled her eyes. "Now who's naive? Knowledge isn't contained by a book. Ever hear of our oral history?"

Shadows darkened her face. "This goes a lot deeper than you realize. The Arcanes behind Billy's kidnapping want to kill Phantom Elementals to take over their extraordinary powers and duplicate them. They're going to create a Dark Lord."

A few harsh intakes of breath from all the Mages. Alarm filled Shay. Hell, she had to be wrong.

Curt gave her the penetrating look he used to interrogate tangos, but it looked more thoughtful than menacing. "There hasn't been a Dark Lord in three hundred years."

Rogers looked uneasy and then scoffed. "We have kept close watch over every Arcane through a regular sweep of

ID cards. Until now, not one single Arcane has stolen Elemental magick."

Shay shifted uncomfortably. Curt glanced at him. "You're wrong, Senator. There was one twelve years ago. We have no proof, though. He vanished off the radar."

A small, cruel smile played on the Mage's lips. "I forgot. Your father, Denning. You're just like him."

"I am not my father," Kelly said, fire flashing in her eyes. "I save children. I'm about justice, unlike you. Just because you're Elementals doesn't make you better than me. Are you going to listen to me, you pigheaded fool? The real threat is still out there!"

"Really, Robert. Are you going to let her talk to you like that?" Mrs. Rogers studied a manicured nail.

Kelly gazed at Rogers without fear. Shay felt a surge of admiration. Same Kelly. Always standing her ground.

Rogers raised his hands, power humming in the room. "I will tolerate no disrespect. Especially not from an Arcane. You will give me answers."

The senator sent the energy ball sailing toward Kelly. As it struck her, she cried out and flew backward, hitting the wall.

Shay lost it. All his male protective instincts surged. Senator or not, Rogers could not treat a woman that way. *You try talking without a tongue, you bastard...*

As Shay lunged forward, ready to leap over the desk, Curt reached out an arm and yanked him back. Waves of calming magick pulsed from the Mage. "Steady, Shay. Take it easy," his CO murmured. "Not here. Not now."

Releasing Shay, Curt scowled at the senator. "I told you, interrogation by the rules. One more violation and I'll toss you out on your ass myself."

Shay struggled to keep a civil tone. "Since when did we allow torture? We're better than that."

"They're both right. Do that again, Robert, and you're leaving the base," Admiral Byrne said quietly.

Rogers laughed. "You can't do that. I'm a U.S. senator who sits on the Armed Services Committee. I'll cut the funding to your precious team of navy SEALs."

Byrne's mouth twisted. "Don't get into a pissing contest with me, son. You'll lose. I'm fifteen hundred years old and can reduce you to ashes before you can say 'defense budget.'"

Ignoring them both, Shay crouched down by Kelly, who rubbed her side where the energy bolt had hit. A small, charred hole showed in the yellow print fabric.

Their eyes met. A jolt went through him at the intense blueness he saw in her eyes. Shay reached out a hand, clasped hers. An internal shudder raced through him. So warm and soft.

Up close, she smelled great, her delicate floral scent cutting through the ozone stench of energy Rogers had tossed at her.

Shay cleared his throat. "You okay?"

As he helped her stand, she gave a rueful smile.

"I'm fine. That jolt works better than a shot of espresso. Maybe I can hire him to roust me out of bed in the morning."

Still the same Kelly, putting up a brave front. Shay studied her face. A bruise shadowed one perfect cheekbone. He touched it and she winced. His temper began to rise.

Those blue eyes, once clear and sparkling as a summer sky, clouded with worry as she caught his expression.

"I'm fine. I mean it. Thanks, Sam," she said softly.

She brushed off her jeans, nodded at the gray folding chair. "By the way, need that? Is it special? Other than for serving as the hot seat for suspects?"

"It's just a chair," Shay told her, puzzled.

"Okay. Let me show you something, Senator."

Digging into her jeans pocket, Kelly retrieved a silver necklace and draped it around her neck. She closed her eyes and extended her slim arms skyward. "Earth, earth, earth, water, water, water, fire, fire, fire, air, air, air."

Shay's blood ran cold. The ancient chanting spell used by Arcanes to gather power from the elements. But they needed a secondary source to properly channel the power, such as an enchanted staff, a wand or an amulet, and all those had been banned....

The three swirls on the pendant around Kelly's neck glowed. White light suffused her body, the energy pulsing steadily. Then she opened her eyes and flung out her hands toward the chair.

KA-POW!

The chair was a mangled, crumpled mess of metal. The little secretary taking notes gasped and stared at Kelly, who calmly regarded Rogers.

"I can take care of myself. I chose not to attack you in return. You're not dealing with a weak Arcane you can bully like you've bullied others."

Rogers sputtered as his wife gasped.

"Where the hell did you get that power?" Rogers demanded. "Did you kill other Elemental children?"

"If I had, would I allow you to hold me prisoner? My powers come from another source, a source for good."

Awareness shone in the senator's eyes. "A triskele. No Arcane has one." He approached Kelly and seized the pendant. It sizzled, and he jumped back with a yelp.

"I put a spell on it so the humans couldn't find it when they searched me. Oh, and enchanted it so any Mage trying to steal it will get burned." Kelly gave a serene smile. "Oops. Forgot to mention that little fact."

Blood drained from Shay's face. The triskele... Damn. She still had the pendant he'd given her. Now she'd learned to use it as a weapon.

If the council found out Shay had illegally helped an Arcane... *My ass is toast,* he thought grimly.

"Do you know who I am? I'm a U.S. senator and an Elder on the Council of Mages." A vein throbbed in Rogers's temple.

"I know who you are. You're Billy's father," Kelly said quietly.

Silence draped the room.

"He's a very brave little boy. He needs you."

Rogers swept his gaze around the room. Looking for support, maybe? None came from the grim-faced SEALs, the four-star Admiral Byrne or the silent Curt.

His wife sighed. "Are we done yet, Robert? I have a hair appointment and we have the Society of the Arts gala tonight. This visit wasn't on your schedule, and it's taking far too long."

Shay focused on Kelly and saw that her elegant, long fingers were rubbing against her torn and ragged jeans. She did that to hide hands shaking in fear.

She'd done it the first night they'd made love, until desire surfaced and then…

Damn, someone had to stand up for Kelly, and no one around here seemed willing. He faced the senator. "You have no right to hold her. Under Mage law, she's legally free within twenty-four hours, unless you can prove she's a direct threat to another Mage. And there is no hard evidence she hurt anyone, including your son."

He leveled a look at the older Mage. "Until then, she walks."

A muscle ticked in the senator's jaw. "You're a soldier, Chief Petty Officer Shaymore. Not a policy maker. Stay out of this."

"I'm a Phantom Elemental Mage whose family has held a seat on the council for the past five hundred years. And still holds one." Shay got in the man's face. "I'm not staying out."

Tension bristled in the air as Rogers clenched his jaw. Finally he gave a gruff nod. "We'll call it even, Chief, because you saved my son's life. But interfere again and I'll be forced to use my powers against you."

Try it, he thought grimly. The senator had no idea of the full extent of Shay's magick. *I'll send you flying into next week. Put that on your schedule, you bastard.*

Kelly flashed him a grateful smile. Even with her long hair tangled, clothing messed and dirt on her face, she was lovely.

The senator turned to Admiral Byrne. "Tag her with the new GPS security chip, the one you use for your SEALs. She's too dangerous to release to an unsuspecting public."

"Take her to the infirmary," Byrne told Sully.

"No." Rogers gave a nasty smile. "I want to see it for myself. Do it here."

Shay's anger rose again. But he kept silent as his teammate left and returned with the injection gun. Sully cleared his throat.

"Um, I'm sorry, but I insert this in your hip."

Color flushed her face, but she unzipped her jeans and pulled them down her right hip. Shay couldn't help looking at the curve of her hip, the mint-green panties she wore with tiny pink roses embroidered on the waistband. She stared straight ahead, not wincing as Sully injected the miniature device.

Then her gaze met his, and he saw the anger dancing in her eyes. Anger, not humiliation, as she zipped up her jeans.

"New security chip? This something you're tagging all my people with, Senator, so you can watch our movements? The ID card isn't sufficient enough?"

"Your people are like cows. Branding keeps all the strays in line." Rogers gave her a cold, hard stare. "As Elder on the council, I order you to remain in your home. If you leave the country, you will be arrested and interned."

When the senator, his wife and his assistant left with the admiral, Curt rubbed the back of his neck. "Miss Denning, I'll drive you to the airport. You have a reservation on the eight-o'clock flight, courtesy of our esteemed council."

The words *esteemed council* were followed by a derisive snort.

Soft with longing, Kelly's gaze centered on Shay. She stood straight and tall, a hint of pride in those slender shoulders. "It's not necessary, but thank you, Lieutenant Commander Curtis."

"It's necessary," Curt said.

Kelly turned to Shay. Her soft pink mouth parted. She blinked back moisture gathering in her clear blue eyes.

"Sam, I'm sorry…about everything."

A wave of emotion pushed at him. If only they could turn back time and go back to how things had once been. If only her father had not killed his family…

Shay rubbed his chest, feeling his heart constrict. *I don't know who you are anymore, Kelly.*

A whistle from behind caught his attention. Renegade jerked a thumb toward the door. "Yo, Shay. Bunch of us are grabbing a few beers at the Dive Bar. Ya in?"

Drinks. With his teammates, friends. Even friends who shifted into wolves and bit were safe and familiar. Comfortable and predictable. Not a woman who spun him around into emotional knots, who looked at him sadly, as if he were the center of her universe and that particular universe had shattered. Shay gave Renegade a rough nod.

When he turned around, Kelly was gone.

Chapter 3

Kelly had to find Sam. This wasn't over.

In a dingy bathroom, she splashed water over her face to fight fatigue. Forty-eight hours without sleep and only an energy bar for food. After a support staff member had dropped her off at the airport, she'd hopped on a bus and gotten off at the nearest gas station.

She tried to clean her dirty clothing, blotting the worst of it with brown paper towels. Finally she gave up.

Not winning any beauty contests tonight, for sure. That wasn't important. Getting Sam to listen to her, and believe her, mattered most.

Beneath the distrust and doubt in his hazel eyes, she'd seen taut sexual awareness. Old feelings were still there. Even though he believed her father responsible for the deadly fire, she knew.

Cedric Denning couldn't shoot a bolt of current if a 220 line fell on him. Her father was innocent. She knew it.

Rubbing her palms against her jeans, she banished the past. It was too late for Sam's little brother. Others needed her help.

Before being escorted out, she'd overheard the SEALs say they were going to the Dive Bar. Kelly counted her money and called for a taxi.

The first driver refused. He'd seen her on television tonight when the newscasters reported her arrest in conjunction with the kidnapping of Senator Rogers's son. Two taxis later, she finally found a driver willing to give her a ride, for double the money. But he seemed confused. He didn't know any bar named the Dive Bar. Never heard of it. Finally she had him drive up and down roads near the base.

Night settled over the coastal town before she saw the flickering sign in the distance.

"There it is!" She gestured to the sign.

The driver snorted. "That's no bar. That's an old bait shop. Been closed for years."

Kelly counted the bills, gave them to him and then climbed out. Driver must be confused. Plain as day, the blue neon sign boasted the Dive Bar.

Well, at least it wasn't a four-star gourmet restaurant. Here, with her dingy clothing, she might fit in. Noise throbbed from inside, the pulsing beat of loud music, the cacophony of conversation and laughter.

Gathering her courage, she pulled open the door. An old-fashioned jukebox warbled a country-Western tune as two men played pool at the room's far end. Squinting in the dim light, she let the door shut behind her. And then, as she watched a customer wave a hand and a bottle floated toward him, the realization hit her.

Every single person inside was a paranorm.

No wonder the cabdriver had never heard of it. The bar must have a magick shield around it to dissuade humans.

Worn buoys hung from the ceiling next to fishnets and two

large plastic sharks. Old dive masks adorned one wall. It was a seedy, run-down and funky bar, the type she usually enjoyed.

People turned to examine the new arrival. And then all conversation ground to a halt. The jukebox shut off abruptly.

Uh-oh. Not exactly a welcoming crowd.

Silence descended, thick as morning fog. Even the bartender washing beer mugs in the sudsy sink stopped his work.

She swallowed hard, wiped her palms against her jeans and then finally placed her hands on the counter. A SEAL she recognized from the compound flicked a hand, the gesture filled with contempt. A half-filled mug of beer exploded, showering her blouse in suds and shards of glass. Kelly jumped. She brushed off her shirt.

"I guess happy hour is over," she said. "Because it looks like the drink's on me."

More silence, broken suddenly by a deep male laugh, the rich timbre rubbing against her like soft fur.

Sam.

As the conversation gradually resumed, and the jukebox kicked in, she stayed still, gauging her former lover.

He sat in the middle of the circular bar, flanked by the SEALs who'd been in the room as Rogers questioned her. A dark blue T-shirt stretched over his muscular chest, rode tight against his well-defined biceps. A hank of sandy-brown hair hung over his forehead. His mouth was set in a firm line.

Seeing him made her blood tingle and her heart race in anticipation. Breath caught in her throat. He was more wiry than muscular, with a deadly edge. The shadow of boyhood was gone, replaced by a virile man.

A pretty blonde in a red dress edged close. Sam gave a charming smile and began flirting. Kelly's heart sank to her stomach. Always the womanizer, until the time they'd become lovers. Kelly silently pleaded for him to look at her. Finally he glanced over. But only cold speculation showed on his handsome face.

She rubbed her hands again, wishing for a change of clothing, a change of scenery. Anything but this cool hostility. But Sam was her only hope. She needed his help to stop the rogue Arcane Mages before they stole more children—and this time killed them.

Finally, as the woman moved off, Kelly skirted the bar and stood behind Sam. "Sam, we have to talk."

Those broad shoulders tensed. He did not turn around. One of the SEALs glanced at her, growled a little. A Draicon werewolf. Wonderful. Sam's friends had tried, judged and convicted her. But the muscular SEALs didn't matter. Only Sam did.

"Please," she said softly and placed a hand on his arm.

Sam picked up his beer and led her to a corner booth. A bowl of peanuts sat on the table. Her stomach grumbled. Kelly picked up a peanut and ate it. Suddenly ravenous, she devoured one after another. Sam looked at her, his mouth a narrow slash.

"You okay? That was a nasty bolt of energy Rogers tossed at you."

"I've felt worse." The two Mages back on the island made Rogers's jolt of energy feel like a tickle.

His expression softened. "You're hungry."

Sam waved a hand. The bartender came over, his expression grim.

"I need a burger, medium rare, fries and a…" Sam cocked his head at her, his expression amused. "Still into root beer?"

"I can handle something stronger. What you're drinking. Domestic, right?"

A ghost of a smile. "Tom, give her a Bud."

Silence from the bartender.

Sam's expression tightened. "Well, Tom?"

"You, I'll serve. Not her."

Anger flared in Sam's eyes, the green sparking like fireworks. "I don't like your tone."

"I like you, Shay. But I've got two young daughters. They

mean everything to me. I don't serve no stinking Arcanes..." The word was spat out in disgust. "Especially Arcane bitches who steal kids just so she can suck out their powers for herself."

Guess good news travels fast. Kelly's appetite fled, the peanuts turning into cardboard in her stomach.

"I didn't do it," she protested.

Sam's jaw worked. He drank his beer as the bartender left. Everyone was looking at her. Humiliation poured over her.

"Sam, please." Kelly struggled to find the right words. After twelve years, she felt at a loss. What did you say to the man who once loved and now probably hated you?

He dug into his back pocket, pulled out a wallet, fished out some bills and laid them on the table. "Here's enough money to get dinner and get a flight out of here. Go home. You'd better leave, Kel. We're all pretty tight, and the guys can be very reactive. And they don't like what they heard about you."

"They heard rumors I steal children."

"They heard what your father did to my family."

Torment haunted his eyes as he looked up. "Don't force me to take sides. Because this time, I can't stand with you against my teammates."

Her throat was suddenly dry. She tried to calm her shaky nerves. "Coming here was a bad idea. I should have known I was up for the pitchforks-and-torches routine. Now what? Do you give me a head start before sending the mob after me?"

"I would never hurt you," he said softly.

"I didn't kidnap Billy. Just because you believe my father killed your family doesn't make me exactly like him."

There. Out in the open. Sam's jaw clenched hard as stone. Sparks leaped from his fingers. "Damn."

Kelly stared. "Sam? What's going on with your powers?"

"They're a little haywire lately."

Sparks sizzled in the air. The lights flickered as Sam's

hands glowed white. Uh-oh. She recognized the potent surge of power....

As she glanced at the bar to see if anyone noticed, a woman stared at Sam. Her expression was both sad and hopeful.

Sam raised his hands and flicked them toward the ceiling.

The lights flickered again, and Kelly glanced at the bar and the burly man standing by one of the SEALs. She stifled a gasp and looked away. Surely that could not be...

Her gaze cut back to the man. Suddenly he was gone. Replaced by...

Evil.

As the lights went out, Kelly shrieked.

Chapter 4

Shay jumped up, the beer bottle spilling. The lights flickered back on as suds spread over the table. Blood drained from her face, Kelly stuffed a fist in her mouth, staring at the bar.

She was okay. He ran to her, his fingers curling around her slender shoulders. "What is it?"

"I saw…" She closed her eyes and then opened them, the fear gone. "A Death Mask. The skull face of a Mage who's slaughtered another Mage to gain his powers. The first step to becoming a Dark Lord."

Conversation around them quieted. His teammates stared at him and then at Kelly. Someone muttered a curse.

"Impossible." Tom shook his head.

"I know what I saw. He's here. Or was." Kelly craned her head to peer past Sam. "He's gone now. Left when the lights went out."

Silence draped the bar. Shay studied Kelly's tight expression and could tell her pulse was galloping. She was scared but resolved. Her gaze scanned the room.

Tom spoke, his voice tight with anger and fear. "You're lying. Get out of my bar."

Unease rippled through the room. Two burly support staff from Team 21 cracked their knuckles and got off their stools.

Whispers and more stares. Shay glanced up and saw Renegade and the other SEALs tense. It was going to get ugly fast. Fear did crazy things to people, even paranorms. The crowd would fast turn into a mob if Kelly didn't leave now.

She turned to him.

"Sam?" A shallow breath and whisper. "You believe me, don't you?"

A razor's edge of silence. He studied his former lover's face, and then her hands. Steady and resolved. He drew on all his instincts and inhaled the air.

He smelled a tinge of something familiar…and foul, as if evil brushed the air and then fled.

"I believe something nasty was here."

Turning, he glanced at his teammates, his friends and Tom. He'd known Tom for years.

"We don't," Tom said flatly. "She's lying. Get out of my bar."

Two lines furrowed Kelly's brow. He recognized the look. It would take force to remove her. "I know what I saw. And I'm not leaving until I search every inch of this place and see where he went."

He turned and saw his teammates maneuver around the bar, getting ready to intercept.

"Shay," Sully said quietly. His teammate nodded toward the door.

Right. As Kelly slid out of the booth, Shay got out and scooped her over a shoulder as if she were a sack of flour. She let out a startled "Oomph." He ignored it as he jogged toward the door Renegade held open.

As the heavy wood door banged behind him, Shay set her

on her feet. He hated her stricken look, as if he'd killed her favorite kitten. A knot of barbed wire cinched his guts.

She was dangerous and outcast. He should send her far away before he got involved. Too late, he thought dimly.

"Sam, you have to let me back in there."

Leaning against the door, he shook his head. "Kelly, I've had a bitch of a day. Watching you get your head torn apart by dozens of drunken vampires, werewolves and Mages is not how I want it to end."

"He's in there. I have to find him. Someone's hiding him, Sam, and you're not standing in my way."

Her fingers flexed. He felt the quiet hum of power in the air. Behind him, the door rattled on its hinges. Sam's own powers surged.

"Back off," he said quietly.

She dropped her hands, her luscious pink mouth trembling. "So that's it. Now what? Go to a motel? No one will rent me a room. My name's been flashed across every television screen in America as a suspect in the kidnapping of Senator Rogers's son. There are no flights until morning. Where am I supposed to go?"

"Home with me."

This new steely, conservative Sam Shaymore still harbored a hint of wildness. It roared with the big, shiny chrome Harley he rode.

Clinging to his back, Kelly closed her eyes as the big bike rumbled beneath her. Wind slapped at her cheeks. The ride was exhilarating and one she'd have enjoyed—if not for the tense male driving.

She hooked her arms around his muscled waist. Sam had always been fit, but the navy had turned him into granite. As her thighs nestled against his long limbs, she felt a jolt of pure sexual awareness. The sharp leather scent of his jacket and his own masculine smell sent her female hormones surging.

Bad timing.

Sam turned a corner onto a quiet street lined with trees and trim, tidy homes. He pulled into a driveway before a two-story white house with green shutters and cut the engine.

Ever the gentleman, he helped her dismount. Kelly pulled off the helmet, smoothing down her tousled hair.

Sam quietly studied her, his full, sensual mouth drawn in a flat line. Unreadable, his expression shuttered.

"You don't live on base?"

"Team 21 has off-base privileges. This is our street. I'd tell you who all my neighbors are, but it's classified."

"And you'd have to kill me," she joked.

"No, the base security officers would." His gaze was even and unblinking. As she gulped, the ghost of a smile touched his mouth. Sam touched her nose. "Gotcha."

The tension between them eased. Kelly breathed a sigh of relief and followed him inside.

Sam had always had taste, but the modest living room surprised her with its plain but comfortable furniture. This was more a home suited for someone like her.

She trailed him into the kitchen, a more elegant room with gleaming granite countertops and stainless-steel appliances. Dumping her pack on the floor, Kelly sat on a stool at the breakfast bar. Sam needed time to download and process before she hit him with the heavy-duty artillery.

He grabbed two bottles of beer and offered her one. Kelly sipped as he hunted through the fridge, setting bread, deli turkey slices, lettuce and Swiss cheese on the countertop. He frowned and braced his hands on the counter, studying her a long minute.

"Do you have any memory of where you were two hours ago?"

Confused, she nodded. "At your base, SEAL Team 21's compound. You're all paranormals, aren't you?"

"Curt didn't take your memories right before you left the

base," Sam said softly. "I'll be damned. Civilians aren't allowed on our compound, and any who do have their memories erased. No one is supposed to know about our team. SOP."

"Maybe your commanding officer has more faith in me than your standard operating procedure. He asked questions, but I didn't answer them."

Because I don't trust him. I trust only you.

"Kelly, you're in deep trouble. And these rumors about a Dark Lord aren't helping your case."

"I will discover the truth. I haven't changed."

But you have.

He cut the bread into four neat quarters. "Late-night snack?" she asked.

"It's for you." He slid the sandwich across the bar. "Turkey on whole wheat, lettuce, no tomato, lots of mayo and Swiss cheese."

Emotion clogged her throat. After all these years, he'd remembered her favorite. Kelly nodded thanks as she devoured the sandwich. Sam remained standing, tipping back the bottle and drinking deeply. Muscles in his throat worked as he swallowed, and then he backhanded his mouth. Green flared in his eyes as he studied her mouth.

"You have mayo…here."

He reached across the counter and touched the corner of her mouth with his thumb. Sam brought his thumb to his lips and licked it slowly, his intense gaze never leaving hers. Heat sizzled in the air. Her limbs felt loose and pliant, her nipples tight.

Hot, heavy need surged. She wanted him badly. Wanted to feel him naked against her hot skin, feel those hard muscles rub against her body. Fingertips ached with the need, the yearning to touch him, explore muscle and sinew.

Kelly quivered, her lips parting. The air grew heavy with expectancy, overlaid with sexual awareness.

She jerked her gaze away, staring at the counter. "I'm not

here to rekindle anything, Sam. I followed you because I need your help."

A douse of icy water on both of them. His mouth became a firm slash. He turned, jamming his hands into his faded jeans and presenting her with his rigid spine as he stared out the kitchen window. The moment had vanished.

But for an instant, she desperately wanted it back.

"Kelly, you don't know what you're up against. Rogers has a lot of influence and can convince the council to imprison you."

She sighed. "I didn't know he'd be that rigid and hateful. I'd heard he was more tolerant of Arcanes."

"Yeah, Rogers surprised me. He never was that much of an asshole. Guess when his son got kidnapped, it sent him over the edge. So now the only fair shake you'd get is my uncle, and he's out of the country. So if they wanted to bypass the rules and imprison you, they could."

"Al is still on the council?"

"He's only there because of me." Sam turned, his jaw tightened. "He saved my ass once, and told me if anything ever happened to me, he'd resign. He's not too fond of those stuffed shirts and their bureaucratic ways. Go home, lie low and wait for this to all die down."

"You know I can't do that," she said.

"I don't want anything to happen to you."

"I can take care of myself."

"Against ordinary humans, even other Mages, yes. But not if the council wants your ass."

"You always said it was a fine ass."

Sam closed the distance between them. He stroked the side of her cheek with a single finger, the well-remembered gesture tender. She struggled with the urge to lean against him, absorb his strength.

"And I'd hate to see anything happen to it."

"This is bigger than me, Sam. It's a lot deeper than anyone realizes. I did see the Death Mask. I have the ability."

He looked at her with the same wariness his teammates had shown. She pushed away. "I hate it, but it's part of me and I've learned to accept it."

Ever since childhood, Kelly knew she was different. She sensed things more than ordinary Arcanes could. Fearful of alarming her father, Kelly had set out to learn on her own. She studied ancient texts forbidden to Arcanes, stealing away minutes in the vast Shaymore library under the pretense of dusting the shelves.

And in the library, she'd discovered that a few, very few, special Mages had the ability to discern a Mage who killed another merely to siphon his power, the first stage of transforming into a Dark Lord. These Mages could see a shimmering Death Mask, a skull with glowing yellow eyes, superimposed over a normal-looking face.

Exactly what she'd witnessed at the bar.

"But I can't accept someone is stealing Phantom Mage children to gain their power. An Arcane, organizing other Arcanes to gain magick for a bigger purpose."

"What?"

She dragged in a deep breath. "To gain power, and exterminate your people. All of them. A genocide."

The stunned look on his face would have been comical if the subject wasn't so grim.

Kelly's fingers curled around her bottle of beer. "Now will you listen, really listen to me?"

Eyes narrowed, he leaned on the counter. "Spill it. Everything."

"A few weeks ago, Sight Finders received an anonymous tip about the bodies of two Elemental Phantom Mages reported as missing. It had been assumed the women, who had been divorcing their husbands, were out having a wild time."

"I remember Uncle Al telling me about it. The council made sure the bodies were taken away before human authorities were notified. They didn't want mortals asking questions.

The council investigated, concluded the women were drunk and careless," Sam said.

"They didn't tell you what condition the bodies were found in."

Kelly fished out her wallet and withdrew a small photo print of two shrunken corpses. "They were sucked dry of their magick. We believe this was a first attempt at gaining power from Elementals."

Blood drained from his face. "Where the hell did you get these?"

"The anonymous tipster sent them, along with the location of Billy Rogers."

A muscle ticked in his hard jaw. "Even if this is true, there's no way Arcanes would get close enough to kill us all."

"Not unless they assumed the identity of someone who's trusted, say the son of a U.S. senator who also sits on the Council of Mages."

Sam drew in a sharp breath. "You think that's why they kidnapped Billy. By killing him and assuming his Phantom powers, an Arcane could duplicate him and move freely about."

"Yes. The Arcane can even duplicate his aura. There is no way to tell them apart. These rogue Arcanes are targeting children to imitate them and assume their places. Then they'd kill their parents and from there…"

Kelly set down the beer. "We believe they're smuggling the kids out of the country. Billy told me he remembers his nanny coming into his room. Then he was drugged. Later, when he woke up, the nanny shifted into a man he didn't recognize."

"The kidnapper's real form," he mused.

"We suspect both Arcanes killed the Phantom women, stole their powers and then used the magick to shape-shift into other forms, one being Billy's nanny. The real nanny is probably dead."

"And the Arcane imitating the nanny was the one we took

out on the island. Which means the other who stole the Phantom's powers may still be out there," he mused.

Picking up the sharp knife, Sam began to twirl it like a baton. Kelly watched this new skill with wary eyes. Seeing her expression, he set it down.

"If Arcanes are planning a mass extermination, why didn't you alert the council?"

"And give them an excuse to round up my people like cattle?" Sam never knew the humiliation of having to show an ID card simply to enter a Mage store to buy healing herbs. Or being physically searched by Mage authorities, laughing as they shoved their hands between the legs of her jeans.

"We can't trust them."

Sam narrowed his eyes. "You're hiding something, Kel."

He knew her too well. Kelly hesitated. "It's more complicated than a single kidnapping. The rogue Arcanes have a base in Honduras and someone is leading them. A staff member in my nonprofit's Honduran office found nine Elemental children hidden in Tegus. Shortly after, he was shot and left for dead. Fernando thinks the children were being held until the leader of the rogue Arcanes arrives. And then they will be killed, their powers drained and their magick used to imitate your people."

She paused. "The email said they plan to create a Dark Lord to lead them in exterminating all Elementals. You've got to stop them." She could see the doubt tightening his face. She had to convince him to help her.

"You have to stop this before it turns into war between our people, Sam. You're the only Elemental I can trust. I know how much you care about children."

His steady gaze met hers. So calm and capable, but she saw despair in his eyes. Bad of her to play the child card, reminding him of his beloved little brother, but she was desperate.

"Please believe me," she whispered. "Not for me, Sam, but for those innocent kids. Please help me save them."

Coiled with tension, he stared at the wall. She saw the hardened warrior unleashed, the Mage who would override everything to keep innocents safe.

"I believe you're telling the truth, as far as you know it."

It wasn't enough. If she couldn't convince Sam, how could she convince anyone else?

Trembling, she sagged onto the bar stool. So fatigued, she felt the floodgates open, her tightly held emotions finally cresting in a huge wave.

Kelly buried her head in her hands to hide their shaking. But it got worse as she rocked back and forth on the stool.

"Easy now, Kel." Two hands on her shoulders, holding her steady. He'd always held her steady when she needed him.

"I can't stop…"

She began to hyperventilate. Sam tipped her head up, locking his gaze to hers.

"Look at me. Look. Easy now. Breathe slowly, long, deep. That's it," he encouraged. "Inhale…exhale. Follow the sound of my breaths."

She did as he commanded, matching her breathing to his calm, even inhalations and exhalations. They breathed together as one—just as they had after making love. It was naive and sweetly romantic…

After a minute, the shaking ceased. She flexed her fingers, embarrassed at the loss of composure.

"Sorry," she muttered.

A real smile touched his mouth. He thumbed her chin. "A little shakiness is nothing to be ashamed of."

The slow stroke of his thumb brought a different weakness. Tendrils of desire shot through her blood.

As his gaze zeroed in on her mouth, her lips instinctively parted. A seductive glint danced in his eyes. Those beautiful, sleepy hazel eyes could coax her into anything. He could lure her into his bedroom with a mere glance.

A slow exhale of breath as he stared at her mouth. The

want intensified into aching need. Kelly moistened her mouth, aware of his smoldering hunger. She leaned forward, her mind clouded with erotic promise.

Lifting her chin, she parted her lips as he lowered his head toward her.

She wanted his touch badly, wanted his strong arms encircling her in a comforting embrace that promised all would be well.

"I want to kiss you again, just like before, when we made love until we were both sweaty and exhausted and spent, and then did it all over again," he said hoarsely.

Her gaze lifted to the silky strands of his hair she'd loved to run her fingers through. Sam stroked a single finger down her right cheek. Holding her hands out like a shield, Kelly stepped back. This hurt so much. "I can't, Sam. Please." Her voice cracked. "Don't do this. We have too much between us. Let me have the memories of how it was. They're all I have left of us."

The moment shattered. This man had the power to hurt her badly. She had none. And eventually he would hurt her, because they no longer were on the same side.

His broad shoulders stiffened as he turned away. "What the hell do you want from me, Kelly?"

"Take your teammates and find the missing children before the Arcanes kill them. Stop the slaughter before it starts. Not for me, but for the innocents who will get hurt if this goes down."

"I'll notify my superior. Curt's cool. He's Mage and I trust him."

Not good enough. "I trust you, Sam. Not some military commander who's bound by regulations. You have influence."

"My life's with the team now. It's not just me, Kelly. It's all of my team. I have to follow orders." Cool, clipped words from a man who'd turned from fire into ice.

"You never did before. You were a maverick," she whispered. "What happened?"

White bracketed the lines of his full mouth. "Your father."

Silence draped between them. Kelly's chest felt tight. "I can't undo what happened, Sam. I wish I could. All I can do is go forward and try to eliminate future threats."

Sam turned toward the window. "You have proof? The email?"

"It's back at my office. All I have is my word. And what I know." She touched her cheek, still warm from his touch.

"I'll do what I can."

The military had entrenched Sam in order and discipline. A knife twisted inside her heart. Her former lover was distant and aloof, as if they'd never known each other.

"Thank you," she said quietly. "It's a risk for you, and I appreciate it."

Sam stared out the kitchen window. "If this is running as deep as you say, you're walking into a minefield. They labeled you a child snatcher and broadcast your photo. Perfect fodder to draw away attention from the real threat. It's standard battle strategy. Your enemy finds a weak spot and strikes."

A terrible suspicion surfaced. "Can I use your computer?"

The paneled, elegant study featured an array of complicated electronic equipment. After Sam powered up the PC, Kelly pulled up the Facebook page for Sight Finders. Her throat went dry as sand. Sam bent over to see the screen and muttered a curse.

"They didn't waste time."

Postings on the wall included hateful messages claiming Kelly's nonprofit was a front for child smuggling. She turned away, sucked in a trembling breath and fumbled for her cell.

Carl, her director, was brief. "Jesus, Kelly, they've launched a war against us. The whole damn government is seizing our files, taking our hard drives, saying we're child traffickers."

He lowered his voice. "They took your laptop. They claim

our office in Honduras is a front for smuggling children and selling them."

Her mouth dry, she managed to ask, "Did you get an IP address on the anonymous email?"

"Some internet café in D.C. I locked away the hard copy of the email. But what does it matter? No one will believe us."

Heart pounding, she spat out the emergency phrase. "The wolf's in the barn."

Carl would alert the others, and they'd go deep underground.

She thumbed off the phone and looked at Sam. "Got a disposal in that nice kitchen of yours? I have to get rid of this phone before they use it to track me down."

Sam took the cell, flipped it into the fireplace and flung out his hands. A burst of white energy shattered the phone and ignited the logs.

She gave a shaky grin. "A fire. Very cozy and romantic. Wish I could stay, but I'm afraid if they find me here, it'll ruin the mood."

Sam followed her into the kitchen as she grabbed her pack. "I'm the target of a witch hunt."

"No, you're the target of a Mage hunt." He rubbed a hand over his chin, lines of tension bracketing his mouth. "Look, Kel, lie low. Stay out of sight."

"I promised my team I'd get those kids out of Honduras. I won't break a promise."

Sam touched her cheek. "I don't break promises, either. And I made one to you, long ago. I'll do whatever I can to keep you safe, Kelly Denning. You know what they'll do to you."

His jaw tensed to granite.

She knew what he meant. The gray, lonely asylum where many Arcanes had been confined…those thought to be seditious and deemed a danger to Mage society. Locked away behind bars…

Never. I'll die first.

"Your team can save them, Sam. Talk to your commander, have him send a team of SEALs to rescue the children."

His expression shuttered. "He'd have to go through proper channels and first determine Elemental children are missing."

Red tape, delays. "It would take too long."

"There are rules. We have to work within the system." Sam lightly gripped her shoulders. "I'm more concerned about you."

She was alone. Kelly's throat tightened.

"I don't need you to take care of me. I need you to convince your superiors of the truth."

Someone banged hard on the front door. Kelly jumped. Blue and red lights flashed outside, stroking over the bushes and the house next door. He muttered a curse.

"I knew Tom wouldn't let this go."

Another hard pounding. "Chief Shaymore, open up," a deep voice called out. "I'm with the security division of the Council of Mages. We need to question you about Kelly Denning."

Sam snagged a set of keys from a peg in the kitchen. "I'll hold them off. Take the trail in the woods out back. It leads to a side road. We have a car stashed for emergencies. Get on the interstate and don't stop. Stay at a friend's house and stay low until the political burn wears off."

She took the keys, her fingers brushing his. "Thanks, Sam. But you know I can't stay low. If you won't help me, I'll go it alone to Honduras. If there's a chance they're still alive, I'll take it."

He turned away, his broad shoulders a brick wall. "Don't leave the country, Kelly. Because if they send me after you, I will be forced to do what I must."

A man filled with resolve, his deep voice stating every word with hard conviction. Kelly drew in a breath.

"Stay safe, Sam." The knife in her heart twisted hard. "Don't come after me unless you plan to help. Because I will be forced to do what I must."

As he went to the front door, she slipped out the back, heading into the cover of night. Putting distance between the man she'd once loved fiercely, and feeling the aching regret that they'd lost something precious and wonderful. She wouldn't make that mistake twice.

Never again.

Chapter 5

Leaving the country when you were a suspected kidnapper was easy enough, if you were a Mage who could shape-shift.

Homeland Security took a look at her fake passport, glanced at the gray-haired woman with the sour face, and nodded her through. No Mages stalked her. The flight was uneventful, aside from the landing. Years of travel to Honduras had conditioned her to the wild corkscrew landings the skilled pilots executed to avoid the rugged mountains ringing Tegucigalpa.

After getting her luggage from the crowded carousel, she headed for the restroom and used magick to change back her appearance.

Kelly inserted the international SIM card she'd bought into her cell phone and made a call to the Council of Mages. A bored man answered.

"This is Kelly Denning. I'm in Honduras. Tell those stuffed shirts if they want me, they'll have to get off their fat butts and find me."

Envisioning his stunned look, she laughed and thumbed off the connection.

When Sam's team arrived, she'd convince them to find the missing children. The SEALs stood as the only neutral force able to stop a full-scale war between Elementals and Arcanes.

Risking her life was worth it to save those of her people, and Sam's.

Weighing the cell in her palm, she considered the gamble. What if they simply chose to haul her back to the States? Brought her into Mage custody, where she'd suffer an "accident?" *Oops, didn't mean to discharge enough power to fry a city block.*

Sam wouldn't allow it. Another gamble.

Nausea boiled in her throat. Once he'd been insouciant and spontaneous. Now he'd turned into a man she no longer recognized.

A blast of humid air encased her as she went outside. The warm breeze ruffled her turquoise silk shirt and teased tendrils of hair escaping her ponytail. Kelly flagged down a cab and gave precise directions in Spanish.

The black-haired driver looked at her. "*Señorita?* You sure you want that house, that neighborhood?"

"Positive."

As he pulled into traffic, he glanced in the mirror, his dark gaze somber. "It is dangerous there. Even for one filled with magick."

Kelly went still. The driver pulled down his shirt collar. His skin had been branded with a dark red circle with a slash through it.

The mark of an Arcane branded for subversion.

"You're one of us," the driver whispered. "I sensed it when you asked to visit that neighborhood. Many Arcanes live there."

Not letting down her guard, she shrugged. "I know someone there. A friend."

"You are one of us."

At a red light, he turned. "You need not be afraid. Are you here to find refuge? Many of our people have moved here to hide."

"I'm here to visit a friend," she repeated.

The man's mouth flattened. "Elementals have pushed our people into dark and dangerous corners. No place is safe from their influence. One day we will be free from their kind, and they will know the same suffering they forced upon us."

Seditious talk, the type that landed Arcanes in prison. She hesitated.

"It's misguided to judge an entire race by the actions of a few and ignore the ones who are kind, good and courageous."

The driver snorted. "All Elementals are bloodsucking scum who think themselves superior. They demean us because we have no power. But they are fools, for some of us are more powerful than they realize."

True. Kelly fingered the triskele, feeling the metal warm beneath her touch.

Buildings passed by in a blur as her heart pounded hard against her chest. Headed into heartache again. She knew what she'd find. Rubbing a spot on the window, she stared outside, seeing nothing.

The taxi jerked to a halt midway down a steep hill. Kelly started. Gray water gushed down a gutter before an aging brick building.

"I can wait for you," the cabbie said.

"No need." She wanted out of the cab quickly. Something about the driver raised her suspicions.

When she stepped out, rucksack slung over one shoulder, he drove off slowly. Kelly shivered in the light rain.

The hallway was long, dark and eerie. Water dripped from a leaky roof. Once the hall had been white, but now paint flaked off like confetti. A woman opened her door, peered out and slammed it shut. Kelly shouldered her pack and stepped into a square courtyard. On each side were two doors leading to apartments. Rain fell steadily onto the stained concrete courtyard. Sagging plants in cracked flowerpots were scattered about the ground in an attempt to provide color. Clothing hung on a wire strung between the two buildings, someone's laundry forgotten in the rainstorm.

She went to the turquoise door on the left and knocked softly. Two solid raps, then a succession of three.

Hilda opened the door.

Kelly gave the small, dark-haired woman a tight hug. "How is he?"

Moisture gathered in the woman's brown eyes. "Holding his own," she whispered in English. "But you know what will happen…"

The home was small, with peeling yellow paint. Rain dripped in a steady patter on the tin roof and into a pot near the door as Kelly stepped inside. On a double bed crammed against one faded wall was a man hooked up to a catheter. He was thin and pale, his eyes closed as he rested on a worn pillow.

She could not heal him. No one could. The knife in her heart twisted with a vicious yank.

But when Kelly approached the bed, the man opened his eyes. Life flared there, bright and angry and resilient.

"Fernando," she said softly, setting down her pack and sitting on the chair by the bedside. She gently took his hand. So thin, the knuckles cracked, the once-strong fingers now weakened from disuse.

"You came back. I knew you would. Everyone else has forgotten us."

"Not forgotten. They're in hiding. I broke free of the watchdogs." She gave a little smile, her heart breaking at his pale face, the wasted limbs. "You and Hilda must move to a safer house, a better house."

Hilda shook her head. "We cannot risk moving him. And this is our home. Fernando wants to stay here, he wants to..."

Bleak resignation on her face told her the rest.

"Enough talk of me." The man tapped the piece of paper he held in his lap. "Memorize the map. The village is in the south. They mobilized and moved the children and have taken over. My contact said the rogue Arcanes are waiting to siphon the children's powers."

"Waiting for their leader to arrive?"

"Yes, but something else, as well. They are planning something bigger, Kelly. Something far more sinister."

She didn't want to imagine the possibilities. "Where is your contact now? Can I meet with him?"

Shaking his head, he pointed to a newspaper on the bed. The headline blared news about a body found by locals near the capital. Drugs were suspected.

"They got to Carlos, too," he said.

Fernando shifted his legs on the quilt and winced.

Eight bullets. He'd been taken down by eight bullets, pumped into him by gang members in a "war act." But it wasn't a turf war or drugs. The gang had operated under dark enchantment. Fernando had been shot deliberately after he'd located the children. He belonged to her team of Arcane Enchanter Mages operating out of Honduras.

Kelly squeezed his hand, took the map and committed it to memory. Using the matches Hilda provided, she burned it on the rusty stove that no longer worked. "Go, rescue the children, Kelly. I do not know how much time they have left," Fernando said, and his voice was strong.

Tears gathered in Hilda's eyes. "You're the only one left who can save them, Kelly." Hilda glanced at the silver triskele. "You have powers we lack. Make right this wrong before the Elementals judge all Arcanes as guilty and kill us."

Hatred punctuated those words. Kelly placed a gentle hand

on her friend's arm. "There are good Elementals. Not all are so unreasonable."

The dripping rain slowed and stopped. But a steady tapping came upon the battered roof. Fear flickered across Hilda's face. She and Fernando glanced upward.

The sound of claws skittering across a metal roof, accompanied by a distinct, foul smell. Only one creature could emit such a nauseous stench....

Kelly's heart dropped to her stomach. She pointed at the ceiling. "Ilthus," she whispered.

Blood drained from Hilda's face.

Fingers tight around the triskele pendant, she headed for the door. Hilda grabbed her arm.

"Don't go out there. It will kill you," the terrified woman whispered.

"I can't let it get to Fernando."

The warped turquoise door creaked as she opened it. Rain dripped on the cracked concrete courtyard, where the soaked wash hung limply on the frayed clothesline. Kelly sang out a chant to gather her powers as she stepped outside.

A foul stench tainted the air, the smell of sulfur and decay. Gagging, she inched backward, trying to peer onto the roof. The skittering sound stopped.

Power hummed beneath her trembling hands. Ilthuses were clever and quick, and they could move...

A harsh screech split the air. As she looked up, a red-and-blue-speckled thing launched itself off the roof.

Scrambling backward, she avoided the daggered claws swiping at her face. Instead, the creature shredded a ragged shirt on the clothesline. The ilthus shrieked again and skittered on all fours. Saliva dripped from its black slit of a mouth.

It came closer, hissing, its lizardlike pupils contracting as it fixed a stare at Kelly, seeing prey, seeing its target up close. A forked tongue shot out of its mouth.

The ilthus opened its mouth and hissed. A steady stream

of gray mist sprayed out of its mouth, the rotten-egg stench making Kelly's eyes tear, her vision blur.

Backing up, she hit a wall. No place to run. *Dear gods, I'm going to die from the smell.* She blinked hard and focused.

The door banged open. Hilda came outside, armed with an iron skillet. The brave, crazy woman!

"Take this, you stinking son of a bitch," Hilda screamed in Spanish as she threw the skillet.

It missed the ilthus, but the distraction was enough. The creature stopped spraying.

"Get back," Kelly yelled at Hilda.

Kelly breathed through her mouth and flung out her power at the creature, and then she dived behind a rusty washing machine.

With a loud shriek, the ilthus exploded, spraying green slime over the walls and the wet laundry.

Hands shaking, Kelly struggled to her feet. She stared at the mess. Hilda stepped into the courtyard, holding her nose.

Rain began falling again. Kelly gave a wry grin.

"Sorry about the laundry and the smell," she said.

Hilda hugged her tight. "You saved us."

"No." She pushed at her long, tangled hair. "I brought it to you. It must have followed me from the airport." She could expect more scouts like this. The rogue Arcanes didn't want interference before they could hide the children in a safe place.

"But who knew you were coming, or where you went?" Hilda looked confused.

Kelly thought of the angry cabdriver. "The taxi driver who drove me here. He's Arcane. Must have been alerted I'd left the country and waited for me at the airport."

"You're fortunate he did not harm you in the cab."

"Maybe he was instructed to notice where I went. They probably want to see how much I know and where I go." Kelly squeezed her friend's hands. "Take Fernando, go visit your sister. Please. For your own safety. He'll be more comfortable there."

The rogue Arcanes were watching her, probably to see if she dared to track down the children. She needed Sam and his team of SEALs. But if they weren't coming, she had to do this on her own. Kelly's stomach churned. She wasn't a courageous navy SEAL, trained to combat evil.

But neither was she a coward.

Chapter 6

In ST 21's ready room, Shay looked at his CO with pure dismay.

Kelly had fled and the Council of Mages gave an official order. They were going down range into Honduras. Hellfire, he could face a squad of vampires armed with RPGs easier than this assignment.

The briefing book lay open before him on the table. In the room, Dakota, Renegade and Sully studied their copies. Using a red laser pen, Curt pointed to a map on the screen in front of the room.

"More than eighty percent of the coke entering the U.S. is shipped through Honduras. Drugs are flown into the Miskito Coast from South America and then transported to the States.

"This is an extremely covert op. Several months ago, U.S. forces joined with the Hondurans and used military outposts, established by the Hondurans, to conduct counterinsurgency against the cartels. The FOL had the Honduran Air Force rapidly deploying to intercept aircraft and boats smuggling narcotics. Brass pulled the plug after bad PR regarding a shooting incident. Now brass wants us to train the Honduran security forces on counterinsurgency and CQC techniques."

FOL, forward operating location. CQC, close quarters combat.

SOL, no explanation needed. That was Kelly's fate, and he was powerless to change it. He'd told Curt what Kelly suspected, but his CO needed proof.

Kelly had none.

Shay squeezed his briefing book, magick boiling in his blood. Sparks of white light began dancing on the table's surface. Sully glanced over and motioned to tone it down.

Deep breaths. He forced his magick to calm. If Curt suspected he couldn't control his powers, he'd order him off this op. And he needed to be there, to ensure nothing happened to Kelly.

"Your mission is nonintervention. Restricted to training the Honduran security forces in counterinsurgency and CQC."

Their CO paused, his gaze steady and unblinking. "That's your official mission. Your paranormal code mission is Operation Flight Bird. Find and capture Kelly Denning to face arrest by the Council of Mages on the charge of kidnapping Billy Rogers. The council is sending a special detachment to escort her back."

So it had come to this. Shay cursed his uncle's sabbatical on a remote island. With Al's lone voice of reason gone, the council moved against Kelly. "So she doesn't get a chance to defend herself?"

"The council will provide an attorney," Curt said.

Shay snorted. "Right. One working for the lynch mob."

Beside him, Renegade shook his head. "The woman's guilty as hell, Shay. You can't see it because you were involved with her."

Flipping him the finger, Shay shook his head. "Everyone is innocent until convicted."

He looked at his CO.

"You know what those bastards in the council will do to her, Curt."

Sympathy flared in the older Mage's gray gaze. "I know, Shay. We're caught in a web of dirty Mage politics, and Senator Rogers is jerking our strings. But she will receive a fair trial, even if I have to fight tooth and nail for her. You have to trust the process."

Trust the process. Right.

"Those are your orders."

He was a soldier in the U.S. Navy. Order and discipline. Even if he didn't like the orders, Shay had to follow them.

Even if the thought of taking his former lover prisoner splintered that rock he once called his heart.

Hours later, they landed at the Palmerola Air Base, where the United States had a long-standing presence. They were joined by Greg Andrews, the new SEAL on Team 21's Phoenix Force. Andrews was a last-minute addition to the op, direct orders from the admiral himself.

Shay knew the guys slightly resented the FNG, the effing new guy, mainly because he took Adam's place. Adam was a jag shifter, killed in Afghanistan when he and Dakota were ambushed by demons.

Shorter in stature, with mild brown eyes and a lean build, Greg studied the old, weathered "hootches" serving as their quarters.

"No running water inside," Greg mused. "Latrines and showers are over there."

Sully took a look at the worn-wood buildings and shrugged. "Beats sleeping in the jungle."

"To each their own, wolf." Greg was a tiger shifter.

They stashed their gear. They had barely finished when Dakota's cell rang and he stepped outside to take the call. Their lieutenant returned to the barracks, his face grim. Shay stopped cleaning his sidearm. He knew that look, disbelief and frustration.

Meaning, some hotshot brass had screwed up the mission.

Dakota ran a hand through his hair.

"Orders have changed. The tracking chip indicates our target is in San Lorenzo, way south of here. We're to capture the target and notify Curt as soon as she's in custody. Then take her to an LZ near San Lorenzo to await a helo, where we'll hand over the prisoner to the Mage council representative. We're traveling as civilians. No weapons. Curt says we'll spook the local police."

Gooseflesh broke out on Shay's arms. "Not even a sidearm?"

"Curt said those are our orders, direct from the admiral." Dakota's voice was tight.

His Mage senses were all but roaring. "What's the deal? He'd never send us out without weapons."

"Damn, I don't like it," Sully muttered.

"Any ideas, Shay?" Dakota gave him an even look.

Shay gazed around the stark barracks. Sweat trickled down his back into the waistband of his cammies. He always followed orders, but hellfire, this order sounded like trouble. He was the team's weapon's expert. "Time to call in some favors." He removed his cell, palming it. "Give me a couple of hours."

It took less than that. The former politician in the Honduran Congress he'd done a security detail for two years ago was happy to help. An hour later, Shay returned to base in a dark blue Range Rover. The other SEALs gathered around the vehicle as he jumped out.

"Vehicle's bulletproof. We'll travel in these."

He tossed five oversize khaki shirts and several pairs of olive cargo pants to Dakota, along with five leather gun holsters. Sully picked his up and whistled. "Sweet. It'll do."

"More goodies in the trunk. Not much ammo. All I could scrounge up at the last moment."

Dakota nodded. "Good job, Shay."

No satisfaction filled him at the praise. Instead, he felt only a sense of unease. Every instinct screamed caution.

A short time later, they emerged from their barracks in cargo pants, the loose-fitting khaki shirts draped over the waistbands. Tucked inside each man's pants was a leather holster carrying a Sig Sauer 9 mm.

"Not bad," Greg muttered. "We blend with the locals. Too bad we can't carry a rocket launcher in our pants."

"Shay always carries a rocket launcher in his pants," Renegade jested.

As they moved to the vehicle's rear, Shay looked around to ensure they weren't watched. He opened the hatch and lifted the carpeting. In a specially designed wheel well were five HK MP5 submachine guns.

"No extra ammo, but fully loaded."

"I always did like fully loaded vehicles," Sully drawled.

Dakota nodded. "Much better insurance for the road than triple A. I'm not going to ask how you got them. We'll take a minimum of gear, plus com equipment, stash it here."

After doing so, they loaded the vehicle with water, supplies and their packs. Shay pocketed flex cuffs he'd laced with his own magick to restrain Kelly once they caught her.

Sitting shotgun next to Dakota, Shay consulted with the miniature receiver that transmitted a steady beacon from Kelly's security chip.

Renegade leaned between the seats. "What if she removed it?"

"She wouldn't. Kelly knows Rogers would send us here. That's what she wants."

Sully whistled. "Why?"

He studied the flashing pinpoint of light. "She needs our help."

Renegade snorted. "Help her? The woman who kidnapped the senator's only child?"

Kelly had trusted him and spilled all her secrets. But she didn't know what a dangerous game she played. Shay's fingers tightened around the transponder. Curt had assured him that she'd get a fair trial. But even the powerful Mage couldn't prevent Kelly from suffering an accident.

Are you delivering her to her death?

He looked directly at his lieutenant. "She didn't kidnap Billy. Kelly told me rogue Arcanes are holding other Elemental children here in Honduras."

Dakota looked stunned.

"She's here to rescue these missing Phantom children. Kelly says a group of Arcanes plans to kill them, drain their powers and use the magick to imitate Elementals to exterminate my people. And they're going to create another Dark Lord to aid them."

Shay's throat tightened. "Genocide of all Elemental Mages."

Silence, except for the rumble of the engine.

"Christ," Sully muttered. "Shades of Rwanda and Bosnia."

"Sounds far-fetched. You believe it?" Renegade asked.

Shay sighed. "I believe she didn't kidnap Billy and that she believes she is fighting for the right cause."

The other, he needed proof.

He glanced at his lieutenant. "And I believe the council is gunning for her, because of Senator Rogers."

Dakota had a white-knuckle grip on the steering wheel. "They're your people, Shay. You know Mage politics better than we do. But we have our orders."

"Let's go," he said, and gave the coordinates.

Trees and shrubs flanked the road, shadowed by the magnificent vista of jagged mountains. Dakota kept a steady speed, except to slow and jerk the vehicle around potholes the size of moon craters. Small, rough-hewn shacks sold colorful handwoven hammocks strung between trees. Two or three times they had to stop and slow for men driving a herd of cattle on the road, waving a red caution flag for vehicles.

Three hours later, they reached San Lorenzo. A faded statue of the saint guarded the town's entrance. Shay's pulse accelerated as he glanced at the receiver.

"She's here. Take the right fork, then the first right."

They drove past a row of buildings and hit a dirt road. Simple wood-and-adobe houses flanked the road, cordoned off from each other by barbed-wire fences. The burning sun in the crisp blue sky baked the landscape.

After a series of turns, they arrived at a white concrete building bearing a sign that read Health Center in Spanish. A few women, babies in their arms, mingled out front as Dakota parked the Rover.

In the dirt road, Kelly kicked a soccer ball to four young boys. Faded jeans hugged her curves and clung to her heart-shaped ass. The cap-sleeved turquoise shirt accented her high, generous breasts and showed arms that were toned and tanned. A clip held up her long red hair, but several tendrils had escaped and curled in the heat. Shouts sounded as the boys chased the ball. She glanced up and saw their vehicle. No reaction.

"She's expecting us," Sully marveled.

Shay removed the flex ties and climbed out as Dakota waited, engine humming. The thick, humid air wrung sweat from his pores as he faced his former lover.

Soon to be his prisoner.

For a moment, he remained motionless. Skin soft and smooth, she was so pretty, life sparking in her big blue eyes. He loved the way the sun glinted off the copper highlights in her hair as the ponytail tumbled past her slender shoulders. Shay drew in a deep breath as a droplet of sweat rolled down the slope of her smooth throat.

He remembered another time when he'd made her sweat.

Shay steeled himself. *You have a job to do.*

Kelly kicked the ball to the boys. "Sorry, guys, my ride's here. You finish the game," she called in Spanish.

As she grabbed her pack, Shay waited. No emotion showed on her face as she walked toward him.

"Kelly Denning, you're under arrest," he said in English.

"Please, don't do this here," she said in a low voice. "Not in front of them. I don't want a scene."

Shay took her arm, led her down a deserted side street, away from curious bystanders. Dakota followed in the Rover.

Before an abandoned adobe building, he cuffed her wrists.

Her skin was soft and warm beneath his fingers. Shay kept his voice steady.

"Kelly Denning, you are under arrest according to the Law of Mages and hereby remanded to custody."

He ushered her into the vehicle, between himself and Greg in the backseat. Dakota glanced in the mirror.

"I made the call to Curt. Helo will meet us at the LZ in thirty minutes," he said in a tight voice.

Her hands shook, but she scrubbed them against her jeans. "Where…" She cleared her voice. "Where are you taking me?"

As Dakota told her, blood drained from her face. "I can't leave the country."

"You have no choice," Shay said almost gently.

She pulled at her cuffs to no avail. "I won't let you do this."

Shay placed a hand on her arm, feeling delicate bones beneath her soft skin. "We're under orders, Kelly."

"Whose orders? Your commanding officer?"

When he nodded, she looked paler. "He's a Primary Elemental Mage, isn't he?"

"Yes." Shay looked out the window.

"Those orders are bogus."

From the front seat, Renegade snorted. Dakota glanced at Shay in the rearview mirror as they headed south on the highway.

Kelly turned to him, her expression fierce. "Your CO isn't

who you think he is. He's been replaced. The extermination of your people has already begun, Sam."

The others said nothing, but their faces said it all. Kelly was a desperate prisoner who'd do anything to escape.

"You think I'm making this up. But for the sake of your people, and mine, listen to your instincts, Sam. You know this isn't normal."

"We're SEALs and paranorms. Nothing is ever normal," he said drily.

Shay studied the landscape as they turned off the highway. Dusty trees, ragged shrubs and rugged hillsides flanked each side of the Rover. They bounced up and down like bobblehead dolls as the vehicle drove through the rough dirt road.

"LZ is an empty cornfield ahead, three klicks," Dakota mused. "Be there in a few."

Every sense on alert, Shay scanned the area for signs of an approaching helo, or any other military. Nothing, except a small child herding a small group of cows with a long stick.

"Dakota, keep sharp," he muttered.

As they rounded a curve, his senses kicked into turbo. In the middle of the road lay several leafy branches arranged in a pyramid.

"Disabled vehicle ahead. Or maybe the road's bad." Sully shook his head. "Not that this road could get worse."

"That's the marker for the LZ." Dakota stopped and cut the engine.

"It's a trap," Kelly said, sitting forward.

To their right, a swath of rocky land rose to a steep hill covered with trees. A barren cornfield was to their left.

Odd place for a landing. Shay's suspicions grew.

"She's right," he said. "It smells like a setup. Let's gear up."

"Do it," LT murmured.

Sully reached into the wheel well and retrieved the MP5s, handing them out, along with five sets of fingerless gloves. Kelly's eyes widened as each man checked his weapon. Shay knew what she thought. The compact submachine guns meant business.

But then she exhaled, a sound of pure relief. "I knew I got arrested by the right people."

Renegade looked up from slipping his radio into its case. He gave a quick but friendly grin. Another surprise. Shay adjusted his bone phone earpieces and checked his throat mic, hoping the wolf's changed attitude would be the only surprise they faced.

They waited. No sound of an approaching helicopter. The air inside the SUV grew oppressive and hot.

"Helo overdue by fifteen minutes." Sully tapped his watch. "Anyone see her ride?"

"I'm checking it out." Shay readied his weapon.

Leaving the door open, he slid out of the vehicle and scanned the area. Those hills were a perfect place for an ambush.

Shay narrowed his eyes. A flock of blackbirds suddenly scattered from the trees on the ridge. Metal glinted in thick bushes on the ridge.

He hit the ground even as a bullet splintered a nearby rock. "Incoming!"

Gunfire crackled, bullets piercing the dusty ground. One hit the windshield. It cracked but did not shatter. Another hit the back tire. It exploded with a burst of rubber. Shay crawled back to the Rover and used the door as cover as he fired back. The other SEALs did the same, aiming at the ridge.

"Shit," Sully yelled. "We're sitting ducks."

The vehicle was designed to take a hit and then drive off, not endure a hailstorm of ammo. Shay glanced backward and saw Kelly lying on the seat, her gaze wide.

"Keep down," he ordered.

A distant scream as they kept firing at the ridge. No return fire. Movement from the bushes to their right. More movement to the right.

Sully grabbed his binocs and scanned the ridge. "Two active targets, Oscar Mike." He gave the locations.

Dakota nodded. "Greg, stay here with the prisoner. Shay, take the forward location. Sully, Renegade, flank to the right. I'll cover the left."

They moved out as a team, a horseshoe encircling the enemy. Shay fought the urge to protest. Greg, the FNG, was barely a SEAL, and if something happened to Kelly…

Using rocks and trees as cover, he gained the ridge and settled behind a thick tree trunk. Shay clicked his radio twice to signal he was in position.

A branch cracked nearby. His KA-BAR was sheathed at his ankle. If he had to, he'd go hand to hand.

A muzzle flash exploded like sparks. Shay stayed low as bullets sprayed haphazardly. The shooter was a total amateur. Then he heard a low curse, someone trying to jimmy the trigger.

Jammed.

Pointing his weapon, he stepped from behind the tree, knowing they needed the assailant alive for questioning. The air went out of his lungs as he stared at the assailant in shock.

The shooter was a duplicate of himself wearing green cammies and carrying an older-model submachine gun.

Shay kept an instinctive grip on the MP5, training it on his twin. In his hands, his gun always remained steady. Always.

"Who the hell are you?" he said hoarsely.

Nothing but a guarded look.

Fine. Shay fired a spray of bullets at his doppelgänger's feet. The man jumped and yelped. A dark stain spread on his groin, the ammonia smell of urine hitting Shay's nostrils.

"Next time, I aim higher. Who the hell are you?"

The man seemed to struggle with his composure. Then he gave a slow smile, as if the neurons in his brain finally began to fire and connect.

"I am what you were. The charmer. The smooth ladies'

man. The man who let down everyone he loved, everyone who counted on him."

The other gave a cocky grin Shay had seen in the mirror. A dizzying sense of unreality began fogging Shay's mind.

"I am the man who cares only for his own pleasure. The man who let his little brother die. Call me…Mr. Dark Side. I am you, Samuel Jackson Shaymore."

A kaleidoscope of memories swirled. In the other, he saw everything he'd been; the carefree man who'd easily seduced ladies, who used his powers to get what he wanted, the youthful boy-man who thought only of the erotic delights Kelly offered…

The person who failed to see the truth of what Kelly's father was, what Kelly's people were, and adhere to his first duty—protect his family.

The man who'd failed to save his little brother.

Waves of pain shocked him, the memories so thick he wanted to claw them away. Once again he heard the chant that echoed through his mind after he'd fought the flames, desperate to get to Pete, his parents….

You can't save them, you can't save them...

"Such a sweet little brother. He died calling your name," the other murmured.

The other was him, the man who'd failed time and again. The self who was failing now as a SEAL, couldn't control his powers, would soon get kicked off the team…

Then he heard Kelly's voice, clear and strong, override the chiding self-incrimination.

"You're my only hope, Sam. Not because you're a navy SEAL, but because I know the strong, dependable man who wouldn't let a raging fire stop him from storming into a burning house is the only one who can stop them."

Chin up, hands steady as he jerked his gaze forward. To his target. Himself.

Who was now running away, zigging and zagging through the forest. That little interlude gave him time to escape.

"Mr. Dark Side, meet Mr. Bullet." He fired.

A hail of bullets spat out of the MK5, hot shell casings coughing out of the gun. One skimmed his neck, burning him. But it was too late. The doppelgänger vanished into the forest.

Dammit. He broke radio silence. "Alpha One, this is Bravo Two. Over."

Dakota's voice crackled. "Sitrep, Bravo Two. Over."

Recovering his composure, he spoke harshly into his throat mic. "Code red, hostile is paranorm. Doppelgänger."

He paused and added, "Bastard knew my history. Over."

LT's voice crackled in his ear. "Roger that. Smoke-check 'em? Over."

"Negative. Target is Oscar Mike."

He hadn't killed the enemy but had let him escape. Dammit, he was a good operator and no stranger to surprise. He was a SEAL.

The radio crackled. "Charlie Mike. Rendezvous at the SUV. Over," Dakota said.

"Roger that. Bravo Two out."

Dakota gave the green light to tail the SOB's ass. Knew he could find him. Shay squatted down, studied the ground. If he shape-shifted into a wolf, he could more easily track the enemy. Tension knotted his stomach. Already filled with adrenaline, he feared the results of shifting. Uncontrollable. Feral. A beast who would not stop, could not stop.

The stench of urine mingled with the heat, decaying vegetation and the dust. Shay focused on the ground, opening all his senses. Each broken branch and disturbed leaf alerted him to the direction his twin had taken.

The man might look like him, but he sorely lacked the ability to mask his trail. Not a SEAL, that's for damn sure, Shay thought.

He followed the trail as it snaked through the woods downward to a stream. The radio crackled into his ear. "Alpha One, this is Charlie Three. Target acquired, ready for download by Bravo Two," Sully said, giving the coordinates.

Dammit. But the team needed him. Shay gave up the chase, moved down the hill and joined up with Renegade and Dakota. "Find your twin?" Renegade asked.

Shay shook his head. "How many targets?"

"Three, including yours and Sully's. Smoke-checked one." Dakota looked around. "Kelly was right. We were set up."

By their own commanding officer. Shay's stomach roiled. The game had changed, and they needed answers. Now.

Chapter 7

They headed downhill through the trees. In a clearing, Sully trained his submachine gun on a very frightened bald man in military fatigues. Not a duplicate.

The SEAL scowled. "Stupid rock can't even shoot straight. Tried to fry me with magick but missed and hit the tree."

"Where are the others?"

"Dead, except for Shay's doppelgänger," Dakota said. "Is he talking?"

"Only to cry for his mama."

"Question him, Shay," Dakota ordered.

Keeping his gun pointed at the prisoner, Sully and the other SEALs backed off. They knew what he was about to unleash.

Shay closed his eyes and released his magick full bore, for the first time in months. Power rippled along his forearms to his hands. Blazing white with energy, his palms pulsed with magick. Sparks sizzled from his fingertips like Fourth of July fireworks.

If he released too much, he'd trigger an uncontrollable inferno of magick. But this time, he knew he could control it. "Who are you, and who sent you?" Shay asked.

The man's wide blue eyes filled with hatred. He lifted his hands as if to surrender.

"Elemental filth," the prisoner muttered.

Then he began a chant of ancient Celtic words Shay remembered from summer solstice rituals. He glanced upward at the darkening clouds. Virulent hatred etched his face as the man began shouting the chant. Clouds scudding overhead turned black and threatening. Thunder boomed.

Oh, hell, not this. Shay's Mage senses tingled.

"Sully, kneecap," Shay ordered.

The SEAL shot the prisoner. The man screamed and yanked his hand downward. Shay's jaw dropped as a black ribbon of pure energy from an overhead thundercloud slithered downward, directly into the Mage's hand.

He was a SEAL. Nothing ever surprised him. But this…

"Die, you Elemental bastard," the prisoner howled.

The man threw back his palm as if to pitch a baseball. Shay tossed out a portion of his magick. Power exploded through the air, a white ball of energy hurling toward the prisoner. In a brilliant flare of sparks, white energy collided with the black electrical charges the Mage tossed at him. Then the black energy absorbed Shay's pure white magick, converging and forming an orb that pulsed and glowed.

Shit! Arcane magick was weak at best. This was something he'd never encountered.

Shay threw more power, only to watch the newly formed orb consume it. Sparks crackled as the glowing ball drifted toward him. His own damn magick was working against him. If the orb touched him, he was dead.

"Shay, kill the son of a bitch," Dakota ordered.

"You need him alive." He sidestepped, and the orb floated through the air, following him.

"I need you alive more," his lieutenant said.

Two could play this game. Shay gathered more power, flung it outward at the orb. Like a child tapping a floating balloon, his magick pushed the orb toward the Mage. His magick then absorbed the ball, shooting ribbons of powerful energy at the prisoner, who screamed as they touched his skin.

As the Mage reached up to pull more power from the storm, Shay threw all his powers into the orb. It burst apart, covering the Mage with a finely laced net of white-and-dark energy. The net sank into his skin like a knife through butter. The ozone stench of energy twined with the slick, coppery scent of the Mage's blood as Shay's magick ate into his flesh.

The man screamed and thrashed on the ground. Then he turned to Shay, his eyes glazing over.

"You'll die. All of you," the Arcane whispered, blood bubbling from his parted lips. "We won't stop until every drop of Elemental blood soaks into the earth."

Shay squatted down beside him. "Who the hell sent you?"

But the Mage was dead, his open eyes staring sightlessly at the sky.

Shay turned the man's head and saw a familiar red brand with a line slashed through it. He searched the Mage's pockets and withdrew a cheap plastic wallet. Inside was a laminated card. Shay handed it to Dakota.

"Arcane ID card. Andrew Jones, ex-prisoner and Arcane. Jailed for sedition."

The other SEALs stared solemnly at him.

"I thought Arcane Enchanters weren't powerful." Dakota looked stunned.

"They're not. This is something new. He must have absorbed his powers by killing an Elemental." Shay gave his teammates a meaningful look. "It's already begun, just as Kelly said."

Plan A had failed. Plan B wasn't looking hot, either. But they were SEALs and knew how to improvise.

He caught Dakota's worried gaze. "Now you know what

we're up against. Curt gave you the orders to proceed to the LZ."

"Curt would never betray us," Renegade protested.

"It wasn't him," Shay said in a clipped tone.

"I know him, it was his voice." But Dakota gazed around the wooded hillside. "We can't trust anyone now."

"Except ourselves," Sully muttered.

Sunlight dappled the thick trees as they returned to the Rover. When they arrived at the vehicle, Shay saw horror shadowing Kelly's blue eyes. She slid out of the backseat as Greg lowered his weapon.

"I heard screams," she said.

"I did what I had to do," he said shortly, checking his weapon. "You were right. Rogue Arcanes are gathering forces and aim to kill all of my people."

"Your people against mine. Sam, I saw that storm. They're gaining powers your kind can't fight. What if they win?"

Rage boiled through him. "Every last criminal Arcane will die before that happens."

"Including me? You just arrested me. Are you throwing me into that group, Sam?"

Guilt filled him at her woebegone expression, those big blue eyes looking as if he'd do exactly that. Greg patted her shoulder awkwardly. "You're safe with us," the tiger assured her.

Shay reeled in his emotions and the surge of male protectiveness that nudged him to shove aside the tiger. He could take care of his woman....

His woman? Who the hell was he kidding? That was in the past. He had no claim on Kelly Denning.

Kelly held out her wrists, still tied with flex cuffs. "Answer me, Chief Petty Officer Shaymore. I'm Arcane. Are you going to kill me, as well?"

"Gods, you don't think I'd do that." Shay felt ill.

A breeze teased tendrils of her red-gold hair. Her expression was guileless, but her hands shook slightly.

"No. But now you believe the threat is real. And it's not me."

Silence for a moment. The men glanced at each other.

"Are you still taking me in? I get the impression there is no helicopter coming to take me to the airport."

Her voice lowered. "The answer is simple. Help me find the missing children, and you find the nest of Arcanes organizing this. Without those kids, the Arcanes can't fuel their powers to carry out their plan."

Nothing about this mission was simple. It was FUBAR, fucked up beyond all repair, complicated by the woman standing before him. Trusting him to do the right thing, and storm the castle. They knew how to deal. But they'd never faced duplicity from their own commander.

Never been tasked with stopping a genocide.

"What's your plan?" Kelly asked his lieutenant.

"For now, seeing everyone gets hydrated. Miss Denning, you, as well. Shay, see to her."

Shay fetched a bottle of water and brought it over to Kelly.

"You look hot," he said softly. He removed the flex cuffs and handed her the water.

She took a sip and handed it back. He drank deeply. Her gaze traveled over his body, and a flush ignited her cheeks. Sexual awareness hung in the air, current as powerful as the magick he'd tossed at the prisoner. Adrenaline pumped through his body, making him hard as a rock. Or maybe it was the woman standing before him, the faint scent of her floral perfume teasing his senses.

"I'm glad you're okay, Sam. When I saw that storm, I worried."

Kelly smiled, the action chasing away the shadows from her eyes and making her look damn pretty. Sheer longing stabbed him. Made him wish for a brief moment that he could turn back the clock. Go back to those innocent moments when they were lovers and thought nothing of tomorrow.

Until it came crashing down upon them.

His gaze narrowed as he watched the other SEALs grabbing water out of their packs. "I knew it. Bastard's doing it again."

Kelly turned and saw Renegade pull out a bottle from a pack with Shay's name on it. "That's yours!"

"Yup. Bastard lightens his load by taking my water when I'm not looking. Not this time. This time, I packed one bottle and left the case in the trunk. Watch."

The shifter took a long pull and choked. Coughing, he dropped it and wheezed, his face turning red.

"What the hell is in this?" Renegade sputtered.

Shay grabbed the bottle and dumped out the contents. "Jalapeño juice. Stay out of my stuff."

Renegade glared as the others laughed.

"Enough," Dakota ordered, tossing his empty into the trunk. "The mission's been compromised. Our CO is a Primary Elemental Mage. We can't be certain Curt hasn't been killed and his identity taken over by an Arcane."

"What the hell are we going to do, LT?" Sully crushed his empty bottle into pulp and let the fragments drop like snowflakes.

"Follow the orders we were given. We stay here, continue the training mission as planned, but send one of us home. That person will work covertly, off base, gathering intel so I can determine a course of action."

"I'll go," Greg offered.

LT shook his head. "I need a shifter, but not you. Renegade, book the next civilian flight, hook up with Stephen and have him meet you in Virginia. We'll need outside help on this one."

No one said anything, but the looks were enough.

"Right. I'm the FNG, so the rest of you don't trust me."

Greg snorted, shuffling a boot in the dirt, as if his tiger pawed at the ground.

"FNG?" Kelly asked.

"Effing new guy," Sully answered. He shook his head. "Tiger, Stephen's former military and an eight-hundred-year-old vampire. If he doesn't like you, he'll eat you for breakfast and use your bones as a toothpick."

Claws began to emerge from the hand Greg held up. "Not before I turn him into shredded wheat."

"Cut the crap, Tiger. You'll get a chance to prove yourself later," Shay said.

The shifter scowled but sheathed his claws.

"The rest of you, with me back to base." Regret filled Dakota's eyes. "Shay, secure transport for the prisoner to return to the council."

"Kelly," he said suddenly, aware of her sliding away. Shay grabbed her arm and yanked her to him. "Where do you think you're going?"

"You know what will happen. They'll toss me into prison and toss away the key. And the real threat's still out there." She struggled in his grip. "I can rescue the kids on my own."

Dammit.

Holding her arms to her sides, he immobilized her. She kicked and struggled. Magick cuffs wouldn't restrain her, and he couldn't risk her escaping. He knew what he must do.

Chest tight, he released her but laced his fingers through hers. Kelly stared, stricken into silence as Shay grabbed her triskele and summoned his powers. White energy pulsed from his body, into the silver medallion and into a stunned-looking Kelly. Burning pain laced his palm, but he held on.

"Sam, what the hell are you doing?" she cried out.

Lifting his face to the sun, Shay chanted.

"Spirit of Air, Spirit of Fire, Spirit of Water, Spirit of Earth, I call you to send forth your powers and bind my spirit and flesh with this woman. Seal us together so none may part."

As he continued to chant, Shay felt aching regret. The ancient bonding rite was originally intended to seal together lovers in the flesh and spirit. The custom died out when females grew more independent, resenting males who tethered them to their sides.

No one used it anymore. It was thought the words were long forgotten.

Shay had not forgotten. If she'd agreed, he'd intended to bond them together on Christmas Day as proof of his fidelity. Not even his father's cold disdain could break the seal.

Now he uttered the words not to bond in love, but to bind in captivity.

Finally the glow died. He opened his palm and released the now-cold medal. Shay displayed his palm and the brand of the Celtic medallion his magick had burned into his skin.

"We're tied together, Kelly. Only I can break the bond. Your life force now mingles with mine."

Kelly wrenched free and ran. Pity filled him as she made a desperate break for freedom, dust kicking up beneath her heels. She'd hate him for this.

He did not blame her.

"You letting her go?" Dakota asked.

Shay said nothing. Minutes later, she returned. The team watched in silence.

"We're tied together now. Separated by more than a half mile and you're compelled to return to me," he said quietly.

"Sam, please, break this. Don't do this to me."

Her whispered plea tightened the knot in his chest. "I will, when you're returned to the States and in custody. I'll make sure you're taken care of, Kelly."

Backing away, she closed her eyes and chanted. Shay looked skyward. Cold sweat streamed down his spine at the gathering storm clouds. She was summoning the elements, something no Arcane could do without a conduit.

The triskele around her neck pulsed white. His teammates raised their submachine guns, their expressions grim.

"Stop it, Miss Denning," Dakota ordered.

Suddenly a streak of lightning shot down straight into her outstretched palms.

Jesus. Kelly had the same powers the rogue Arcane possessed. White energy glowed from her bunched fists. Stretching out her hands, she looked straight at Dakota.

"Let me go, Sam, or I will hurt him."

Sully, Renegade and Tiger inched closer, training their guns on her. Shay motioned for them to stand down.

"That's it, Kel? You going to fry LT? Sully? All of my team? What about me? Kill me and you'll die, as well."

Her hands shook.

"I don't want to hurt anyone. But you're not giving me a choice."

"Let it go," he said gently. "C'mon, Kel, let it go and we'll talk."

All the while inching closer to her, close enough to touch.

Shay grabbed her. The white energy gathered on her hands flared but did not burn. Concentrating, he inhaled it into his body. The glow faded from her hands.

The other SEALs lowered their weapons. Shay turned over her palms. Not dark energy, like the rogue Arcane. Kelly hadn't turned to evil.

Enraged and relieved, he clasped her slender shoulders. "Where the hell did you learn to do that?"

Wide blue eyes met his. "You taught me long ago, that night in the meadow. The ancient spell to call forth the elements."

Shit. He groaned.

A harsh sputter of laughter from Sully. Shay turned. "Shut up. LT, give us a moment."

As the others drifted away, he squeezed her shoulders, feeling delicate bones and soft flesh. Impulsive as ever, she disregarded the rules and stormed ahead, regardless of the consequences.

"Are you crazy? My guys would have killed you. You like risking your life?"

"If this turns into war, my life is over anyway," she whispered.

He looked at her, feeling something implode inside his chest, bright and hot and pressured. Kelly didn't know anything about war and death. She didn't know about suicide bombers and how a dirty bomb could shred your insides like glass. He'd seen men fall beneath the onslaught of enemy bullets. Heard the grinding trill of machine guns. Those times, a man had to turn cold and emotionless, because when all hell broke loose around you, all you had was your damn brains and your training to survive.

He never wanted her to see the brutal ugliness he'd witnessed. His stomach twisted at the thought.

Dropping his hands, he cursed softly. "I promised I would not let anything happen to you. Let me take care of this."

"I'm no princess, Sam. I can take care of myself."

"You don't know what you're tangling with. We train constantly. And we don't storm into a sitch without knowing what could lie ahead. We're briefed as a team, function as a team. Tell me where the children are, and I'll find them."

"Not without me."

"Blackmail doesn't suit you," he grated out.

"Neither does a cold Elemental prison cell. I've already been in one, when they arrested me after the fire, and I'm not going there again. Join me, Sam, and help me find them. Forget your team. I need you more than they do."

Challenge flared in her gaze. *Take sides,* she urged, the wordless plea flaring there as if shouted.

Shay knew what would happen. If he took her side, all his hard-won control would vanish. All these years of being a

SEAL would wink out with a flutter of big blue eyes pleading with him.

Join with me.

He risked losing everything. Because he knew he could get lost in those baby blues…swim in their sensual depths, awash in a sea of sexual need and the communion of two people who once knew each other's secret hopes and dreams.

Hopes and dreams were for romantic fools. He was a navy SEAL and valued duty and honor.

He'd already taken a side, and not even Kelly Denning would sway him from his commitment.

Until she spoke in a pleading whisper.

"Give me a few days, Sam. I know where they are. How many Elemental children must die before all this is over? How many must be sacrificed because of your obeying orders?"

Oh, hell, not fair. But resolve crumbled. He glanced at the road.

Renegade cupped his hands to his mouth and called out. "Yo, Shay. Stop trying to make time with the pretty lightning lady."

"Shay, what's the 411?" Dakota asked as they returned.

He looked his friend, and commanding officer, straight in the eye. "I'm not taking her back. Not right away."

Gratitude shone in Kelly's eyes. The other SEALs muttered.

"You defying an order?" Dakota asked.

"Amending it." He dragged in a breath. Rules and orders had kept him in line for years, even though he'd pushed the boundaries several times. Now he was going to bulldoze them.

"I'm going with Kelly to find the children."

But Dakota shook his head. "If Miss Denning isn't returned to the Council of Mages, everything is shot to hell. They'll know something's up. We can't risk it."

"Buy me some time. Radio in that the LZ was compromised

and we still don't have the prisoner—I don't care. You're creative, you make the excuse. Those kids deserve the chance."

He saw the struggle on Dakota's face. No man ever got left behind. And Kelly Denning was still a prisoner wanted by the council.

"Tell me where they are," Dakota told Kelly. "Shay and I will conduct the search."

"Right. While your men return me to Mage custody. No dice. Either I go or no one finds them. If you send me, you're not just saving lives, Lieutenant. You're screwing with these Arcanes' plans. They'll have to find new, equally strong Phantom children to replace the ones we'll free."

If nothing else, her plan bought them much-needed time.

"It might be too late. The kids could be dead," Dakota pointed out.

Shay shook his head. "We have to take the chance."

A heavy sigh from Dakota. "Four days. That's all I'm giving you, Shay. If your ass isn't back on base by then, you force me to report you as UA and you'll be subject to disciplinary action."

His friend looked grim. "There's too much at stake here, and we can't afford a political battle with the council and Senator Rogers. Not when we may be needed to stop an all-out Mage war."

UA, unauthorized absence. A mark on his permanent record. He could even get kicked off the team. A heavy weight compressed his chest.

The team meant everything to him.

But innocents were at stake.

The lieutenant's gaze never wavered from Shay. "And you maintain constant radio contact. If I don't hear from you in four days, we're coming for you."

The significance of that look said, "But I can't help you."

No one could. They were on their own.

* * *

Sam never changed his mind when he presented The Chin. Firm as granite, stubborn in his commitment.

The men formed a semicircle, talking in low voices. All five SEALs carried the biggest, baddest-looking guns she'd ever seen, using them with smooth skill. They carried themselves with confidence, knowing they were the biggest, baddest weapon against anyone crossing them.

As they broke up the group, Sam loaded his pack with water and supplies. A hank of his sandy-brown hair fell across his forehead and he automatically brushed it aside.

Kelly's fingers tingled. The gesture was intimately familiar. Once she'd done the same, running her fingers teasingly through the silk.

Now he'd become a stranger, as intense and deadly as the gun he carried. She'd seen another side of Sam as he'd dropped to one knee, firing with fierce concentration at the shooter on the hill.

He'd help her. That was all that mattered. Kelly wished she'd never dragged Sam into this, risking his career as a SEAL. After all that he'd suffered, she did not want to cause more pain. Sam didn't deserve this. But she had no one else.

"Thank you for believing me," she told him as he handed her a bottle of water.

Green blazed in his hazel eyes, searing her with heat.

Wary, she took a step back, her gaze falling to the heavy pack on his shoulder. Her breath faltered.

"Are you afraid of me?" he asked, his voice husky.

Kelly shook her head. "Wary, perhaps. Cautious. I'd be foolish if I weren't, after what happened."

"I wouldn't hurt you."

"It's not your gun that I'm afraid of," she admitted. "It's being with you, remembering what we once shared."

For a single moment suspended in time, everything between them evaporated. They were once again bonded, this time by mutual agreement for a cause.

"I'm not going against my principles or values, or asking you to surrender yours. All I ask is for you to set aside your past feelings so we can work together."

Sam closed his eyes, long dark lashes feathering against those lean cheeks. When he opened his eyes, his gaze was stark. "That's just it, Kelly. It's tough as hell to set aside my feelings when it comes to you."

Her heart did a crazy flip-flop. He still cared. But his look stated the blunt truth. *I will, because I must.*

Just as she had to do what she must.

Something inside Kelly shattered. Her throat closed. She forced a calm smile, despite the ripping feeling in her chest. "I'll make it easy. I have no more feelings."

Liar.

I want you, Sam. I want the man who made love to me, who laughed and held me tenderly, the man I could trust with my life.

As the others attended to the flat tire, he took his pack, checked it and then removed his shirt.

Her breath caught in her lungs.

An intricate tattoo of ancient Celtic runes swirled from the front of his right shoulder around to his back. Making a circle around him, she studied it. Beneath the blue ink was a large, puckered scar.

She pointed to it.

"Bullet," he murmured.

"Engaging the enemy?"

"Dakota shot me." At her incredulous look, he gave a lopsided grin. "We were in Grenada, tracking down a voodoo priestess who was using the locals in her rather nasty ceremonies. I tangled with her, and she tried sucking out my life force."

He touched another scar on the same shoulder, this one with

teeth marks. "Here. I couldn't think, couldn't breathe, totally immobilized. Dakota saw what was happening, took the shot. Blew her away and blew a hole in my shoulder."

She couldn't fathom the dangerous assignments he undertook, putting his life on the line every time he deployed. Not only facing enemies armed with metal weapons, but some with fangs, claws and dark, evil magick.

"How did she get so close?"

Sam's jaw tightened. "Was taking her into custody, barely got the zip ties on her when she started…coming on to me."

He looked away. "I looked into her eyes for the barest moment and was lost. Next thing I felt was the pain from the bullet Dakota sent sailing into my body. If he hadn't shot me, she would have killed me. And I wouldn't have felt a damn thing except this bone-jarring pleasure."

Horror filled her. She traced the tattoo with her gaze, shuddering at how close he'd come to death.

"Got inked as soon as I healed. The runes are protective, ancient symbols."

"The knots are a reminder of your heritage," she said softly.

His expression hardened as he shrugged into an olive-green T-shirt. "They're a reminder not to lose my head over a woman. Pack up."

That was Sam, navy SEAL. The colorful Hawaiian shirts he'd worn, the crooked smile, all gone. All replaced now with cool, calm efficiency, like that shown by the soldier who had handcuffed her.

Shouldering his pack, he tested the weight. Kelly stuffed water and rations into her pack, knowing that a subtle shift had occurred. He was now in charge. It didn't matter that she knew this area. Sam had taken over, and he led the way.

Kelly released a deep breath. Sam was with her, her brain sang. And even though he wasn't committed to the cause, he was trudging along the dusty road in his heavy boots, committing to the journey.

Whatever they encountered when they reached their destination, they would face together.

Chapter 8

"How are we getting there? The village is south, at least fifteen miles from here. We can take a chicken bus, but the closest stop is a mile away," Kelly told him.

Focusing on cutting a hole in the leather holster, Shay didn't answer. He finished and slid the Sig into the holster. He put on the khaki shirt. Untucked, it would serve as a jacket, hiding the gun.

The others had left after changing the tire on the Rover. Dakota had ordered Shay to sanitize the scene. So he'd burned the bodies with magick, erasing any evidence of a firefight taking place, just in case some happy locals chanced upon the place.

And then he took a powerful magnet he'd tucked into his pack and ran it over Kelly's hip. Senator Rogers had no way of knowing the GPS chip had been designed so the SEALs could easily disable the transceiver if they needed to. Because sometimes the Phoenix Force couldn't risk being found and have norms come after them.

Just like he didn't want anyone else right now coming after Kelly.

"Going to hump it until we can swipe a vehicle. We're too visible for public transport." He shrugged into his pack and glanced at her widened blue gaze. "What?"

"Hump it?"

"Hoof it. Military slang."

"Ah, got it." She removed the hair clip, finger-combed through the strands and secured her long hair. "You've changed."

In some ways. But not others. The old pull of sexual attraction still hung between them, crackling like a live wire. Shay wiped his face with his shirtsleeve. He didn't know if the heat was making him sweat or the woman standing a few feet away.

Probably both.

A hint of shyness lingered in her blue gaze, contrasting with her confident demeanor. She intrigued him, this Kelly who was both courageous and intelligent. No longer the bashful girl whose sweet kisses had inflamed his blood. She'd grown into a striking woman, features and manner stamped with purpose.

He'd thought he could forget her. But this new Kelly fascinated him even more, whetting his sexual appetite in ways he'd never anticipated. The primitive male urge to chase and conquer flared to new life.

She wanted nothing to do with him.

He wanted to do everything to her. With his hands, and his mouth.

Sex was out of bounds. Shay tamped down the stray thought. *Concentrate on the job, and pretend she's a guy.*

Bending over, Kelly rummaged in her pack. The move pulled her jeans tight over her deliciously rounded bottom. A sharp spike of desire hit like an arrow. He'd loved cupping her ass when they'd been together, holding her close as they kissed. Once he'd hoisted her up against the wall of his father's elegant study, holding her beautiful bottom steady as he'd driven into her, Kelly's tiny, excited cries bouncing off the stern portraits of his ancestors.

Shay bit back a hiss. Okay, thinking of her as a guy would not work.

But he was a professional, and this was a mission. He could deal.

Kelly knelt on the ground and spread out the map she'd retrieved. "The village is supposed to be here…." She pointed to a small pen mark closer to the border of Nicaragua and rattled off the latitude and longitude.

Despite circumstances that would rattle the nerves of a strong man, Kelly remained calm and focused. She was single-minded in her determination.

So was he. They had a job to do.

He consulted his GPS. "We're going to follow the river we passed on the way here. There's a footpath along the banks. We'll avoid the main road, head into the woods and go south."

"Can't we just hitch a ride?"

"Locals gossip. Strangers create talk, and we need to lie low, keep the villagers from knowing we're coming."

"Locals are less trouble than what we might face. The more time we spend in the woods, the more likely our trail will get picked up."

He went instantly alert. "By who?"

"By what. An ilthus. One followed me to my employee's house. I killed it, but when there's one…"

"There are others." He thought all they faced was a hard trek to the village in rough and unknown terrain. Now there could be creatures on their tail. What a total GF. "Dammit, Kelly, why didn't you tell me before?"

Kelly flushed at the rough, commanding tone he used when pointing out royal goat flusters to other SEALs. "Excuse me, I guess it slipped my mind when you handcuffed me."

Whoa, okay. Shay dialed it down. Way down. He softened

his voice. "Tell me everything you know about these things. I've never seen one."

"An ilthus is a creature transformed from a normal animal. It's a mutated creature, created by dark magick. It's twisted and malformed by power, its mind melded to do the bidding of the one casting the spell."

"Deal. Give me the 411. Small, or large? Are we talking moose or squirrel?"

"Think squirrel with big teeth and a malformed body. They don't like using domestic animals, because those have a connection to humans. Smaller animals are easier to manipulate, and less obtrusive. Mostly they're sent as scouts to sniff out the trail of a target."

He glanced around the deserted roadway, the high rise of ground and the forest. "So if I see a cute, furry rodent armed with teeth the size of dinner knives and an attitude, I'll know to feed it peanuts and bullets."

The ghost of a smile touched her mouth. "They prefer pistachios."

Shay checked his sidearm and screwed on the silencer. "I should have read my horoscope. 'Be sure to pack enough ammo. You will run into deranged mutant squirrels and lightning bursts from crazy Arcanes with ego complexes. Oh, and be careful crossing the street. Make sure to look both ways for oncoming evil overlords.'"

A laugh that sounded suspiciously close to a sob tore from her throat. "Bullets won't help much. Magick does, but you drain your powers trying to fight them, and before you can recharge, whap! The evil Mage overlord throws you under the bus. Or in this case, down the stairs. Thump, thump."

Insight hit him. "That's how they got you, isn't it?"

"I was on the yacht, trying to free Billy. Nearly made it, but I ran into a little problem. Oops," she whispered.

"When your team raided the island. I wasn't suntanning.

I heal in sunlight and was dumped out there to heal, so they could…"

Bile rose in his throat.

"They could what?"

No answer. Shay clasped her shoulders, forcing her to turn and meet his gaze. "Kel, what did they do to you?"

Shadows haunted her eyes. "They wanted my contacts. I wouldn't tell them. They found them anyway. And they kept…beating me. They'd dump me into the sunlight to heal and then start over."

Rage filled him. His hands shook with the urge to kill the Arcanes all over again. Kelly was innocent. And she'd said nothing about the beatings, the torture. He gently cupped her cheek, feeling soft skin beneath his calloused palm.

"Hell, I had no idea. The triskele didn't protect you?"

"I'd given it to Billy to protect him. I could take what they gave me. Until the last time. Billy gave it back because I guess I looked a little worse for wear."

Kelly had taken the brunt of the beatings. The gorge rose in his throat, along with protective rage. He wanted to hold her close, whisper promises that no one would ever hurt her again.

"I got through it thinking of you. The times before, when we were together. I remembered how much you cared, and then I remembered how much I missed you," she whispered.

Red suffused her face.

"I thought you had no more feelings for me," Shay said quietly.

Kelly struggled to contain the moisture brimming in her eyes. But a tear slipped free and cascaded down her cheek. It dropped onto her shirt, a splash of acid on his heart.

She turned around. Shay gave her shoulders a comforting squeeze. He wanted to enclose her in his arms and promise no one would ever hurt her again.

But he couldn't. Because eventually, he'd have to turn her over to the Mage authorities. And this time, he'd be the one hurting her.

Chapter 9

The harder Kelly tried to fight her emotions, the more tears slid down her cheeks. *Yeah, I have no more feelings for you,* she thought humorlessly. *Every time you touch me, I want to fall into your arms. But you're a damn land mine, Sam. And I've come too far to get blown up.*

Feeling his gentle touch, she stiffened. Tears always got to Sam and brought out his masculine tendencies to comfort and protect. She couldn't risk emotions around him.

You don't want him to see you still care, because it hurts too much.

Searching through her gear for something to wipe her streaming eyes, she kept the backpack as a shield between herself and Sam. And then a clean blue bandanna dangled in her face.

Muttering thanks, Kelly wiped her face and then stuffed the soggy cloth into her backpack.

"Always keep a spare. Never know when Renegade is going

to have one of his weepy moments. The wolf cries at Hallmark commercials and specials on Animal Planet."

He winked.

"Let's go." Enough of the waterworks.

But he caught her wrist. Kelly felt his physical strength, but his touch was absolutely gentle.

"Listen, I won't let anyone get to you, okay? I'll keep you safe."

Long ago, he'd made the same promise and then vanished. It hurt too much to think how shattered he'd left her. "I'm fine, Sam. Those days are behind us. I don't need you. Not as my bodyguard. Just get me to the village, help me bring those kids home and…"

With a hard tug, she freed herself and dusted off her hands. "Your duty is done. What we had between us is long gone. And I never want it back. I'm sticking to my own kind after this."

The tender look vanished. Sam shouldered his pack. He set off at a steady clip, the broad expanse of his back rigid as brick. Hoisting her pack, she followed him as he hugged the road's edge and headed into the woods. Despite his heavy boots, Sam made little noise in the undergrowth. She became painfully aware of each branch crackling beneath her soles, every snapped twig.

Intense heat stripped her energy. Sweat dampened her shirt and molded her jeans to her body. When they reached the wooden bridge spanning the river, he glanced upward at the sun and turned south.

A narrow dirt path flanked the steep riverbank. Her sneakers were worn and slipped in the mud. Kelly brushed away a tendril of hair, hating the silence between them, but knowing it was best.

With every step Sam took, she felt him slip emotionally away from her. The SEAL was fast, moving quickly. He wasn't a Mage, she thought grimly. He was a damn Pegasus, the mythical horse with wings.

"Can we take a small break?" she asked, gasping.

Sam turned into a small clearing in the woods. When they were off the path and out of sight, she sat down and unscrewed her bottle of water. Sam uncapped his, drank deeply and then wiped his mouth. His flat gaze studied her without emotion.

"How long have you done this?" The silence between them was too thick, too tense.

"Long enough. You ready?"

Kelly replaced her water. Sam peered into her pack with a frown. "You only packed two bottles of water."

"I have a small drinking problem. I'm trying to cut back."

"Always pack enough water. You never know how long you'll be on an op. I'll save a bottle for you. I thought you were smarter than that."

Kelly's temper rose. "Excuse me, Petty Officer Shaymore. I didn't take army survival training like you. I got a little side-tracked trying to rescue Mages."

"Navy. I'm navy. And if you're going to use titles, it's chief petty officer. I worked damn hard to study and pass the chief's exam for enlisted men."

Kelly trudged after him on the path as he took off again. "Enlisted? Why? You're college-educated, Sam. You should be an officer."

"I am an officer."

"Noncommissioned."

No reply.

"Maybe being a commissioned officer was too tough? Doesn't seem so. You enjoy being in charge and giving me commands."

The taunt worked. He stopped hard and turned. Kelly took a step backward.

"It's different when you're a SEAL. I signed up to spend time in the field, not behind a desk. Being enlisted meant more time in action, as an operator, not a paper pusher. It meant discipline, training and learning to control my emotions."

He took a deep breath and then blew it out, as if struggling with those emotions. "The navy saved my sorry ass. I was mindless with rage and grief over what your father did to my family. If not for the navy, I'd be dead by now."

Guilt twisted her stomach. Kelly couldn't skirt the issue lying between them like a land mine. "There are no words to say how sorry I am about what happened to your family. But my father didn't do it."

Sam's mouth became a narrow slash. "This is a bad idea. You. Me. Teaming together to find lost children. Let's go back. Dakota and I will find them. Wolf's a damn good tracker. I'll cut a deal with him. He'll keep you safe on the base until we return."

The shock of his words ripped her like a blade. Trying to get rid of her, before they even started. "Your lieutenant doesn't know their names, and they'll be moved before he can even draw close. They need me."

"Let's get this straight. They don't need you. You need them. Saving these children will redeem what your father did."

The words stung, because they rang of a truth she couldn't admit. "I'm doing this because I'm committed to saving all Mage children."

"But saving Elemental children looks good, keeps the record clean."

Her own temper rose. "You make them sound like a commodity, as if I'm using them."

Kelly's hands tightened on her backpack straps when she saw his raised eyebrow. "Dammit, Sam, I don't need to prove anything."

"Then back off and let us handle it. You have enough trouble on your hands. Stop trying to save the world and save yourself. Don't be a martyr."

She drew in a deep breath, counted and released it. "Are you done with the lecture? We're wasting time."

He didn't speak again but set off on the pathway. After one

mile, Sam stopped and crouched down. She squinted and saw a faint indentation in the mud.

"Path's been used recently." Sam stood and scrutinized her appearance.

"You need to blend. You look too American," he muttered. He pointed at her bright blue shirt. "Got less obvious clothing in your pack?"

"All my clothing is Arcane sackcloth. What all martyr fashionistas are wearing," she shot back.

Sam gave her a level look.

"All right. No. Nothing that can pass for local stuff."

He scanned the area. "I'll have to improvise. That path must lead to a house. There'll be something there we can buy. And that hair has to go."

Sam had tied a black bandanna with a skull and crossbones around his head. With his scuffed boots, cargo pants and shirt, he looked like a rugged college student backpacking across Honduras.

Not her. The designer jeans were torn at the knee, and the shirt was smudged with dirt, grime and sweat. She looked like a refugee from a war zone.

"Some covert operator I'd make." Kelly sighed.

His expression softened. "I'll take care of it. I don't see smoke up ahead, so either the homeowners aren't there or they don't have enough food to bother with a cooking fire. I'll do the talking."

A pathway wound up the mountain, giving way to a cornfield where stalks grew waist-high. The rough-hewn mud-and-stick house sat beside the field. Tied between two palm trees was a faded blue-and-yellow hammock where a woman rocked a skinny toddler in her arms. Lines bracketed her weary mouth, but her eyes were kind, her expression curious.

Sam spoke rapid Spanish. Kelly hid her surprise. Even his accent was impeccable, as if he'd lived here many years.

The woman introduced herself as Rosa. She set down the

sleeping toddler in the hammock and motioned for Kelly to follow her inside.

Small but clean, with a simple dirt floor, the house had two rooms, each with a separate entrance. Newspapers were stuffed into several cracks in the adobe. Inside the bedroom, Rosa poured a pitcher of water into a plastic basin and set it on a wood table. She removed a shirt from clothing that was neatly stacked on a blue barrel and handed it to Kelly while Sam hovered outside.

When Kelly expressed her thanks, the woman smiled sadly and left. Sam stepped into the room. As she washed her face, sighing with relief at the cool water, he hunted through his pack and produced a khaki bandanna. "Use this to cover your hair. If it doesn't work, I'll have to cut it."

Regret etched his face as he lifted a strand of her long hair and rubbed it between his fingers. "It brands you, makes you stand out. So soft, smooth, crimson silk."

She took the bandanna. "I'll make it work."

"You always do. You're the queen of improvising."

His intent scrutiny made her flush, the way he looked at her with admiration flaring into frank sexual awareness. Sam was a lethal warrior, leashed strength with a hard edge. The boy she'd adored had turned into a man.

The moment was too intense, too intimate. She remembered another time she'd improvised, when they'd been hot and eager for each other but lacked privacy. The skies had opened up and it poured, but Kelly had tugged him into the woods, sloshing through the wet grass until they reached the forest. Naked in the rain, they'd made love beneath the trees. It had been wild and exhilarating and primitive, his wet skin rubbing against hers, the passion flaring in his eyes as he took her…

Oh, boy. Judging from the heated look on his face, he remembered, as well. Keeping the sensual memories at bay, Kelly dangled the bandanna.

"No pink, not even a hint of mauve? You tough navy SEALs

don't carry a supply of fashionable bandannas? I can't wear this. You never know when *Vogue* will be doing a photo shoot in the forest. I simply need accessories with designer labels."

Kelly redid her hair and tied on the bandanna. She examined the white T-shirt. Ragged and slightly small, but clean. She shrugged off her grimy blouse and folded it, placing it in her pack. Behind her Sam inhaled sharply.

"Lace. You still wear…lace."

She glanced down at her pink silk bra with its scalloped edges of lace. She'd forgotten her famous weakness for pretty lingerie.

He had not.

Sam stepped forward, tracing the outline of the bra's edges with a forefinger. "So delicate," he murmured.

Heat suffused her body as if his touch were a firebrand. Kelly trembled, unable to break the contact, not certain if she wanted to stop him.

He raised his smoldering gaze and focused on her parted lips. This time she did not move away. Kelly moistened her mouth.

With a low sound, he bent his head and kissed her.

His mouth, so firm and yet soft and warm, commanded her with each lazy stroke of his tongue. The Mage knew how to kiss, knew how to take her arousal and hike it up several notches. He kissed her into a drugged oblivion, just like that first time, as if they had all the time in the world. Everything ceased to exist except this man and his mouth working magick on hers.

He tasted like coffee and the promise of sex. He kissed like a man who knew what he wanted and would not stop until he had it. The kiss of a man who intended to tip her back on the bed, spread her legs and love her until the soft rose of sunrise peeked through the windows.

Kelly made a humming noise of pleasure deep in her throat

and slid her hands around the thick muscles of his neck. He muttered something against her mouth and pulled her tight.

She played with the fine strands of his hair, enjoying the silk slipping through her fingers…lost in the sensation of his mouth and his hands on her bottom, drawing her tight against his hips, his erection.

The silk beneath her fingers was much shorter now….

She drew up short and gasped into his mouth. Sam broke off the kiss abruptly. Green flared in his eyes, overriding the brown. Though he was equally affected, his pulse was steady and his breathing unlabored.

Male voices outside. Sam jerked away, alert and aware, his expression hardening. Stunned, she stepped back as he withdrew his gun. She'd known this man for years, had given him her body, had listened to all his hopes and dreams…

Watching him turn from a passionate lover into a dangerous warrior, Kelly realized she didn't know him at all.

She shivered. The focused stranger before her, cupping a pistol in his hands with a warrior's expert stance, was a man she'd never want to call an enemy.

"Stay back," he whispered and crept to the doorway.

Kelly dressed in silence. With the back of one hand, Sam lifted the curtain fluttering in the breeze, his sharp gaze scanning outside. A shaft of sunlight glinted off the pistol's muzzle. Craning her neck, she glimpsed a man outside wearing a stained white cowboy hat and carrying a shotgun.

Sweat streamed down her temples. If she was caught this time, it would be bad, making the beatings on the island feel like kisses.

They'd do far worse to Sam.

Quiet, so quiet, only the distant cackle of birds in the trees, the hum of insects, the murmur of voices and the rapid pounding of her heart.

Sam let the curtain fall as the voices drifted down the pathway.

His expression was grim as he turned. "We're leaving."

"Who were they?"

"Locals. But they're clearly searching for you, and they're armed. They asked Rosa if she'd seen a woman with bright red hair, shiny like metal. Someone is paying a very nice price to find you."

The curtain jerked aside and Rosa poked her head into the room. She spoke a volley of Spanish Kelly could barely understand. But Sam nodded.

As the woman returned to the yard, Sam shouldered his pack.

"Rosa told the men she heard of a woman with such hair who was headed to the main road, looking for a bus back to Tegus."

"She put them off our trail," Kelly said, relieved.

"For a while. And they're only searching for a woman traveling solo. Not a couple." Sam was grim as he checked his weapon.

"Did Rosa ask who wanted to find me?"

Anger glittered in his eyes. "*El Gran Jefe.* A man with dark eyes like the dead, skin stretched over his skull. A powerful man with whispered magick. He's paying enough cash to keep a village fed for five years."

El Gran Jefe. The big boss. Kelly thought of the shimmering Death Mask she'd seen at the bar. Was this Mage here, tracking her down?

"This bastard isn't taking any chances. He probably hired a few ex-army soldiers to find you, in case the ambush failed."

Digging into her pack, Kelly found a fistful of lempira notes. The money would be enough to buy food for a month for the woman and her son.

Sam would balk. If they left money, whoever was searching for them would know foreigners had been here. But she couldn't leave this hungry family without helping them.

Turning back to explain, she caught his startled expression. Wallet in hand, he'd withdrawn several lempira bills.

Sam gave a sheepish grin. They laughed.

The laughter faded, pinching her hard in the chest. How many times in the past had they shared moments like this? When they did things in secret to amend a situation, only to find out the other one had done exactly the same thing?

"Remember when we tied up my dog because he kept following us, and I felt so guilty about it, I returned later to untie him, telling you I'd be right back, and when I got there…"

"He was already gone and the ropes were in my hand. Oops," Kelly finished.

Sam's deep chuckle filled the room. "You were always one step ahead of me, Kel."

Except the night his family died and he was plunged into the abyss.

"What—" She cleared her throat. "Whatever happened to Whiskey Sour?"

Sam tensed. "I gave him to a neighbor who promised to take good care of him. I had to make sure he had a good home. Whiskey was the only member of my family your father didn't kill that night."

Stung, she stared at him. "I told you before, my father couldn't have set that fire. That wasn't him we saw running from the house that night."

"Sure looked a hell of a lot like the man."

"My father never would have hurt your family. He resented working for your father, but he didn't hate him. But your father…" Damn, this hurt, and she knew it would hurt him, as well. Sam had idolized his father. But he had to know.

"Your father hated me. He wanted me off his property. He offered me money to leave."

Incredulity filled his gaze.

"He offered fifty thousand dollars if my father and I moved

away, Sam." Her voice dropped. "And if we didn't take the money, he'd find a way of making us leave."

Sam shook his head. "He'd never do that."

"He made the offer to my father the night before the fire. I overheard them talking. They were both angry."

"You never said anything to the authorities." A line dented between his brows. "Why, Kelly? Because you knew it would implicate your father? It looks like he had a damn good reason for getting rid of my family, before they got rid of you."

Her hands went cold and clammy at the fury flashing in his eyes. "If I'd told them, they'd have used it to lock me up for good. I wanted to tell the truth." Kelly drew in a trembling breath.

"You didn't tell me," he said slowly.

"You'd already been hurt enough."

"No, Kelly. You didn't trust me. After everything we'd shared, you thought I'd turn you in. Because I'm an Elemental, the race your kind has been taught to loathe and fear."

Silence draped between them.

"Blood ties." Sam gave a bitter laugh. "How the hell could I be so damn blind? You chose your people over mine, after I was willing to give up everything for you."

"Don't judge me. You're the one who left."

He went still, watching her with a guarded look.

Her voice dropped to a whisper. "Maybe I didn't tell you right away, but you never gave me the chance to try. You didn't stick around long enough to say goodbye."

His chest heaved, as if he struggled to contain everything inside him. Sam turned. "I couldn't."

No more words. Words got them mired in a past they both wanted to forget. Kelly glanced around for a place to hide money for Rosa.

The bed was a pile of boards covered neatly by a hand-stitched quilt. He stuffed his money beneath the cloth. When she went to do the same, he shook his head.

"Keep it. There's enough to buy food for a month and get herself a little business. If something happens to me, you'll need money to get out of trouble."

Rosa gave a real smile as they left, the lingering sadness gone. Sam's manner was professional, and when he told her about the money, he said it was in exchange for the clothing. Nothing to make her feel humbled. Rosa straightened. In her stance, Kelly saw a pride previously lacking. She went to a woodpile, removed a machete and handed it to Sam.

"Use this as a weapon," Rosa said. Anger filled her brown eyes. "Those men, they are not bad men. They only want to feed their families. But hunting people like animals is not the way. I'd starve before turning over another. My husband would not approve of men hunting others. He survived the war in El Salvador, and he saw what humans can do to each other."

"Where is your husband?" Sam asked gently.

Moisture filled the woman's eyes. "He fell ill from disease. By the time we found enough money to take him to the hospital, the doctors could not save him. I fear sometimes that the same will happen to Miguel. I don't know how I'd survive if I lost my son."

Kelly pressed the woman's hands. They were thin and bony, bearing the scars of a hard life. "When we are safe, we will return and check on you and your little boy."

Rosa hugged her and gave Sam directions. She waved goodbye as they took a barely perceptible pathway behind her home. A shortcut through the forest, Rosa insisted. It would lead to a road seldom used by anyone but villagers on market day.

The thin ribbon of worn grass wended through a thatch of banana trees and scrub. Sam used the machete to hack through the bushes. It was slow, and knowing there were desperate, impoverished men after her made Kelly even more anxious.

She glanced around at the sadly neglected field, the dying

and dead banana trees choked by dust and drought. No wonder men were willing to turn her over for money.

"Money makes life easier. You don't live in fear of being evicted, or making a mistake and losing your job. My father sometimes said…"

She bit her lip. Sam didn't want to hear about his enemy.

"What?" Sam sliced another banana leaf. "Are you telling me now that blackmail wasn't all my father did? Because my father was an Elemental who hated your kind?"

The sarcastic tone stung.

"You don't know, Sam. You're not an Arcane, you've never faced discrimination or lived with the fear of getting kicked out of your home or losing your job. Your family did treat us well enough. But…"

He turned and looked at her. "But what?"

Kelly shook her head. "Doesn't matter."

Sam sighed. "It matters to me. I want to know."

"Leave it. It's in the past."

"I need to understand, Kelly. We're facing issues a hell of a lot larger than the two of us. A war that could wipe out both our people."

He cut a few leaves, and they moved forward again.

"Arcanes have no rights. Your family was kind, but it was still your land, your home." Kelly held down a branch so Sam could cut it. "We had no voice if your father decided to turn against us. I was taught if I didn't obey an Elemental, he could have me tossed into prison. Our lives were always on the edge because of what your father could do to us."

He turned to look at her, his expression fierce. "I'd never have allowed it. If I knew, I'd have fought tooth and nail to keep you there."

Her heart skipped a beat at the determination in his husky voice. She believed him. But now circumstances had pulled them apart for good. Sam was a dedicated soldier, calling the navy and his SEAL teammates family now. He'd managed to move on with his life.

Kelly just wished she could, too. But no matter how hard she'd tried, he still remained in her heart, a small ache in the night.

Chapter 10

Sweet gum, elephant's ear and mango trees peppered the wooded hillside, but the brush slowed them down. Cutting through the overgrown bushes frustrated Shay. He itched to move faster, get to higher ground. Too many threats. Though he spared the amount of cuts he made, he knew they'd left behind a trail obvious as a billboard.

Sam only hoped the peasants trailing them were more desperate than skilled.

"Am I slowing you down?"

He flicked away a mosquito. "We're doing okay."

His first concern was getting Kelly to safety. And that meant risk.

She's survived just fine without you these past years, his inner voice mocked.

Burning curiosity made him ask the question. "What happened after you left the estate?"

He had to know. All those nights roaming the forested mountains out West, his heart shattered, he'd never ceased worrying about her. When the stars came out, he'd lie down in a grassy meadow, hands fisted beneath his head, and gaze skyward. Wondering if Kelly saw the same stars, felt the same desolate loneliness.

Finally, he'd shifted into a wolf, trying to forget his pain. Forget Kelly, the sweetness of her mouth on his, the feeling of absolute peace after they'd made love and lay tangled together like entwined branches.

He'd shifted into a wolf because he'd lost not just his family, but her. And then he'd gone feral. Losing control to the animal side of his wolf finally dulled painful emotions.

Stupid. It hadn't made him forget. Instead, he'd turned into a phantom roving in wolf skin. Not living, just existing.

Kelly ducked beneath a low branch. "I headed south to Florida. Drifted from job to job for a while until I knew what I wanted with my life. I settled in Miami and opened Sight Finders, hired staff and we began rescuing Mages who needed help."

"It takes financing to start a nonprofit. You had the money I gave you to start over again. Did you use it to start the agency?"

"I gave your money to another charity. I had to do it on my own."

Perspiration coated the machete's handle. Sam raised and lowered the honed blade with a vicious downstroke. Had to watch himself, if he didn't want to cut his thigh.

"I gave you the money to take care of yourself, Kelly."

"The money tied me to you, Sam. Things were so completely severed between us that I felt like a hypocrite using it."

Guilt stabbed him. Lowering the machete, he took the silver triskele between his fingers, feeling the humming power in the pendant. "But you kept this. My gift to you."

Her expression blank, she tugged it away and then removed the necklace, pocketing it.

"I kept it as a memory to cherish what we once had. Not as a reminder of what we'd lost. And that we separated for good."

Despite the sweltering heat, she looked pretty and achingly sexy, her red hair hidden by the bandanna, Rosa's shirt plastered to her breasts and flat stomach. Even sexier was her relentless spirit, that damn refusal to give up and the drive to keep going despite the incredible odds.

Sam admired stubborn people who persevered. He had the same ability, and it got him through the intense training all SEALs endured.

But hell, he'd never intended for Kelly to face hardship.

This damn heat, it was sucking out every drop of moisture. Or maybe it was emotion turning his throat dry as desert dust.

"We're together now," he said. "Until I remove the bond, I'm taking care of you."

"It's not necessary," she began.

Shay put a finger to her lips, feeling their warmth and softness. "It is."

Grimly he focused on blazing a trail. *Concentrate on the mission.* Nothing else mattered. *No emotions. Forget what you once shared.*

It worked for a while. Sam used his intense concentration to forge ahead. These woods seemed safe. Dark, but unused.

An odd, foul stench filled the air. Suddenly a hissing sound came from their right. The bushes parted as a creature jumped from a low-lying mango branch and landed on Kelly's head.

Don't scream. Screams would echo through the hills, alert whoever stalked them. Bile rose in her throat as she fought the creature pecking at her head, its claws raking into her skull.

The stench closed around her throat like a fist. Bending over would enable her to see it, but the claws sank deep, making her eyes water from pain.

"Stay absolutely still."

Kelly struggled against the impulse to fling away the creature clawing at her head. Sunlight glinted off the pistol Sam pointed at her head. Her blood pressure plummeted. If he missed…

"Trust me," Sam told her.

Closing her eyes, she did.

Slime splashed over her face and shirt. The creature's claws sunk into her skull. Sam came over, helped her pull it free and flung the remains to the ground. He squatted down and examined it. Once it had been an ordinary black crow, but now what was left of the bird had daggered claws and a nasty hooked beak.

"Ilthus?" he asked, glancing up.

She nodded, studying the gun he held with practiced ease. A tube protruded from the barrel.

"Why the hell did you put away the triskele? It couldn't have hurt you if you wore it around your neck," he scolded.

Kelly flushed and put on the necklace. His gaze softened.

"You're bleeding." He holstered his weapon and fished out first-aid supplies from his pack. Sam steered her over to a swath of sunlight. He wiped her face, removing the creature's slime, and then packed away the stained gauze. Sam gave her an apologetic look as he soaked fresh gauze with antiseptic.

"This'll sting. Sorry. But you can't risk infection."

Kelly winced as he swabbed her wound. "Good point. Always when wounded by something that smells like a sewer, apply disinfectant. A gallon should suffice."

He smiled as he dabbed the lacerations. "The cuts aren't that deep. How long do you need sunlight to heal?"

"Not long. Good thing you've got a steady hand. I must admit it was a little nerve-racking, having you point a loaded gun at my face. Of course it's not as scary as the stench that thing emits when it gets really going. If I had to keep breathing that, I'd have wished for you to shoot me instead."

Pinching her nose with a thumb and forefinger, she made a face.

A quiet, deep laugh from Sam. "Kelly Denning, you're something else."

She touched her head, feeling the wounds starting to knit together beneath the sun's healing rays. "Your gun doesn't make much noise."

"Ah, the suppressor. Sweet little tool. Keeps everything nice and quiet, so no evil overlords can hear."

"And their little smelly minion nasties." She gave a brittle laugh. "No evil overlord would be complete without one or two. I guess we know for sure they've got my trail."

Kelly hesitated. "Maybe you'd be better off heading out without me. They're after me, not you. Break this spell, Sam. Untie us. It could be your only chance of rescuing the children."

He tapped her nose. "Nice try, Denning. I'm not breaking the bond. You and I are stuck together."

"Sure you want to be stuck with me, Sam?" she whispered. "You don't know what lies ahead."

"We never do. All we can do is adapt and survive. We'll get through this. I'll see to it."

Confidence burned through him. For so long, she'd been on her own, shouldering heavy responsibilities. It was incredibly tempting to let him carry the load.

With a sigh, she leaned back and let her weary body absorb strength from the sun. Posture military erect, Sam stood guard, scanning the woods. So strong and assured, a hardened warrior. He hadn't even blinked at the ilthus, just took the shot.

Fear threatened to claw up her spine again. Too much danger in these woods, too many threats lurking behind the dense brush. She began humming a favorite song.

He glanced over one shoulder. "You still like to sing?"

"Chases away the boredom of waiting to heal. I'm not very patient. Can't sit still for very long."

Sam turned and grinned. "You should try recon. Stinking

hot and thirsty, waiting for hours for that scumbag target to move so you can take the building."

"Staying still for hours? You? Mr. 'Let's go, let's do something, move it now'?"

"I can be very patient, especially if the reward is worth it," he said, green dancing in his suddenly hot and hungry gaze, his intent clearly shifting from scumbag targets to something deeper and more sexual.

Flushing, she refused the bait. Legs feeling like jelly, she stood and brushed off her jeans. "We need to get going. I can't guarantee another mutant bird thing won't attack. Or a zombie. Never know when the zombies will surface. Though I think I can fend off a zombie attack. All they care about are brains, and according to Elementals, Arcanes have none."

Sam gave her shoulders a gentle shake. "Chill it, Kel. No more talk of Elementals or Arcanes. It's just us, and we'll get through this."

"I can't bear for anyone else to get hurt because of me," she whispered.

He laid a finger across her lips, his touch gentle. "They won't. I'm a trained navy SEAL, and if this doesn't work—" Sam gestured to the weapon holstered at his side "—then I always have this." He pointed a finger like a gun and aimed at a tree. "Bam. Magick bullet. All zombies are all dispatched, milady."

Warmth filled her as he kissed her hand in a gallant gesture. Kelly managed a small smile. "I've missed you, Sam. I've missed us."

Sam's expression shuttered. "I need to bury this." With the toe of a boot, he poked at the dead ilthus. "I can't risk drawing more attention by frying it with magick."

Hiding her small hurt, she helped him dig. *Bury this.*

When he really wanted to bury old feelings.

After they finished, he gave her a critical look. "That thing found you because it picked up your scent. We need to disguise your smell."

She touched her sticky hair. "I smell more like dead ilthus. Any chance we can find that river again? I heard water up ahead."

They pushed on through the forest until reaching a tributary that fed into the river. Kelly walked along the edge until reaching a deeper pool. Then she dropped her pack on the bank and ducked her head into the water, scrubbing away the slime. But if these things had her scent…

After shedding her jeans, socks and sneakers, she waded in and submerged her entire body. Kelly sighed with relief as the cool water touched her hot skin. As she waded out, Sam stared at her.

"What the hell are you doing?" he asked in a thick voice.

"Disguising my scent."

A pulse ticked in his throat. "She should have given you a darker T-shirt. And panties, as well."

Glancing down, she saw the wet fabric plastered to her skin. The soaked silk bra turned transparent, along with her lace panties, showing…everything.

Body taut, he clenched his fists, the green in his eyes flaring. Sam looked as if he struggled to contain himself.

"Cover yourself," he ordered harshly.

Not moving, she gave him a defiant smile. "You look hot, Sam. The creek is nice and cool. Go for a swim."

With a strangled sound, he removed his outer shirt and then tugged his T-shirt over his head. Whoa.

"Stop that," she told him.

"Can't go swimming with my clothes on."

Sweat streamed down his back, and coated his face, the angles and planes glistening in the sunlight. The curve of his smooth biceps flexed as he tossed the shirt aside. Beneath Sam's mocking, cheerful charm lurked an edge of controlled wildness.

Reaching for the zipper of his cargo pants, he met her gaze. She gave a small squeak.

"You wouldn't dare."

Sam unzipped his pants and, in a swift move, pushed his pants and boxers down. Baring his body to all.

Her startled gaze met his heated one. Kelly glanced at the dark, curly hairs covering his sculpted chest, marching in a tempting line down his muscled abdomen to…

Not going there. She finally found her voice. "You don't play fair."

"Never did, sweetheart."

"Sam, put your clothes on!"

"Do you really want me to?" he asked softly.

Need spiraled through her. Sam had been a tender, considerate lover.

He would not be so now. If they came together again, he would be primitive and possessive. Images shot through her mind: naked, tangled together, their bodies sweat-slicked as they surrendered to the overpowering desire and made love. Her gaze shot downward, past the ridge of muscle at his lean hips, down to his long, sleek limbs and then up to…

Whoa.

Straining upward from the dark hair at his groin, his thick penis was erect. Moisture gathered between her legs, her sex pulsing in natural response, her nipples tingling and hardened.

Oh, gods, she wanted him so badly.

The harsh sounds of his breath twined with the rush of the gurgling stream. Sam kicked off his pants and boxers and waded in. Her hungry gaze riveted to the smooth muscles of his taut ass.

Sam ducked beneath the water and turned over, his smoldering, predatory gaze riveted to hers.

Kelly's heartbeat kicked into turbo as her breathing hitched. The space between her legs felt aching, open, her core pulsing in response to his naked body. She envisioned those strong hands holding her fast as his thick cock pushed deep inside her.

He wanted her, and she wanted him equally. Time had erased the emotions they had for each other, but it could not vanquish the searing heat. Circumstance and sorrow had dampened but not extinguished it. Now the same desire sparked into life once more.

All she had to do was shuck her clothes and join him. Their joining would be intense, passionate and blazing. Sam need only touch her and she'd have one shattering climax after another.... It had been so long since she'd had sex, too long since anyone had held her close....

Now Kelly did cover her breasts, hugging herself.

Not make love. Have sex.

Hot, steamy, deep-thrusting, clawing sex. Sex that would leave her feeling empty and alone afterward. The fire inside her died.

She couldn't let this man grow close. Too much had happened, too much pain and regret. They would become lovers again, and then he'd hand her over to the Mages.

"Hijo de puta!" she snapped.

Sam stopped swimming.

Biting the inside of her lip, she found her jeans and quickly dressed, her back to the stream.

Water splashed behind her. Sam stood before her, droplets of water from his bent head falling on her skin like tears. His voice was gentle as he lifted her chin to meet his concerned gaze. "What is it, Kel?"

You. Me. We can't do this. We're not the same kids we were, innocent and carefree.

Emotion clogged her throat. She clenched her fists. "Are you ready? Because we're wasting time."

She fussed with her backpack, avoiding his gaze. A damp T-shirt dangled before her.

"Put this on," he said quietly. "It's rank, but it will cover your natural scent when your own clothing dries."

The fabric smelled like leather and sage and Sam. Kelly held it close and inhaled his scent. When she looked up, the predatory look flared on his face once more, as if he liked his shirt, his scent, covering her.

"Let's move on," she said in a shaky voice. "It's not safe here."

Truth was, no place was safe, not with Sam at her side and the ever-burning flame still shimmering between them, ready to sear them both.

Chapter 11

A while later, they found the unpaved road Rosa told them to take. However, either it was market day or everyone decided to go south. It had turned into a pedestrian superhighway. Men drove cattle ahead of them with long sticks. Flocks of women with woven baskets atop their heads gossiped as they walked. Students in plaid uniforms, worn backpacks over their skinny shoulders, headed home from school.

Behind thick bushes, Shay hunkered down, watching the traffic, Kelly behind him. They needed to blend with the locals. He glanced backward at Kelly. With her wide cornflower-blue eyes, delicate cheekbones and soft, smooth skin, she stood out like a living flame.

He remembered how she'd looked at the stream, a lush, red-headed Venus rising out of the water, and he bit back a hard kick of desire. *Focus,* Shay reminded himself.

"Is this the only way south?" he asked.

"There's another, but we have to backtrack and it's much

more popular." Her fingers wrapped around the triskele pendant. "Can we use magick to disguise ourselves?"

Traces of magick would alert other Mages, a neon sign in the darkness. But he worried more about the human posse of shotgun-wielding locals.

"We have no choice. No one would notice me much, but you?" He shook his head.

"I hid my hair. No one can see I'm a redhead."

Shay's gaze swept over her curvy body. "That's not what will draw men's attention. You're too pretty to ignore."

A faint flush colored her cheeks, heightening her sexual allure. Shay clenched his fists. Hell, other men? He worried more about himself.

"I wish you could shape-shift into a man," he muttered.

"Okay."

Closing her eyes, Kelly softly sang notes of ancient Celtic words as she gripped the triskele. Electrical energy charged the air, raising the little hairs on Shay's nape. A vortex of gold and crimson sparks swirled around her body. As he puzzled over the phenomenon, the sparks faded.

His former lover vanished.

A dark-skinned man stood in her place. Gray hair hidden beneath a battered straw cowboy hat, the lanky man wore a faded checked shirt and plain cotton pants.

Shay glanced downward. Thick, hairy toes peeped out from worn leather sandals.

"Meet Juan Hernandez, a visitor to this town."

Even her voice had deepened to a man's timbre.

Suspicion filled him. Only Elementals had the power to shape-shift, and it was limited to Phantoms like himself.

Arcanes gained the power only when they'd killed a Phantom and siphoned all his magick. What if Senator Rogers was right? Was Kelly's nonprofit a front for stealing Elemental children and killing them to enhance their powers?

The thought sickened him.

Shay's hand automatically fell to his sidearm as he studied Kelly's guileless expression. No darkness tinged her aura, only the normal crimson of an Arcane, interlaced with strong gold. Gold because of the triskele, he thought, glancing at the pendant. Either the medallion endowed Kelly with his magick, or the spell binding them together had fueled her with power.

He didn't like this. But other priorities mattered more.

Removing the leather holster and pistol, Shay tucked them into his backpack. Damn, he hated not carrying, but packing would raise a few eyebrows.

Culling his magick, he focused. The change was almost instant, perfected by years of practice.

"Wow." Her gaze widened. "Uh, very Freudian of you."

She fished a small compact mirror from her pack and handed it over. Shay looked.

In the mirror, Kelly stared back. Silky red framing a heart-shaped face, cheeks tinted by a rosy flush. Shay licked his reddened, wet mouth.

What the hell?

"Do you mind? It's very disconcerting seeing you as me."

"I'm suddenly quite tempted to kiss myself."

"Sam, please change into someone else. Anyone else. Even Senator Rogers is better."

This was priceless. Shay grinned. "Hmm. I like this body. Feels nice." He ran a hand over his new chest. "Very nice."

Juan/Kelly's cheeks darkened as he flushed. "Stop feeling me up. Or are you indulging in some private fantasy? One without me because you prefer it that way?"

Shay dropped the grin. "Never," he said quietly. "I'll always prefer the original model in my arms. No magick could ever duplicate her. She's one of a kind."

Kelly turned away, but not before he caught the glint of moisture in her now-dark eyes. Shay steeled himself against the urge to gather her into his arms and give comfort as he'd done in the past. He needed her sharp, alert and unemotional. Sympathy wouldn't snap her out of it.

"Buck up, Juan. Real men don't cry. If you're going to go soft on me, turn back into a girlie girl."

"I'm not crying, dammit." Those thin shoulders tensed with pride.

Atta girl, he thought silently. Concentrating, he envisioned a pretty, shapely brunette. The mirror now showed a woman with dark hair and eyes, cheekbones sharp as blades, the stamp of ancient Mayan ancestry on her features. Shay smoothed his skirts and straightened the white peasant blouse.

Kelly flicked a hand at his chest. "A little much? You like skinny women with huge breasts?"

Far from it. He adored a woman with curves, whose soft body would cushion a man when he lay between her legs. A redhead with deep blue eyes sparkling with laughter and passion would suffice. Kelly.

Hell, no wonder he'd screwed up the shape-shifting.

"It's a distraction. Men like to check out women, I gave myself big assets to draw attention to me and away from you. If we encounter any bounty hunters, most will be too busy staring at my chest to notice you."

"And you know this because…why? You like to stare at women like that, too, Sam?"

He actually did not. Shay loved women, respected them too much. Oh, hell, he'd scope out a woman like other men, but he'd notice other things. The way she laughed, how she moved, how she interacted with others. Aggressive and bold or quiet and confident?

Kelly taught him that. He'd learned to see beyond appearance to the woman beneath. And now when he chose his female companions, never more than for a few nights of pleasure, their biggest assets were inside their heads.

"Call me Maria." He pursed his lips and batted his lashes.

"Sam doesn't go well with this outfit. You're my husband and we just recently married."

"We make a great pair. Like matching salt and pepper shakers."

No, we made a better pair when we were Sam and Kelly, long ago.

But he said nothing as they stepped out onto the road.

The disguises worked. No one gave them more than a cursory glance as they walked to the next town, although Shay had to remind Kelly to rein in her natural grace.

Men didn't sway their hips.

Crumbling adobe buildings with sagging corrugated metal roofs lined the narrow streets. Women sat beneath faded beach umbrellas, selling roasted corn and mangoes. Shay spotted a sign reading El Nuevo Comodor. The restaurant had a cracked window and peeling paint, contradicting its boast of such newness. He checked the sun's position. Time to give Dakota a sitrep. The restaurant was nearly empty.

While Kelly went to the ladies' room, Shay fished his cell from his pack and punched in LT's number. The phone rang. No answer. Either Dakota was out of range or something had happened. He left a voice mail.

When she returned, they bought water and snacks from the restaurant, earning a small smile from the owner. As they made their way down the cracked sidewalk, wending through a gaggle of women selling fruit from woven baskets, a chicken bus stopped. The ancient school bus, painted in wild colors, waited for a herd of goats to cross the street. A man hung an elbow out the bus window, his sharpened gaze raking over the street. The faint red glow of his aura pulsed. Shay tensed, bracing for action.

"Maria, I am very hungry for a delicious mango. Don't these look good?" Juan/Kelly asked in halting Spanish.

The passenger's gaze whipped over to Kelly. He lifted something from his lap. A shotgun.

Juan/Kelly glanced up and saw the gun. Blood drained from her face. Sam squeezed Kelly's arm in silent warning and pointed to the mango basket. She bent her head, examining the ripe fruit. He itched to have his Sig in hand. The weapon was part of him.

But the disguise was more effective. He adjusted the white blouse to show a tantalizing glimpse of generous cleavage. Nearby men began studying him and moved closer to the mango seller's stand. Murmurs of frank male appreciation followed.

The shotgun-carrying passenger in the bus riveted his gaze to Sam's chest.

Give them a show. Sam moistened his mouth and bent over to pull two ripe mangoes from the basket, showing a generous display of cleavage. Out of the corner of his eye, he saw shotgun man lean out of the window, his interest fully engaged.

Juan/Kelly fished bills out of a wallet to pay the beaming seller. Finally, the bus rambled past. Shoulders hunched, Kelly stared at the ground.

She looked too damn scared. Other pedestrians glanced at them curiously. They were drawing attention.

"Juan, I want to buy some tortillas, too," he said, hoping she took the hint.

Silence. *C'mon, Kel, take charge,* he silently urged. *Play the part.*

He pouted, putting a hand on one hip as he'd seen women do. "Another man would give me what I want," he said in a smooth purr.

It worked. Juan/Kelly's head snapped up and she seized his arm, holding it in a proprietary way. "Enough shopping. We need to make it home before dark."

Her Spanish was slow but precise. Shay gave an approving nod.

A brief, stinging slap on his ass made him yelp. “You are too much of a flirt with the men, Maria.”

Glaring, he rubbed his ass. “They like what they see and pay attention to me.”

“They only stare at your body.”

Shay wriggled his hips. “Is it not a body worth a few stares?”

“They will never have you. Mine is the only bed you will ever lie upon. Perhaps I should keep you there naked until I plant another baby in your belly.”

Whoa. This was too weird, the words getting him cranked up.

Beneath the plain cotton bra, his nipples turned to hard points. Shay glanced down in dismay. So this is what arousal felt like for women.

And he thought it was hard to hide an erection…

“Let us go, Juan.” Man, he sure as hell hoped she’d get the hint and stop talking. But Kelly was too into the role.

“When I get you home, Maria, I will give you no reason to leave our bed. You will enjoy the pleasure I give you and forget about all others,” Juan/Kelly continued.

Pleasure…memories flooded his mind. Kelly stretched out beneath him, her fingers interlaced with his, her smoky gaze widening as he lowered his head and encased one taut nipple in his mouth. Those little screams of hers driving him wild, her hands stroking him lower until he wanted to die…

An odd, disconcerting ache pulsed between his legs. Shay felt real alarm. Dammit. “Let’s roll,” he muttered in English.

Grabbing her arm, Shay picked up the pace. The hell with acting like a meek woman. This role reversal was more dangerous than he’d anticipated.

Finally, they reached a deserted side street. Juan/Kelly pulled him into the recess of a doorway, out of sight. “What’s your prob?” she hissed in English.

“You, talking about fucking me. Stop it,” he said darkly.

Those sun-darkened cheeks flushed again. "Sorry. I didn't think..."

"Then start."

Juan/Kelly hugged himself. "I was scared. That man in the bus seemed like he knew who I was. I thought if I got more into the role of a man, it would help."

Shay's anger faded. "It's okay. I overreacted. It's a little unsettling, getting turned on as a woman."

Curiosity flared on her face. "Is it? I've always wondered what it feels like to be a man, you know, when you get aroused. What turns a man on?"

Hooyah, this was getting interesting. *You.*

"Try it," he said softly. "Touch yourself."

"A little kinky. But maybe if I imagine I'm touching you, when you're Sam." Juan/Kelly gave a seductive smile. "Like this."

Her hand dropped lower, over her groin. A single, slow stroke. Now blood began to rush much lower, making the ache turn into a pulsing need as Shay's imagination kicked into overdrive. This was too much to resist.

"Touching me how?"

"All over," she whispered. "The way I used to dream about, after you left. The way we first made love. I was scared, because I'd heard a woman's first time hurts. And then you told me to explore your body..."

He closed his eyes, remembering Kelly's hands touching him, stroking over his naked body, exploring every exposed inch of his hot skin. Then her mouth slowly lowering, those wet, red lips opening as she took him into her mouth...

Oh, hell, this was all wrong. No fantasy could ever suffice. He wanted the real thing.

Shay's eyes snapped open and met her startled gaze. Then she glanced down with a look of pure dismay. He bit back a chuckle.

"Now you know what it feels like," he murmured.

"How do I get rid of this?"

"I find it helpful to think of baseball. The Yankees winning the playoffs works for me."

"This is too weird," Juan/Kelly muttered.

"Right." Shay sobered. "Think of what's really at stake. What we need to be doing instead of standing here like a couple of horny teenagers. What could happen to your people and mine if all this goes down."

Juan/Kelly paled. "That works for me, Sam, because right now I feel scared to death."

"Hey." He ran a finger down one sun-darkened cheek, envisioning the real Kelly beneath the disguise. "I'm not going to let it happen. Trust me."

They moved out of the building and to the main road. Juan/Kelly scanned the area. "So far, at least three humans are after me. The guys back at Rosa's and the man on the bus. Those aren't too bad odds."

"The man on the bus was an Arcane."

"Not possible. How could you tell?"

"All Arcanes' auras deepen to crimson when they're tense. When we're young, Elementals are taught to detect the slightest flicker. It's taught in our schools, to protect Elemental children."

A small, disdainful snort. "How wonderful for your kind. And what about Arcanes? What defenses do we have? Did anyone ever consider we're tense because our magick is weak and we're under constant scrutiny by Elementals?"

Shay fell silent. Kelly had been a victim of suspicion and prejudice long before the night of the fire.

"I'm surprised my aura isn't neon red. They've labeled me a criminal simply because I'm an Arcane. Any evidence of my innocence will be thrown out once I'm brought before the council."

Her voice dropped. "I'll be imprisoned. Or executed."

Acid coated his throat. "No way in hell. Not going to happen, so stop talking about it."

He'd fight to the blood and bone to ensure she was safe. The promise made long ago still held. Even when he'd left her on her own, he hadn't forgotten.

"You won't have any choice. As soon as you hand me over, you're back to your SEAL team. The council will prevent you from interfering."

Shay sighed. "Trust me, Kel. I have influence and power, and I'll be damned if I let those bureaucratic bastards touch you."

But a niggling doubt wormed into his mind. Did the council truly treat all Arcanes like that? No trial, no chance to plead their innocence, just thrown into prison, or worse?

It would get worse. Once the council believed the threat of genocide, it'd act. Spring into action and imprison all Arcanes. Or kill them.

Fair and just Mages like his uncle would stop them.

But fear was a powerful motivator. All it would take was a few whispered words to the right people, and Arcanes would disappear.

Kill an entire population simply because they were different. Couldn't happen.

Right.

Gritting his teeth, he sidestepped a man lounging against a streetlamp. "If you want a normal life when this is over, Kel, you have to give the system a chance to work. Give me a chance."

"I gave you a chance twelve years ago. It's too late."

The hard shell encased his heart once more. He said nothing, only nudged her to keep moving.

Keep moving forward. All they could do. Except with every step forward, Shay felt himself sliding backward into the past.

A past he missed more than he could admit.

Chapter 12

They needed a car.

Sam hunted through the village looking for one to boost, but the town was too crowded. He opted for public transportation instead. La Aurora was too far to walk. And with the increased threat of men searching for her, Kelly knew they had to find the missing kids.

Before a bounty hunter captured her.

They boarded a chicken bus. Afraid to meet strangers' gazes, she looked out the window.

As twilight fell, they got off at a town an hour's drive from La Aurora. As they stepped off the bus, Sam steered her toward a shop that sold sundries and clothing, ignoring her protests.

There, he purchased a plain white scarf and handed it to her.

At her puzzled look, he pointed to a small mirror. "Take off the hat."

Kelly gasped.

The once-gray hair now had streaks of vibrant red. Her

magick was fading. Next she'd start growing breasts and curves and…

"How long does your shape-shifting hold out?" he asked.

She thought of the one previous attempt as she bound her head in the scarf as if her head were bandaged, hiding all her hair. "Two, three hours, maybe. I've never held it this long. Maybe when you bonded us together, it enhanced my magick."

His gaze sharpened as her stomach growled. "You need to refuel. I'll find a restaurant."

"So much for the man being in charge," she grumbled softly, replacing the hat.

Sam gave a soft laugh. "I am."

Bypassing several smaller, quaint restaurants, he selected a larger one with a mixture of Europeans and locals. Sam chose an isolated table against the wall and faced the entrance.

The waitress came and took their drink orders. Sam's rugged confidence outshone her own. Even disguised, he held the attitude of a tough SEAL who could break an enemy's neck with less fuss than a woman breaking a fingernail.

Her nervousness grew. "We should have gone someplace smaller."

"It's safer here in a crowd," he explained, leaning on the table and scanning the room.

Get back into character, she thought. "Elbows off the table, Maria. A lady never slouches."

He shot her a dirty look.

Opening her menu, Kelly considered. "I'll order for you, Maria. You don't know what a woman likes to eat. You have no taste."

"Maybe I don't know what a woman likes in the kitchen, but I sure as hell know what she enjoys in the bedroom. Especially a certain redhead who screams my name when I indulge my palate in a very special way."

A wicked gleam entered those dark eyes. Heat crawled over

her face. He would remember that. "As I recall, that particular dining experience resulted in a few satisfactory exclamations."

"One, maybe," she muttered.

A crooked smile touched Sam's mouth. He held up five fingers. Kelly ducked behind the menu.

"You kept track?"

"Only to set the bar higher," he murmured.

The waitress set their drinks down. Sweat trickled down Kelly's temples as she stammered out their orders. When the woman left, Sam squeezed her hand. "Chill, Kel. You look scared as a rabbit in a wolf den. I'm just playing with you, getting you to relax."

"I can't. Talk to me. I feel like everyone's watching me." She folded and unfolded her napkin. "How did you become a SEAL? Was it as hard as I've heard?"

"Worse." Sam rubbed the back of his neck. "I had a real asshole officer in boot camp. He kept pushing me hard, goading me to drop out."

"But you didn't."

"If I quit, I knew it was a matter of time before I did something stupid, like turning into a feral wolf again. The navy kicked my ass, taught me self-control."

Kelly looked at him with new respect. "You were never one to take orders."

"I learned, especially during BUD/S. Even BUD/S was nothing compared to training after I became a SEAL. More training to join Team 21. I had a werewolf, all two hundred pounds and teeth, nearly ripping my throat out. Was worth it to join the Phoenix Force. Damn best bunch of guys I've ever known."

"Sam, what's going to happen to me when all this is over?"

His gaze was steady. "My orders are to return you to the base first. Erase your memories."

Panic crept up her throat. "You can't do that."

"I have to, Kel," he said softly. "Just your knowledge of the team."

And him. "Please, isn't there some way around it?"

"It's not so bad," he said quietly. "Doesn't hurt. You don't feel a thing. Not like when you remember the bad things."

Like when my family died. The words hung in the air, unspoken. Kelly shifted in her seat.

"Our memories make us who we are, even the bad ones."

Sam gave a very unladylike snort. "Cut the psychobabble. I'd love to erase the past."

"You'd wipe out all memory of it, including me?"

Raising her chin, she watched his jaw tense. "Not you. Your father. He set that fire on purpose because he hated my family."

Sam had every right to his anger. Maybe if she told him the truth, it would help him deal, ease his anger. But what if the truth meant hurting him all over again?

"He didn't hate your mother."

"Right."

"I have proof."

Shock widened his eyes. He slapped his hands on the table, his body quivering, the thin shoulders in the white peasant blouse tensing. "What?"

She hesitated.

"Tell me," he ordered. "Right now."

Swallowing hard, she plunged ahead. "A few weeks after the fire I snuck back to check our quarters, see if there was anything I could salvage. My stuff was all in the trash. The Mage authorities had done a thorough search, looking for evidence."

"Go on."

"The only thing they hadn't thrown out was the policies and procedures manual your father issued all Arcane servants. I was going to toss it but decided to go through it. Sometimes Dad wrote notes in the pages, reminders of stuff to do…"

Her throat closed up tight. "Dad had taped a note to the back of a page. Dated Christmas Eve."

His gaze narrowed. "Handwritten?"

She nodded. "He'd jotted down a task list. Dad was involved in a small, underground group trying to secure equality for Arcanes. FES, the Freedom & Equality Society. And he'd found an ally within the walls of the mansion."

Kelly clenched her fists until the nails bit tender flesh. "Your mother."

Sam went very still. "Impossible. What did the list say?"

"It was just notes. Wednesday night, eight-o'clock meeting, FES, execute plan. Target—Chloe Shaymore." Her heart banged hard against her chest.

He leaned forward. "What else, Kelly?"

"There was a notation. Oil lamp, spill, master bed."

Red suffused Sam's face. He swore in a low voice. "The master bedroom, where firemen said the fire originated. A hit list of the first Elemental to kill. My mother."

"No!" Others glanced at their table. She lowered her voice. "It was a reminder about something. He scribbled those things all the time. Your mother's name was listed because she was conspiring with him and the FES. Once or twice I saw them whispering together. She went with him to a Wednesday-night meeting."

His tight expression warned he didn't believe a word. "Why would my mother, who was queen of the Elemental social set, do something that dangerous? And every Wednesday night she went to her bridge club."

"And who was her chauffeur? My father. At her tea party, one of her friends talked about how they'd had to cancel bridge until finding new partners. She never went, Sam. Instead, she was with my father at a secret FES meeting."

Sam was utterly still, looking as if she'd stabbed him in the gut.

"Your mother was essential to his plans to gain more rights for our people. He'd have fought to protect her."

"He was laughing as he fled. I saw him. Hell, you saw him! Does that sound like a man who wanted to save her?"

"I don't know! But my father would never hurt anyone."

"Why the hell are you telling me this now, Kelly?" Sam looked sick.

"I thought it might help you to know my father didn't hate your family and couldn't have set the fire." Kelly reached across the table for his hand, but he drew back.

Muscles taut, he leaned forward, his gaze glittering. "What did you do with this note? Did you turn it over to the Mage authorities?"

"I burned it. I couldn't risk them jumping to the wrong conclusions and using it to frame him for murder."

"You protected him."

"How could I trust them?"

Sam went silent as their food was served. He picked up the fork, pushing the chicken around the plate. "You could have given it to my uncle. He's fair and just. He's the one who argued for your release and got you out of jail after the fire. Al has been a voice of reason for all Arcanes."

"I couldn't risk it. Elementals aren't interested in justice, only revenge. They're all narrow-minded."

"Does that include me? I'm Elemental," he asked quietly.

"Of course not! I'd never think of you like that. Trust me, Sam."

A snort of harsh laughter. "Trust you? Why should I? You're acting as biased as those windbags on the council, except you're prejudiced against my people. I see whose side you're on."

"I don't want to take sides."

"Too late."

To her dismay Sam booked them a room in one of the town's motels. Kelly barely noticed the polished tile, the freshly painted walls and the bouquet of fresh flowers on the front desk when they registered.

Instead, all she focused on was the fact that they'd be sharing one room. One bed, when an entire town right now wouldn't be big enough to cover the silence hanging between them.

Kelly bit her lip as he counted the money for the room. Gone was the carefree camaraderie between them. Sam had taken charge, assertive in skirts, a no-nonsense attitude.

The red-tiled room had bright blue painted walls, a simple pine desk and one nightstand. An overhead fan lazily swept the air over a small, narrow bed.

She turned to see Sam's glamour vanish. But this time he was dressed in an olive-green T-shirt, camouflage pants covering his long, muscled limbs.

The compassionate, funny Sam vanished, replaced by the efficient soldier known as Shay.

She had taken the man and turned him into a machine. Somehow, she had to reach him again, get inside to find the real Sam.

"We can't stay here. We have to push on to La Aurora," she said.

"It's too late. Time to take a break."

"I don't need a break."

Sam unzipped his pack and withdrew his pistol. "I do. I'm not thinking clearly. I need to calm down. And you need sleep. You're on the edge of collapse."

"But the kids… What if the rogue Arcanes get to them before we do?"

He glanced up, hazel eyes hard. "I know you don't like to take risks, but that's one you'll have to take."

Ouch. Kelly winced as he tossed back her own words. Sam's expression softened. "They won't get to them. I suspect they're more interested in getting to you."

He gestured to her head. "You're exhausted and your glamour is fading. Look."

The mirror on the bathroom door showed a man with reddish hair, soft mouth and…she glanced down to see rounded hips.

"Change back. Then shower and get to bed. I need you fresh and alert. We'll leave before dawn."

She opened her mouth to argue, but seeing his expression, she changed her mind. Kelly closed her eyes and summoned her true form. The mirror now reflected a redhead with sallow skin and purple shadows beneath her eyes.

Sam was right, dammit. She looked exhausted. Yet he was tough as steel and showed no signs of stopping.

Hating the distance between them, Kelly investigated the bathroom, a tiny area where she could barely turn around. Checked tile walls of red, blue and yellow were accented by a bright yellow cabinet. She looked longingly at the miniscule shower.

"Go." Sam sat on the bed with his pistol, turning it over in his hands.

"Aren't you going to shower?"

"You first. I have other priorities." At her expression he added in a hardened voice, "This is a mission. Checking my weapons and the equipment comes first."

An air of danger quivered in the air, emanating from the man on the bed, holding a pistol in an experienced grip. Somehow, she had to break through that reserve, find the Sam she'd glimpsed before. The Sam who once had believed her, trusted and listened to her.

Even though he had no reason to do so.

Kelly dropped to her knees before him, putting a hand on his sleekly muscled thigh. He stiffened.

"Sam, I didn't mean to say that about all Elementals."

"But you can't help but thinking it deep inside. We're all the same. Can't be trusted."

Drawing back, she curbed her temper. "Hard to trust you

when you left after paying my bond, no forwarding address, just a formal letter ending everything."

Sam looked away.

"You left me, because I was an Arcane. No longer just Kelly."

Lacking her father to arrest, the Mage authorities tossed her in jail for twenty-four hours. Sam had paid her bail but had vanished. It was the roughest time of her young life. Missing Sam dreadfully, wishing he were with her, teasing away her fears with his wicked charm and humor.

Too terrified to trust anyone, grieving for Sam's family, heartsick over her father, she finally went to the cabin where they'd first made love...and saw an envelope from him. With eager, fumbling fingers, she'd torn into it, knowing Sam, the man who professed his love, wouldn't abandon her.

Instead, she found a key and a crisp letter directing her to a bank safe-deposit box, along with instructions to use the money to start over and "forget about us." Sam had severed the ties between them with words as sharp as the ax her father used to cut trees.

A heartbeat of silence passed. Sam picked up the pistol, turned it over in his hands.

"I had to leave. Wasn't possible to stick around. Not when I'd lost so much."

"You didn't lose me."

"Wrong," he said quietly. "I lost you the moment you insisted on Cedric's innocence, even after we'd seen him run from the house. The fire destroyed my family, my life. But your fidelity to your father, and your own kind, destroyed everything between us, Kelly."

"I had to defend him. They were set out on a witch hunt. It had nothing to do with you."

"It had everything to do with me. Even though he'd disappeared, you chose him over me. It used to be you and me against the world, and you turned it to your people versus mine."

Torment shadowed his eyes as he stared at the wall. "I felt so alone, trying not to show it. When the Mage authorities showed up that night and kept questioning us, you didn't just insist Cedric was innocent. You ranted at them, saying they automatically blamed an Arcane. You said, 'Because that's what you damn Elementals do. You're all the same, nothing but arrogant, rich, entitled, powerful aristocrats.'"

Tension pulled his muscles tight. "Every insult you lobbed at my people included me."

"Never!"

He ticked off his fingers. "Rich. Arrogant. Entitled. Powerful. Aristocratic. You called me all those once, as a joke maybe, but that night you weren't joking."

Shock punched her low in the gut. Sickened at this revelation, Kelly drew back on her haunches.

"I couldn't deal. Not after my heart was ripped to shreds and all I had left was a crumbling shell of a home and three gravestones. I needed you badly, Kelly. You were all I had left. But you weren't there for me."

"Sam," she choked out. "Oh, gods, why didn't you tell me? I never knew how you felt. It would have changed everything."

"Would it?" His broad shoulders stiffened. "Go take your shower. I'll secure the room."

Trembling, she stepped into the bathroom, closing the door behind her. Once they'd been lovers, had laughed together, planned a future as they lay close, talking long into the night. One night had changed everything, damaging them both.

Her throat constricted as she undressed and stepped into the tiny stall. The shower was cool and refreshing. She stood beneath the trickle of water, letting it wash away dirt, grime and tears.

After placing safeguards on the windows and doors so he'd detect the slightest tap, Sam returned to the bed. His hands curled around his Sig. He hated the hurt look on Kelly's face, knowing he'd put it there.

The steady patter of the shower conjured images he didn't want. Kelly, standing naked beneath the shower, head thrown back as the water cascaded down her breasts, a droplet sliding in between those lush mounds. His body grew tight and hard as he thought about tracing each drop with his tongue, his hands splayed around her hips, the musk of her womanly scent drowning him…

He was a SEAL and trained hard to deploy on the toughest assignments in the world. This was one. Maybe Curt should schedule more training time on how to deal with ex-girlfriends on a mission, he thought humorlessly. Lesson one: close-quarters defense when faced with a woman you badly wanted to fuck.

He'd deal with it. And then what, when he returned Kelly to the States and into Mage custody?

Shay didn't see a way around it. He lived by the rules. They kept him centered and focused when his world had fractured, kept the feral wolf inside him at bay.

Not anymore. She was naked, just a few feet away.

The bed was soft and the sheets crisply white. He closed his eyes, remembering how they had once tangled together in hot, slick need, perspiration glistening on her soft skin as he loved her long and hard.

Shay gave a bitter snort. He loved her once. And then one Christmas Eve everything had shattered, and her loyalty proved exactly how brittle love was.

When she emerged from the bathroom, patting a ragged towel on her hair, a fresh linen shirt damp against her skin, he steeled himself against a hard kick of desire.

"Sam, I'm sorry for everything that happened." Sorrow filled those big blue eyes. "Can you forgive me for not being there for you?"

He could not speak. Instead of answering, he headed past her into the bathroom.

"Do you always bring a gun into the shower?"

Only with you, he thought. The Sig was a hard reminder of his identity, his obligation to the team.

Not to a pretty Arcane who'd shattered his trust all over again.

The door closed behind him with a firm click.

Chapter 13

"It's okay, it's okay, Sam, wake up!"

Velvet-soft voice, urgently calling. A light snapped on. Cold sweat trickled down his temples as Shay sat up, ready to cold-cock the new threat.

No threat. Just memories of the past and the fire that changed everything. Instantly he surveyed the surroundings. Motel room.

Eyes wide, Kelly sat on the bed. "You were having a nightmare. I wanted to wake you up, but you were thrashing around and I didn't want to get punched."

Shay shook off the nightmare visuals. "Smart. Never try to wake me up abruptly. I could hurt you."

She glanced at his hands fisted in the sheet and the curve of his biceps. "Even though you wouldn't mean it."

Kneeling beside him, she placed a soft hand on his tensed shoulder. The thin blanket beneath him was soaked. He'd slept on the floor, giving her the bed. The golden glow from the bedside lamp sheened her face, sharp with worry.

Aware of his half-naked state, the sheet falling to his waist, Shay looked around for his pants. He pulled the sheet around his waist.

"You called my name."

"Um." Embarrassed, he couldn't speak.

"A bad one, huh?" Sympathy tinged her husky voice.

"No big deal."

"I've had dreams. I know how bad they can be." She gave a soft smile and sat on the bed, patting it. "That floor looks really uncomfortable. Come on up. I need to talk to you."

Shay shook his head.

"Please, Sam?"

Damn. Those big, woebegone eyes got him each time. Shay sat, kneading the cords and tendons in his neck. Gods, they felt tighter than piano wire.

"It's okay to need someone to hold you after a bad dream. Do you want me to hold you, Sam? Will that help you sleep?"

Hell no, his brain decided.

Oh, yeah, his body declared.

Brain lost the battle as he gave a jerky nod. Kelly wound her warm, soft arms around him. It felt so good, feeling her against him, her warmth chasing away the black coldness of the dream. Remembering, Shay's heart pounded hard. *Don't go there.* Gods, the thought of losing her as he'd lost his family, the panic clogging his throat as he'd tried to rescue her.

Gently, he pulled away from her and sat back, rubbing a hand over his face. "I'm okay."

She pushed at her tangled, silky hair. "I hate that you're having nightmares. It's my fault. I did this to you, because we fought."

The tightness in his chest increased. Shay waited.

"It was selfish to think only of myself and my father, after you'd lost your whole family. You're right. That night I was judgmental and blind and didn't think about how much you needed me. How much my words could hurt you. I'm so sorry, Sam."

Kelly didn't meet his gaze but stared at the floor. He knew her, knew how it stung her pride to admit this.

"Hey," he said softly. Shay took hold of her chin, lifted it to meet his gaze. "I was wrong, too. It's normal to turn to your own flesh and blood to protect them."

"Maybe. But I neglected you, Sam, and after everything we shared, you deserved so much more." She put a hand on his arm. "Can you forgive me and let us start over?"

Start over? Not possible. Years ago, maybe, when they were younger, but things were too complicated now. "There's nothing to forgive, Kel. Let's get some sleep."

But she didn't move, only looked around the room and shivered, her blue gaze haunted. "It's hard to fall back asleep after a nightmare. I had plenty after I left Tennessee. Sometimes I'd wake up and wished someone would hold me, tell me it was okay, instead of being alone."

So forlorn and sad. He rubbed his chest, resisting the urge to give the comfort she'd never had.

Shifting his weight away from her, Shay tried for levity. "This nightmare wasn't as nasty as waking up to Renegade in the field. That wolf's morning breath could melt steel."

Kelly laughed, an enchanting sound. Mint-green silk flowed over her body, clung to her curves. Her nipples stood out in rigid points against the fabric. He felt a jolt of hard need.

Shay felt fully awake as Kelly sighed and leaned against him. Oh, man, too awake. Especially certain parts…

Kelly nuzzled against his throat, giving a pretty little sigh. "You always know how to make me feel better. Wish I could do the same for you."

Feel better… His mind automatically shifted to sex. Closing his eyes, he buried his face against her hair, inhaling sweet jasmine and fresh raindrops. Need surfaced, chasing away the night sweats.

She lifted her head, eyes questioning. Shay stared at her soft, red mouth.

He brushed his lips against hers, a bare nuzzle. And then she made the sweetest purring sound beneath his mouth.

Hello.

He deepened the kiss, pulling her hard against him, her body so soft and warm, Kelly's heart beating fast as a hummingbird's wings. Losing himself in her sweetness, he drank in the promise of abandon in her lips. Thoughts of loss and grief vanished, driven away by her excited little breaths. Erotic heat spiraled through him as he claimed her mouth and felt her hands squeeze the hard muscles of his shoulders.

Vaguely, he wondered if other lovers had soothed away her bad dreams. The thought bothered him. Shay hated the idea of another man touching her, his hands skimming her smooth skin, his lips pressing against hers.

Mine.

Even though he had no claim, he wanted Kelly exclusively for himself.

All these years, he'd dreamed about touching her again. Caressing her soft flesh, feeling her quiver beneath his questing hands as she did now.

Beneath the insistent pressure of his mouth, her lips grew soft and pliant. Shay kissed her deeper, as if his last breath depended on it, each inhale and exhale feeding him life. Sliding his hands down the slope of her back, he cupped the sweet roundness of her ass, drawing her closer. Kelly climbed into his lap and wrapped her long, slender legs around his waist. With a low purr, she rubbed herself against him.

Torture.

Beneath his boxers, his cock turned to steel, pushing against the warm, wet cotton of her panties. Kneading her ass, he kept kissing her, giving her what she instinctively needed, rubbing his hardened cock along her wet slickness.

So close, he wanted badly to shed the last barrier between

them and slide into her. Banish the nightmare with her soft female flesh sheathing him, the perfume of her scented hair tangled in his senses. Kelly made eager sounds against his mouth as he gently laid her down and straddled her hips. Shay nuzzled her neck, kissing his way down to the slope of her collarbone. His hand eagerly palmed one breast, thumbing her taut nipple. So good, felt so damn good…

"I want you so much," he said thickly. "Kel, tell me what you want me to do."

"I…don't know," she whispered.

Sliding a hand beneath her nightgown, he ran a finger along the lace waistband of her panties. "Do you want me here?"

Shay gently cupped her mound.

"Or something a little slower…" He rubbed a finger along the soaked cotton between her legs. "What do you want, Kel? Whatever you want, I'll give it to you."

A little sob escaped her. "You can't. Because I want what we used to have."

Breathing hard he drew back, staring into the depths of her wide blue eyes. Seeing cold doubt.

Dammit. Coming to his senses, he rolled off and smothered a curse. "Right." Shay ran a hand through his damp hair. "Let's get some sleep. Early day tomorrow."

He switched off the lamp. Back on the floor, he punched his pillow. Lost control. Hadn't done that in years. Not since he'd become a feral wolf, allowing emotions to ride him.

"Sam," she whispered.

"Get some sleep," he said hoarsely.

Shay closed his eyes, telling himself he imagined the sadness on Kelly's face as he'd turned off the light.

It wasn't turning out to be a great day.

First, his plans to swipe a motorcycle turned south when Kelly told him the Honduran police would stop them and ask questions. Two people on a motorcycle broke the law.

"Because that's how drive-by shootings happen. One person drives, the other aims." Her mouth turned down. "It happened to a staff member of mine as he went to open the office. They left him for dead."

A good reminder of the dangers they faced. Hell, it could have been her who took the hit. Shay's guts wrenched at the thought of Kelly innocently turning the key to the building and then facing a hail of bullets....

Instead, they rode another chicken bus. Shay had shifted into the form of a young Honduran in a black baseball cap, black jeans and sleeveless T-shirt. To draw attention to himself, he carried a live chicken, trussed at the ankles.

Kelly's magick had failed when she'd tried to shape-shift. "I'm too drained," she'd told him. "Maybe later, after I've recharged."

Instead, she covered her silky hair with a bright scarf and wore loose clothing. Men still stared and one even boldly propositioned her in Spanish, making her blush. The protective male in him overcame good sense. He'd punched the guy.

As a result, they got tossed off the bus.

The good news? La Aurora was only a mile away.

They began walking along the dusty road. Shay clutched the chicken by its legs, his trepidation growing. He'd heard the whispers in the bus of the haunted village where darkness reigned and no one dared to visit.

Hell, he'd feel better doing this solo. Too much risk for Kelly. The nightmare images from last night seemed too real.

As they drew closer to their destination, an oppressive silence met them. No birds cackled in the trees, no goats bleated, not even a cow grazing on the roadside.

Not even the hum of insects.

"Time to test the air," he muttered.

Shay untied the chicken and set it down. It pecked the ground a minute and then wandered toward the village.

Suddenly the bird flapped its wings and ran in the other direction, squawking loudly.

"It's a sign." Kelly drew in a breath. "Not good."

"Like miners releasing canaries into shafts to check for gas. Looks like our chicken doesn't want to get near the village," he muttered. "Stay alert. I'm going to transform back to conserve my powers."

Afterward, they walked into town on the cracked sidewalks hugging the narrow cobblestone road. The colonial buildings flanking the street seemed deserted. There was no one lingering in the doorways, no women carrying baskets of goods to sell.

No children, either.

Place was a damn ghost town.

Itching to palm a weapon, Shay nudged Kelly to the cracked sidewalk and the shadows. A wood sign creaked in the breeze, a ghostly sound in the seemingly deserted village. Goods and Sundries, it read in Spanish. His Mage instincts tingled. Something nasty had passed through. He glanced at Kelly.

"Evil," she whispered in English. "Whatever was here is evil, but left. I can see the faint traces of white magick. The kids. They were here, as well."

"Let's check it out."

A woman cranked open a window across the street, saw them and shut it, drawing the blinds. Shay tensed. They had to hurry. If she were a spotter, they were toast.

With a faint creak, the door opened beneath his palm. Stale air greeted them inside the store. Metal shelves created two small aisles. On each shelf were glass jars, labeled neatly in Spanish. Canned tomatoes, peppers, corn.

Then he took a closer look. Kelly slapped a hand to her mouth, covering her gasp.

Not canned vegetables. Body parts, swimming in fluid. He detected an eyeball squeezed between bloodied organs.

"They're not human," she said.

"Gods, I hope not." Shay squinted at the spidery writing below one label. "They look like recipes."

"Spells. Black magick spells written in the Old Language. This is the den of the rogue Arcanes."

The hell with this. From behind his jeans, he withdrew his Sig Sauer and then pulled the slide back. Cocked and loaded. Cupping his gun, he turned down each aisle. No one. But the miasma of evil filtered through the air.

"Kelly?" Shay glanced around.

"In here."

She was in a back room, studying a leather-bound book on a dusty counter. Excitement filled her gaze as she looked up. "Look at this! The ancient texts of my Arcane ancestors! This is the book of spells the Elementals hid from us after they killed the Dark Lord three hundred years ago."

"Never enter a room before I check it out first." Shay blew out a frustrated breath and lowered his weapon. "Understand?"

Her face fell. "I'm sorry."

He gave a gruff nod and holstered the gun.

The shop reeked of darkness. Stale air, no signs of life, not even a spider. And his own spidey senses were tingling. Automatically he scanned for an exit. That back door. He unlocked it. The door led to a square of dirt yard.

Leaving the door unlocked, he turned back to Kelly, who used a corner of her shirt to leaf through the pages.

"These are the most powerful Arcane spells, both dark magick and light. If I can find the spell for creating a Dark Lord, we can destroy it before the rogue Arcanes use it. The skull mask I saw at the bar indicates a partial transformation…"

Shay turned and cocked his head. "How do you know so much?"

Color flushed her pretty cheeks. "When I was ten, I broke into the forbidden section of your father's library and read the history books."

He laughed. "I knew you weren't into dolls. So, Miss Lawbreaker, how does an Arcane turn into a Dark Lord?"

"It's a dangerous, lengthy process." Kelly shook her head. "Your father's books didn't exactly give a recipe. But I got the sense the final step includes gathering together several innocents and sacrificing them in a ritual."

She scanned the pages of the book and then came upon a separate sheet of paper, not yellowed with age like the book. "Sam, look! It's the names of the nine Elemental Phantom children, and a record of who their parents are...."

He joined her, reading aloud from the book.

"'Through a ritual killing, an Arcane is able to absorb the Phantom's powers. He can imitate the form of anyone he touches, absorbing their DNA through his skin.'"

She blew out a breath. "I told you, that's why they took the kids. With the children's powers, the rogue Arcanes can move freely among your people and kill them."

It still made no sense. His SEAL instincts tingled. "All warfare is based on deception," he mused. "If your enemy is secure at all points, be prepared for him. If he is in superior strength, evade him."

Kelly gave him a questioning look.

"Sun Tzu. *The Art of War.*" Shay rubbed the back of his neck. "These criminal Arcanes want to destroy my people. Imitating key players and infiltrating our ranks, yeah, that would work. But once we discovered the deception, it's over. All Arcanes would be thrown into prison, the war over before it started. The enemy is weak in numbers. They'd need superior strength to defeat all my people...."

"By creating a Dark Lord, they'd have superior strength," Kelly pointed out. "The last one, who was executed three hundred years ago, wiped out entire towns before several Elemental Mages managed to combine their powers and destroy him."

Sudden insight struck him. He stared at the yellowed parchment, scanning the spidery writing. Gorge rose in his stomach as he read the brutal, graphic details. "Oh, shit. This is not good."

"Sam? What did you find?"

He met her worried gaze. "The final spell for creating a Dark Lord. Using the dead, ah, body of a Mage possessing tremendous courage…and the blood of ten innocent Mage children."

Horror stole over Kelly's face.

"Once a Dark Lord is created, other Arcanes can absorb his strength and powers by declaring allegiance to the Dark Lord and drinking his blood."

It all made sense now. Shay's heart raced as he imagined the possibilities. "These rogue Arcanes want to kill a group of Phantom children and a brave Mage to create a Dark Lord and in turn, he will create an army of Dark Lords."

Her voice dropped to a shocked whisper. "Unstoppable. Their powers so great, even the strongest magick couldn't destroy them."

She covered her face with her hands. "The children may be already dead."

"Steady," he soothed, squeezing her shoulder. "They must still be alive or we'd never access this shop. The barriers would be too strong. And you said these Arcanes had stolen only nine children."

At her nod, he felt a surge of relief. "That's why they haven't killed them yet. They have to wait to capture the tenth. Someone is leading them. They're not working alone on this, but through someone's instructions. And they need a Mage to complete the ritual. Courageous. Not exactly something you can buy at the local grocery store."

Kelly stared at him. "Sam, you're a courageous Mage. You're a navy SEAL."

Oh…shit.

Realization struck with a sharp punch. "My twin didn't want me dead. He wanted to capture me."

And the SOB was still out there, waiting.

"Sam, he must be the Mage I saw at the bar. He took your DNA when you were there and followed you here!" Kelly's mouth quivered. "Take this. Protect yourself. You matter more. If they destroy you—" she slipped off the triskele and put it around his neck "—I'd want to die," she whispered.

The selflessness of the gesture deeply moved him. Shay took her hand, emotions churning inside him, and kissed it.

"No one's dying today. Let's get out of here." Shay glanced at the window.

Trembling, Kelly lowered her hands. The letters on the ancient parchment began to twist and turn. They blackened, forming an indecipherable smear, and then puddled into a sticky mass of ink.

A droplet rose from the book.

"Don't touch that," he yelled.

As Kelly's hand brushed the page, the black slime leaped onto her fingers. Screaming, Kelly clawed at it, the goo sinking into her skin like acid.

Summoning all his powers, Shay directed a streak of white energy at the form.

White energy severed the black mass in half, but the glob on her hand remained. Shay balled energy in his palm and touched her. White sparks crackled and surged into the black mass, shooting fiery current. Kelly began to convulse.

The electrical shock was killing her.

Shay pulled back his powers. Now the mass began to crawl up her forearm, eating into her skin.

Sobbing, she scratched at it. Shay fumbled to remove the triskele and dropped it. The silver pendant rolled on the floor, beneath the table. He dropped to his knees, fingers combing the dusty floor.

"Use your magick," he yelled. "Fight, Kel!"

Got it. Shay scrambled to his feet.

A glow of golden light suffused Kelly, crimson sparks

attacking the sticky black goo. Face twisted in agony, she chanted ancient words as her blood dripped onto the floorboards.

Shay laid the triskele on the black blob on her arm. The gelatinous substance parted, forming a mouth. An unholy squeal filled the air, hurting his eardrums. Glowing with white light, the triskele sank into the mass, turning it smaller and smaller…

Until it vanished with a soft pop.

With a small cry, Kelly fell back against the wall. Shay draped the pendant around her neck. Gently, he grasped her injured arm. Ugly, bloodied wounds scored the flesh. She offered a brave smile. "It's not too bad."

Shay touched her cheek with a finger, marveling at this woman's courage. "Let's get outside, so you can heal."

Her gaze shot to the store's front. "Someone's coming."

He tugged Kelly toward a stack of boxes to hide. Cupping his pistol, he peered around the cover.

The front door opened and closed. A middle-aged man stood in the doorway. He had brown hair and skin tanned by the sun, and he wore chinos and a plain white shirt. He looked ordinary, a man sent to the store by his wife to fetch a jar of peppers.

Only what were in the jars weren't peppers.

Kelly stole a look. "Arcane," she whispered. "One of the men guarding the stolen children. I saw him in the photographs Fernando took."

They needed to get the hell out of here. He motioned to the window and then helped her climb out.

Racing down the alleyway, he herded her toward the end. It opened onto another narrow, cobblestoned street leading to a small village square and a whitewashed church. Voices drifted from the square.

He tucked away the weapon, found a stone bench in the sun and sat her down. Kelly leaned back, her face pale as she absorbed the sunlight. Standing guard, he scanned their surroundings.

This section of the village seemed untouched by darkness. People went about their business. Women sold vegetables in small stands on the sidewalk.

The wounds on her arm stitched together. Shay ran a finger over the pink flesh, marveling at her healing ability.

Kelly gave a wan smile. "Stupid of me to remove the triskele."

He knelt beside her. "But not the reason you did it. For me," he whispered. Shay kissed her hand. "Thank you, Kel. I needed to hear that."

Swallowing hard, she nodded. "You hungry?"

"Ravenous."

Shay spotted an open-air restaurant and motioned her toward it. He seated her at a table covered with a tablecloth embroidered with tiny pink flowers.

Anxiety shone in her eyes. He took her hand and squeezed it in reassurance.

A young waitress came with a pad to take their order. She had large brown eyes, a hesitant smile and rounded cheeks.

He almost missed the shine of terror in those dark eyes.

Shay set down the menu and leaned back, smiling with the air of a man intent on flirting. "What do you recommend?" he asked conversationally in Spanish. "My sister brags her *pupusas* are the best, but I tell her she should not be boastful. Shall I try yours?"

The pad shook in the girl's hands. She nodded.

"Two, and lemonade cut with soda."

When the waitress scurried away, Kelly raised her eyebrows. "Flirt much?"

"I need information," he said in a clipped tone. "Let me do my job."

He'd gathered intel before. He was good, chatting up the friendlies, assessing the area and enemy movement. Sometimes he did it in the local bar, offering drinks and making contacts, using his charm with the ladies. It amazed him how women liked to spill secrets after sex. No need for magick, just good, solid insight into human and paranormal nature.

Unfortunately in this village, he sensed he couldn't pry out information with a crowbar and the Jaws of Life. The pall of fear layered the air, threading through the delicious smell of grilled meat and fried peppers. And the idea of using seduction to gain intel turned his stomach.

Especially when the only woman he really wanted in his bed sat two feet away.

"Look around." He lowered his voice. "I need your eyes and ears. Tell me what you see."

Scanning the area, she shook her head. "Everyone's too cheerful, too fake. They're sweating, nervous. I don't see any little ones. There are always children, no matter where you go."

"No kids, even in the streets." He dipped a tortilla in the mixture of beans and cheese the waitress brought to the table and ate it. "Odd for a country where the average age is below thirty."

It was as if the villagers kept their children hidden, out of fear of someone stealing them….

They ate quickly. Shay excused himself and headed for the restroom, using the opportunity to scan the café.

In a corner table, a man sat alone, a glass of yellow foaming beer in front of him. The man glanced up with dead, cold eyes.

A chill snaked down Shay's spine. But he detected no dark aura. Just a nasty-tempered villager?

Someone to keep eyes on.

When he returned, Kelly's attention was riveted to a child in the street. Shay's heart skipped a beat.

From this distance, the towheaded boy in a rumpled blue shirt and navy trousers could have been his little brother trudging home from school. Pete. The name hovered on his tongue.

Pete was dead.

Shay shook free the memory and focused. This child carried a red backpack, hurrying along the sidewalk and glancing over one thin shoulder with a frightened look. Kelly stood as if entranced.

"Oliver," she breathed. "One of the missing Phantoms."

Shay tossed a few lemps on the table. "Hold on. We follow, but from a distance."

Tailing the child, Shay kept Kelly behind him. The narrow cobblestone street ran straight for a few blocks and then curved to the left. Garbage littered the gutter. Inside an open door, two men played dominoes.

The boy vanished around a corner.

Shay's instincts tingled. As they turned the corner, he motioned for Kelly to stop at a lamppost.

"What?"

"Not sure. Something."

The child ran into an open doorway.

The street was deserted, not even a stray dog sniffing at the garbage-riddled gutters. Shay hesitated. Every cell screamed to leave Kelly there.

"Glue yourself to this lamppost. Don't move. I'll be back."

He removed his sidearm and cupped it, holding it low.

"I need to see, make sure it's him," she protested.

"I'll bring him out to you."

Kelly lurched forward. "Sam, don't stop me from doing my job."

Shay gave her a gentle push back against the lamppost. "Don't stop me from doing mine. Now, stay here, or do I get out the cuffs again?"

Slumping against the post, she gave him a sullen look.

The open doorway was an invitation. Too easy. He checked right and left and ran across the street. No noise, no sounds inside. For the first time, Shay cursed the bond he'd put between himself and Kelly. If he got into trouble, she couldn't run for it.

Culling his magick, he prepared to fire, bullets or energy.

His senses tingled as he crept inside. Light from a small lamp burned from a back room. Making no noise, he stole through the room and saw an abandoned red backpack on the floor.

Soft, snuffling sounds, like crying. Shay's guts kicked. Couldn't stand hearing a child in distress. Poor kid. He advanced slowly.

Checking the corner, he saw the little boy sitting at a table. Cradling his head in his arms, he sobbed loudly. Shay's throat closed tight. The kid had the same vulnerable air as his little brother.

Then he raised his head, tears streaking his grimy face.

"It's okay," Shay soothed, lowering his sidearm. "Who are you?"

"I'm Oliver. I escaped when they weren't looking. I'm so scared. Please don't shoot me!" the boy beseeched. "The bad men pointed a gun at me."

Shay checked the room and sensed no danger. He set the gun on the floor and stepped inside.

Heavy chains fell upon him. Burning pain like acid. This wasn't a Phantom child in trouble, and he'd walked directly into a trap.

Chapter 14

The silver stung his eyes and ate into his clothing, searing his flesh. Shay instinctively put his hands in front of his face to shield his eyes, holding the chains away.

"It hurts," the little boy said in a singsongy voice. "But the hurt goes away after a minute. I know because I tested it on myself."

The pain eased and Shay opened his eyes. The child shape-shifted in an eye blink. Into himself.

With all his might, Shay fought the chains.

"It's about time you arrived. For a navy SEAL, you sure are slow." His twin gave a cocky grin.

Shay aimed a bolt of energy at the bonds but emitted only a few sparks. His powers were bound, as well. Dammit.

"We used your DNA, figured out what could hold you. Works good, huh?" His twin gave a mocking grin. "I set others at the café to keep an eye on you. Nice touch, flirting with the waitress. She's a pretty piece of ass. I'm sure you'd enjoy fucking her, had you the chance."

A distressed cry outside. Kelly! Frantic, he fought the bonds. If only he could shape-shift. But the chains stripped his magick.

"You thought you could hide." Shay's twin laughed. "I have your DNA. I know you, Chief Shaymore. I know your scent. As for the shape-shifting..."

His twin pushed into his face. "Two words, Elemental scum. Didn't. Work."

Shay's mind raced. Had to get to her...

"You can't break free, Phantom."

Going still, he examined the bonds. Silver, but the chains weren't steel. Some kind of alloy laced with magick.

Finding one of the links with his fingers, he tested it. He pulled harder, keeping his gaze on himself. How weird this was, listening to the lies and bragging while looking his twin in the eye to keep his attention from Shay's hands.

There. Pulling at a link, he felt it give slightly. He analyzed it. In layering the chains with alloy, the idiot had weakened the links.

Three men entered the room. Shay recognized the brown-haired one from the shop. "Move him into the back room," Shay's duplicate instructed.

Shay didn't fight, because he couldn't risk expending energy. The concrete floor came up hard as they tossed him into a whitewashed room. Dust motes danced on sunlight streaming from a window near the ceiling.

The room resembled a bomb shelter or a basement. The floor sloped toward a trench and a drain. His pulse kicked up as he saw the spigots jutting out from the wall. He inhaled. A sharp, coppery smell. Blood.

A slaughterhouse.

A length of similar silver chains wrapped around her body, Kelly was tossed into the room, landing on her side. Her mouth was sealed with duct tape. Shay growled at the Arcanes laughing as they hovered in the doorway.

Inching over toward her, he bent his head. "You okay?"

Eyes wide with fear, she nodded.

He wished he could touch her in reassurance. "Hang in there," he said softly. "We can beat this."

His twin smirked as he leaned against the doorway. "The mighty Phantom, big-shot navy SEAL. Now look at you. Trussed up like a chicken before the chopping block." The smirk turned into a dark smile. "Except we're not going to cut off your head. We need your body whole for the ritual. The less damage, the more pure the power."

Shay said nothing, watching Kelly's eyes widen as she studied the Arcanes.

"You're a disgrace, Shaymore. You can't stop us. We're gathering our forces, and soon we'll have enough power to blast the strongest Elemental to the netherworld."

"Let her go." Shay jerked his head at Kelly. "She's one of you, and there's no need to kill her."

Something flickered in the other's eyes. "She's not one of us. Kelly Denning chose the wrong side when she rescued Billy Rogers and fucked up our plans."

But a pulse jumped in his jaw. Shay's heartbeat accelerated. Damn bastard was lying. Why?

The doppelgänger gave a chilling smile. "All it took to capture you was the right bait. You're such a sucker for saving children. Especially little boys. I am you, and I know everything you know."

Not going there, bastard. You think you're me, but you're everything I struggled to change about myself.

"Wrong, asshole. I never miss a shot like you did on the ridge. And I never wet my pants when someone's firing live rounds at me," Shay taunted.

A Mage standing in the doorway snickered. The doppelgänger reddened and then turned and backhanded the Mage hard across the mouth. "Shut up. All of you, turn on the water.

Then get the car and head to Tegus to await the arrival of our leader."

Vehemently, Shay hoped the bastard's plane crashed.

"What about the tenth child?" one of the Arcanes asked. "We need one for the ritual."

"Soon. We located one in the States."

"What about the villagers? Kill them?" asked the brown-haired Mage.

An odd look entered his twin's eyes. "Don't touch them. They'll keep existing in their dream state."

Two of the Mages went to the faucets and twisted the spigots. Another plugged the drain. Water gushed onto the floor and ran down the trench.

Shay struggled to a sitting position, nudging Kelly to do the same.

"Have a nice swim," his twin sang out.

The door closed behind them.

Forcing himself to relax, he waited until the chains loosened enough to give him room. Shay snapped the first link with his fingers. Then he snapped another and another until he could wriggle his fingers and then his right hand through the hole he'd made.

"Bend over and I'll remove your gag."

Though he tried to be gentle, she winced as he ripped off the duct tape. "Sorry, sweetheart. I know that hurts."

Returning his attention to the links, he concentrated on breaking more.

"I guess these guys are really bad." She gave a small, shaky laugh. "Because the triskele isn't working against them."

"They've discovered a way past our magick. Stripped my powers, too."

"If they did that, how can you break your chains, Sam?"

"That son of a bitch may have my looks, but not my brains or strength. A baby could break these links."

Snap. Snap. The water began rising up the trench, to their toes.

"Hurry," she begged.

Too slow. Taking too long. With a last burst of strength, he focused and pushed with all his might.

Silver links burst apart, clinking on the floor. Shay ran to the door. Locked. Skimming the door with his hands, he looked for a weakness. None. The door was steel.

Searching the pockets of his cargo pants, he found a small tool. He picked the lock, turned the knob and pushed. They'd bolted it from the outside.

"Are you sure your powers are gone?" Kelly asked.

Without the chains binding him, his abilities might have returned, he thought. Shay closed his eyes and culled his magick. Feeling his powers surge like currents of electricity, he summoned them into his hand.

Opening his eyes, he looked at his palm. The faintest of sparks glistened and then died.

The door. But brute force wouldn't budge it. After body slamming it a few times, he gave up. Water rose to his ankles as he went to untie Kelly.

"Try your powers. Use the triskele," he urged.

Maybe without the silver binding her, it would work. Kelly grabbed the medallion but nothing happened. Her panicked gaze searched the room. "I don't understand."

Shay went to one wall and ran a hand across it, feeling a slight tingle. He swore. "Bastards lined the walls with a shield that negates all magick."

"They planned for this," she whispered. "They needed you and knew you'd come here to rescue the children with me. I'm sorry, Sam. If it weren't for me…"

His heart gave a lurch at her woebegone look. Shay stroked a finger down her cheek. "Don't. I make my own choices, and this is one I won't regret. Help me search the room. Look for weak spots, cracks, anything that might help us get out of here."

Kelly ran to the faucets to shut off the water, but the Mages had broken them.

His gaze shot up to the window and then to Kelly.

"I'll give you a hand up." Crouching, he cupped his hands as a step and lifted her up as she climbed onto his shoulders. Kelly supported herself against the wall, but her fingers barely touched the bottom of the windowsill.

Shay caught her in his arms and lowered her. Wide-eyed, she studied the room. "There has to be another way out. We can't reach the window."

"Then we'll have to swim for it."

Drowning was not a good way to die, Kelly thought as the water rose to her knees. Swim for the window? They'd die before opening it.

"I was kind of hoping you could shift into a seal. The animal kind, not the navy kind."

"Listen, sweetheart. You're going to have to trust me. Look at me, Kel." He pointed to his eyes with two fingers. "Focus. Right here. Focus on me."

"Okay," she whispered.

"We can only reach the window when the room fills up with water. I need you to concentrate and stay calm. Panic uses up air. We're going to float in the water until it gets too high, and then you'll fill your lungs with air and hold your breath as the water covers our heads. Take a deep, deep breath."

"Like Rose in *Titanic?*"

Shay smiled and stroked a finger down her cheek. "Just like Rose."

"I don't know if I can."

"You will," he stated. "I believe in you, Kelly. I'm your Jack and I'm telling you, hold on to my belt and swim out with me. I'll keep you safe."

"You can't hold your breath that long. Neither can I."

Kelly ran to the sunlit window. Flexing her fingers, she tried summoning her magick with a chant. Nothing worked.

Water rose to their waists now, sloshing around them.

They weren't going to make it, Kelly thought. Despite Sam's confidence, she knew it. Her breath came in little gasps.

"We're going to die," she choked out.

So strong and dependable, he looked calm.

Shay squeezed her shoulders. "No one's dying, sweetheart. Thanks to my training, I can hold my breath for a long time."

"So you're giving me a crash course? Did I ever tell you I'm not a great student?"

His hands were warm against her cheeks. "You're a terrific student," he murmured, smiling. "I remember those lessons I gave you in the cabin and how much you learned so quickly."

A flush heated her cheeks, and she laughed a little. Their lives were in jeopardy, and Sam made her think about sex.

Amusement and smoldering heat danced in his gaze. "I'm looking forward to teaching you more, Kelly. We're going to get out of this, because we both have too much to live for."

Gently he stroked her cheek as the water crept above their waists. "I'm not going to die until I make love to you again."

Gathering her courage, she looked down. "There's still time now. I heard sex in the bathtub is kinky but fun."

Sam kissed her gently, almost reverently. "I'm here and won't leave your side. We'll swim upward until we meet the ceiling. Then I'm opening that window, and we'll climb out. It's a long drop, so I'll go first and catch you."

"I'm not a good swimmer. Remember that time when you saved me in the creek?"

"I won't let go," he repeated. "Strip down to your underwear. Clothing weighs you down, and you need to be buoyant."

Following his instructions, she stripped. Sam gave a cocky grin as he removed his pants, shirt and boots.

"I lied," he said suddenly.

Kelly licked dry lips.

"I only said that about the clothing so I could watch you undress."

She sputtered and then splashed him. Flinging droplets from his hair, Sam laughed. "Good," he said softly. "Now you're smiling. Keep that smile on. I want to see it in the sunshine."

As he instructed, she began breathing deeply, learning his hand signals for when they could no longer talk. With every breath, Sam centered his warm gaze on her. His sheer affection fed her strength.

She, too, wanted to live so they could make love again.

Together, they began to breathe in rhythm. When the water reached her chin, he motioned for her to float. At first she sank, but he grabbed her hand.

"Remember what I taught you in the creek that day? You did great. You're doing great now, Kel. Hold on to me."

As he treaded water, she wrapped her arms around his muscled waist. "That's it," he encouraged. "This is only a big pool, and I'm your giant noodle."

Daring, she slid her hand a little below his waist. "Giant noodle. That's a new name for it. As long as it isn't limp."

Sam laughed again. His attitude eased her fear. Confidence began returning. He was with her, and she could do this. As the water rose, she let go, treading water. Sam reached out and squeezed her hand.

With him at her side, she could make it.

Kelly believed it, even as the ceiling drew close.

"Remember, don't panic and follow my lead." Husky and reassuring, his voice was a life raft.

"Please don't let go of my hand."

"I have to, just to open the window. Hang on to my waist and you'll be fine."

Water filled the room. Now they were only a foot from the ceiling, high enough to reach the window. Sam tugged her toward it. Legs kicking hard, heart beating fast against her chest, she followed him.

Sam grasped the window and pulled upward.

Nothing happened. He didn't have enough leverage.

Not going to panic. Sam could do it, even open a window that probably had been nailed shut. He was strong, a SEAL…

Water covered the window.

Panic pushed at the edges of her mind. Refusing to surrender to it, she clung to her belief in Sam.

"I have to let go, Kel. Take a deep breath while I open this damn thing," he shouted.

His hand felt so strong and assuring. Oh, how she hated to let go. But she did and then watched him dive beneath the water and fumble with the window.

The ceiling approached. Sam swam upward, took a tremendous gulp of air and dived back down.

Water covered her lips, her nose. She nearly kissed the ceiling and took one last, enormous breath.

Think of something else. You and Sam making love. So good. He was tender and gentle and considerate...we never wanted to leave that cabin.

She blew out a few bubbles. The window was still jammed.

Her lungs burned. Kelly's vision blurred. She opened her mouth to get air and gulped down water. Her airway shut as a terrible burning began in her chest.

Darkness engulfed her. She fell into its welcoming embrace.

As Shay kicked at the wooden window frame, he felt something nudge at his back. He glanced over one shoulder. Kelly floated, silky red hair wreathing her grayish face. Shay pushed back panic. *Don't think. Concentrate.*

His lungs began to protest, but he grimly kicked again.

The wood cracked this time. Sam kicked harder. Aided

by the pressure of the water, the window finally gave way, crashing outside.

The suction nearly pulled him outward. Sam swam back and grabbed Kelly's hand.

No time to consider the actions of such a fall. Broken bones could be repaired. Legs first.

He'd need his arms and hands to revive Kelly.

Holding her against his chest, he spilled outside, aiming for the ground so his body hit first. Sam gasped, dragging air deep into his lungs, sputtering as he fell, never letting go of Kelly.

He hit the ground first, his body cushioning Kelly. The hard fall was broken by a stack of firewood. Pain exploded in his right leg, but Sam ignored it as he rolled off the stacked firewood and tumbled to the ground.

Kelly's limp body followed.

He grabbed her and threw her on her back in the dirt. Adrenaline pumped through his body.

She lay pale and still, the pink lace of her bra and panties a bright splash of color against her grayish flesh. He opened her mouth and began CPR. With each compression and between breaths, he talked, urging her to live.

"Come back to me, sweetheart. C'mon, Kel, you can do it. Please, Kel, come back, come back, dammit. You're not leaving me now. Think of the kids. You have to get to them, keep them safe."

Tears blurred his vision. Not responding, she lay still and lifeless. One more compression. "I promised you we'd make love again, and goddammit, I don't break my promises."

Heartbeat.

She coughed. Sam quickly turned her on her side, letting her vomit out water. She coughed and coughed.

"Easy now," he soothed, stroking her hair. "You're here. It's okay. It's going to be okay."

Blue eyes the color of cornflowers met his. Kelly gulped down air as he continued soothing her.

"I drowned," she said between coughs.

Unable to find his voice, he nodded.

"You revived me."

Throat tight, he nodded again.

"I did it on purpose…" She drew in another beautiful, glorious breath. "Just so you'd kiss me."

He laughed shakily. Shay wiped tears with the back of one hand and then lifted her into a sitting position and drew her into his shaking arms.

He kissed her hard, never wanting to let go again.

Chapter 15

Sam's wet mouth trembled against her lips. He held her tight, his kiss frantic and urgent, reaffirming that she lived.

Closing her eyes, she clung to him as joy surged through her. Life was a precious gift, handed back to her by the man who'd refused to let her die, whose very mouth had breathed her back to consciousness.

Cupping her face, he kissed her harder, drinking in her mouth as if he were the drowning victim, drawing in her every breath as his own. A desperate kiss filled with passion, reminding her of the times when they'd made love until a scarlet dawn broke over the treetops. Sweaty, desperate, clinging love, each one never wanting to let go.

When they broke apart, he stroked a trembling finger down her cheek. Shadows darkened his hazel eyes. "I was so afraid I'd lost you. All because I had to let go."

Her heart lurched at the pain in his expression. Kelly brought his hands up and kissed his scarred knuckles. "I'm here now. I trust you, Sam. I knew you wouldn't give up on me and let me go for good. Besides, you promised to make love to me again."

He gave a slight smile. "Right."

"You kissed me like old times, Sam." She brushed a lock of wet hair back from his face. "The way you once kissed me, when we swore to each other that we wouldn't let anything come between us."

As if she were his next breath, his entire world.

The familiar guarded look dropped over his face. As he shifted his weight, Sam flinched.

"You're hurt," she cried out.

"Just a small break. I can walk."

"On a broken leg. Nothing serious. Sam!"

"I've had worse."

Now she noticed the odd angle of his leg, the lines of pain bracketing his mouth.

"I'll splint it, and we'll get on our way." He looked around the yard. "We have to get moving before those bastards return."

Kelly lifted her face to the burning sun. "Let me try something. I can heal in the sunlight. You bonded us together. Maybe I can combine my powers with yours to heal your leg. Will you let me try?"

A rough nod. Water beaded his dark lashes and clung to the tip of his strong nose. His mouth was a firm slash, indicating just how much he hurt.

With one hand, she clasped the triskele, her other hand gripping his. Kelly began the lyrical chant her father had taught her.

Soothing light and warmth filled her as the sun's healing rays surged into her body. Stunned, she watched the triskele pulse with white light. A glow suffused her body and traveled down her arm to their linked hands.

As the light touched him, it brightened to white, becoming

stronger. Gasping, he shuddered as the warm energy pulsed down his torso to the wounded leg.

After a few minutes, the glow faded. Sam ran a hand over his calf.

"I'll be damned," he muttered.

Beaming, she touched his leg. "It's the bond. Alone, we are not strong enough, but together we are practically invincible."

Sam narrowed his eyes. "How did you do that? What exactly are you, Kelly?"

Stricken, she drew back. "It's me, Sam. I'm just an Arcane. It's the triskele. It works as an amplifier."

"Not even the triskele can turn an Arcane into a healer. The power has to be within the Mage first."

"Are you calling me a liar?"

Sam's jaw tensed. "I'm saying your ability to heal isn't normal. We'll talk about it later. Right now, we need to get the hell out of here."

She'd thought they could regain what they once had. Forget they were Arcane and Elemental. But the suspicion on his face threw up new barriers.

They found their packs on a shelf in the front room and swiftly dressed into a spare change of clothing. Sam retrieved his pistol from the shelf where the Mages had placed it. Kelly slipped into a pair of sandals, glancing at the still-flooded back room.

"Those were my favorite sneakers."

"I'll buy you a new pair." Sam tucked the gun into his waistband. "Time to go hunting."

"For what?"

A ruthless look entered his hazel eyes. "The son of a bitch who wears my face."

Finding his duplicate proved easy.

From a shadowy doorway across the street, Shay watched

the restaurant. His twin sat at an outside table, downing a bottle of suds. Several bottles sat on the table before him.

Same brand Shay enjoyed.

His hands itched to hook around the bastard's throat and snap his neck. Shay curbed the urge. He was a SEAL and was used to waiting. Waiting to deploy. Waiting for the enemy to surface.

Waiting for Kelly to open her mouth and breathe again.

Waiting for Kelly to close her mouth about things he'd rather not discuss.

That kiss *had* been special. And kissing her had brought out all his fears about losing her. Damn if he could bring himself to admit it.

The old chemistry still flared between them. But taking it further was dangerous because deep inside, he still had feelings for Kelly Denning.

And then there was the little matter of Kelly's very unusual powers. Shay wondered about that. Maybe it was the triskele, as she'd suggested.

The same waitress who'd served them earlier approached the doppelgänger with the wariness of a sheep serving a wolf.

Laughing, the fake Shay swatted her bottom. "Nice ass." The words were a drunken slur.

As the girl backed away, his twin pulled her into his lap and began fondling her. Stark terror pinched the girl's face. Patrons in the café turned their heads.

Bile rose in Shay's throat. Why was everyone ignoring this?

"What the hell is wrong with those people?" he muttered.

"They're enchanted," Kelly said. "They don't care about anything. It's as if everything they cared about has been erased from memory. Including their own values."

The frightened waitress pushed at his chest as his twin slid his hands beneath her skirt.

"If he takes her into the back, I'm going to be sick." Kelly bit a knuckle.

Shay shook his head. "All he cares about is screwing her. And he thinks he's my exact duplicate. That's not me."

She glanced at him. "No, it's not. But you once were obsessed with women. Your reputation was well-known even among Arcanes. Oh, you had too much honor to do that," she said, flicking a hand at his twin. "But all the servants talked about Master Samuel sneaking lovers out of the mansion when dawn broke."

Guilt pricked his conscience. "House gossip. Rumors."

"That's what I said, until I cleaned your room and found boxes of condoms in your closet."

No condemnation, just resignation. Stricken, he stared at the mirror image of himself, remembering his twin's mocking words. Kelly was right. And he still was a womanizer. Everyone knew it, from his tight unit to the support staff on ST 21.

I'm not like this anymore.

Yes, you are. After the fire, the old ways were comforting and familiar.

It sickened him to see tears rolling down the young waitress's cheeks as the fake Shay nuzzled her neck.

Shame gnawed through him. "He's got my DNA stamped into his body. He's like me. He uses women for sex and then moves on."

"Did you ever force a woman?"

"No!"

"This one seems intent on it. And that's not you, Sam. You may have been a womanizer, but you're no bastard. If you were, I'd never have become your lover."

"Why did you?"

Her soft gaze met his. "Because I believed in you, not your reputation. It wasn't the sex. It was your kindness, your generous nature and your compassion for others. You always treated everyone, even the lowest servant, with great respect. And you saw me as a woman, not an Arcane."

She looked at him tenderly, as if touching the broken pieces inside him, willing them to mend. Too overwhelmed by her deep faith in him, he could not speak. Reaching up, he caressed her cheek with a finger.

Then he dropped his hand and glanced at the restaurant. "We've got to get him away from her. I have an idea."

Two streets away, he turned onto a deserted street. Shay scanned the area and saw an abandoned hotel. He picked the lock and opened the door. A waft of stale air greeted him. The lobby smelled of mildew. Shay ran a finger over the dusty front counter. How long had this village been enchanted?

"How fast can you run?" he asked.

"I'm a good sprinter."

"You don't have to go far. Go back to the restaurant, lead him here and I'll be waiting."

"I can outrun him, but not if he calls on his Arcane magick," Kelly said.

"He's too damn drunk to remember how to use his powers."

"Ah. I guess…it's a good thing you know him so well."

Guilelessly she looked at him. Sam's heart kicked hard. So pretty, and honest. Honesty was something he valued, because in his job, he sometimes had to lie.

And in your personal life, too, the little voice inside him added.

"If he looks like he's going to use magick, start screaming. No one will care but me."

"Be careful." Kelly touched his arm.

He hesitated, desperately wanting to kiss her and hold her against him as he had before. Shay nodded, watching her jog back.

Hovering by the doorway, he cupped his pistol and waited.

A few minutes later he heard the sound of footsteps in the street running fast. "Tag, you're it," she sang out.

Shay pointed his Sig and aimed.

"Can't you run faster, you drunk monkey? Twenty feet behind me, and you're ready to fall over."

She'd given her pursuer's position. *Good girl.*

Kelly hooked a right and ran toward Shay. His twin was on her heels. Seeing Shay, Kelly dropped and rolled clear. Shay fired at his twin's left thigh.

The Mage screamed and released a string of curses Shay knew too well as he clutched his leg and fell down.

Shay dragged him into the hotel lobby and searched his quarry. Kelly ran inside and shut and locked the door.

"Draw the curtains," he ordered. He trained his gun on the fake Shay. "Where the hell are those kids?"

"I don't know." His twin was cursing as blood seeped between the fingers pressed against his leg. "Goddammit, that hurts, you bastard."

Placing a foot on the man's groin, he aimed the pistol at his other leg. "A shattered kneecap hurts worse. First, another bullet in your thigh, right into the muscle. Then a kneecap. I've got time and ammo. Tell me where the children are."

Panic flared in the man's hazel gaze. Shay felt disoriented, as if looking into a mirror image of himself.

It's not you.

"You've got ten seconds. Nine, eight, seven..."

"They aren't here," the twin burst out. "They're not even in the country!"

Behind him, Kelly gasped.

"Where. Are. They?"

"The master refused to tell me. My orders were to find you both and kill you but not damage your body too much. Her, it didn't matter." Shay's twin pointed to Kelly.

Frustration and anger snaked through him. "Are they in the United States?"

No answer. Shay fired a bullet into his other thigh. The man screamed. Kelly paled but remained silent.

"Yes, but I don't know where! Only the master knows."

"Who set us up at the LZ? The admiral? Curt?"

"I'm just like you. I'll never tell."

Holding on to his fraying temper, Shay shook his head. "You're too weak to pull this off alone. No matter how much you look like me, you're not."

"Fuck you."

Shay retained his cool. No way would this bastard get under his skin. But the man's expression shifted and turned crafty. A chill snaked down his spine. He knew the expression, knew what it meant. Had used it on the enemy before to interrogate. Find the weak spots…

"I may look like you, but I'm stronger. I'd never let a stupid yearly tradition weaken me. Sentimental rubbish."

Shay went still.

"The one time of year when the big, bad navy SEAL turns to mush." The other tilted his head as if listening. "I can hear the Christmas carols playing now. The favorites, of course. So pathetic. A ritual for rotting corpses."

"Stop it," Shay ordered. The knife in his heart gave a vicious twist.

"Pretty, shining, sparkling tinsel," he murmured. "So festive, fluttering in the wind. His favorite. You couldn't save him because you were too busy fucking that slut, so every year you invade the stores like the other losers. But you're all alone, Samuel Shaymore, so sad and alone, celebrating a holiday no one will celebrate with you. Your father would be so ashamed…."

Fury and grief collided together, adrenaline shooting through his body. Shay pointed his weapon at the man's face.

"Good thing he's dead and you can't disappoint him anymore."

"Shut up," he screamed.

"Sam, don't let him do this to you."

Shay glanced at Kelly and saw the pity and anger tightening her face. "Kelly, get back, now!"

"You went from rebelling against the old man to trying to make him proud. Do exactly as he would have wanted. That's the only reason you became a SEAL. You rescue others but couldn't save your own little brother."

A beseeching look from his twin. "Please, Sammy, save me. Please, it's hot. It's so hot, and you promised to sing for me. You promised, you lied…"

"Oh, Sam," Kelly whispered.

"Oh, Sam," the other mocked. "You saved yourself and let them die."

"Don't listen to him. This bastard wanted you as a sacrifice because of your courage and honor, remember?"

Shay's fingers curled tightly around his weapon. Courage. Honor. He was a U.S. Navy SEAL and a powerful Phantom Mage, not some ass-kicked whimpering fool….

He was a soldier, and no one caught him off guard….

Goddammit!

"Kelly, down," he yelled, spying the move, seeing the stiletto the fake Shay fished out of one boot.

Shay dropped and fired as his twin threw the knife. The blade landed in the wall, where Kelly's chest would have been.

Blood dribbled from the hole in his twin's forehead as the man stared sightlessly at the ceiling. Shay put a finger against the man's neck and checked his pulse to make certain.

This is what I'll look like dead.

And then the corpse shimmered and shifted into a square-jawed man with features nothing like his, a body that had gone to fat. The duplicate's true form.

Taking a deep breath, he expunged the grief and shame, purging it from his system.

"Sam, are you okay?"

"Fine," he snapped. "Next time, listen to me when I tell you to stay back. Do I have to save your life twice?"

Hurt filled her wide blue eyes. Shay rubbed his nape. "I'm sorry, Kelly. But you need to listen to me when I give an order."

Her gaze fell to the dead man. "We have to bury him before someone finds the body."

"No need," he said curtly. "Stand over there, by the door."

Summoning his powers, he directed a sizzling current of energy at the corpse. It imploded, leaving behind a mound of gray ash. He went to the wall and leaned against it. Gods, he was exhausted.

Kelly placed a reassuring hand on his arm as he holstered the pistol. He hated how she kept looking at him as if expecting him to break down and cry.

Not him. That was saved for one precious day every year.

"We need answers," he muttered, more to himself. "Someone here has to know something."

"Even if we could question the villagers, it's useless. They're enchanted. There's no way to break the spell."

He remembered the book of spells. "Maybe there is."

A hardened soldier walked beside her, gaze scanning the area, his muscled body tensed and coiled for action. When they reached the shop, they found the book of spells still open on the counter, and Sam slid on black gloves he'd found in his pack. With extreme care, he turned the pages. "The spell to enchant them has to be in this book, so the counterspell must be here, as well."

Kelly shook her head. "You won't find it like that. Every Arcane spell has a counterspell, but they're hidden."

She pointed to the spidery writing. "This is a book of darkness, so the opposite would be…"

"Light," Sam finished.

Outside, he placed the book on the ground in the direct sunlight. Nothing happened.

And then she walked around the book to read it upside down. Faint writing appeared around the edges of each page.

"Here."

Sam squinted and shook his head. "Singing chant. I can try this, but I'm no Arcane. I can't carry the correct notes."

"I can."

Lifting her hands skyward, she closed her eyes. Power hummed through her body. She recited the spell, calling on the good, strong light to cast away the darkness of sleep holding the townspeople hostage.

Kelly opened her eyes and caught Sam's sharpened gaze. "I felt something in the air. Let's see if it worked."

"Wait." He knelt down and leafed through the pages. "We need to find a spell to contain this book, keep the dark magick at bay."

Sam scanned the pages and tapped the parchment. "Here's a locking spell. Try this."

Stunned, she stared at him. They'd been in such a hurry before, she'd failed to notice.

"Sam, this is a book for Arcanes. How can you read the spells? They should be obstructed to an Elemental. My ancestors guarded this book from your people."

He glanced down. "I'll be damned."

Expression guarded, he touched the book. "Doesn't matter now. Chant the spell and lock up the book. We need to take it with us."

After, they gathered their packs and went into the street. People looked dazed as they stumbled down the sidewalks, shaking their heads as if dispelling a long sleep. Sam went still and swore.

Kelly's heart dropped to her stomach.

The dark enchantment holding the townspeople hostage had cloaked them, as well. People of all ages and races walked the streets. Dark-skinned. Pale. She glimpsed a redheaded girl about her age accompanying an Asian boy. They looked like college students.

A golden haze surrounded each person. Kelly gasped.

"They're not locals. They're Elementals. How did they get here?"

His jaw turned to granite. "The rogue Arcanes probably rounded them up to make the mass extermination easier."

Kelly stopped a woman wearing skinny jeans and a scoop-necked yellow shirt. She looked American and about eighteen years old. The girl hoisted her backpack, looked at her and smiled.

"Are you an Elemental?" Kelly asked in English.

The girl beamed. "You headed to the festival, too? Sweet. I heard there's a record number of attendees this year. This town rocks. None of those slimy Arcanes for miles."

The insult stung. "I'm an Arcane," Kelly said.

Immediately the girl squinted, as if examining Kelly's aura. Her expression changed. "What the hell do you want, bitch? I'm late meeting my friends."

"Whoa." Sam pushed himself between the girl and Kelly. "Easy now. We're looking for answers. What brought you here?"

The girl's eyes narrowed as she scanned him. "I can see your aura. You're one of us."

Wrinkling her nose, she skirted around Kelly. *Okay, I'm not back in elementary school and this isn't the popular girl tossing eggs at me.* Still, it stung.

"It's the Festival of Summer Solstice. We heard it was held in this town this year and decided to visit."

"Then what?" Sam demanded.

"After backpacking across Central America, Bob and I came here. We joined up with friends from school, got a hotel and went to the restaurant for dinner. That was last night."

The girl looked bewildered. "Wasn't it?"

Sam smiled. "Go meet your friends. It's fine now."

As the girl rushed away, he gave Kelly a meaningful look. "The annual festival of the sun was four weeks ago."

Her mouth went dry. "They've been here that long. Gods, how many weeks have these Arcanes planned this?"

"Maybe months, even years."

"My agency never got any missing persons reports." Kelly pointed to the girl scurrying away from them. "I'm sure she has parents who are worried about her."

"Unless the parents are here. It's a big village, and it's an important festival to Mages."

"Elementals," she corrected. "Your people cull power from the four elements of earth, sun, sky and water. Mine can't. Mine don't celebrate the summer solstice."

Sam's gaze hardened. "And mine do, which made it easier for these rogues to lure them into a trap. Goddamn Arcanes. Damn them to hell."

His words sliced her, jabbing deep. Seeing her face, he softened his expression. "I'm sorry, Kel. Spoke before I thought. Not all your people are like that."

"For a moment, you sounded as if they were. And I'm one. What your people consider the enemy."

His voice went husky. He stroked a finger down her cheek. "Not you."

Kelly closed her eyes, relishing the tender touch. Remembering what they once shared. Time had crushed all her young hopes, replacing them with cold reality.

Her eyes snapped open. "Not me, Sam? Even though I belong to the group targeting your kind?"

Bleakness shadowed his face. "Sometimes I wish we could go back in time, when it was you and me, not Arcane and Elemental. Life was easier, Kelly."

"But it isn't now. We're on opposite sides. When everything is said and done, I'm still Kelly Denning, Arcane."

A hollow ache settled in her chest. "Always the enemy in the eyes of your people."

His palm cupped her cheek. With a gentle thumb, he stroked over her skin, arousing feelings she tried so hard to bury. "Screw the labels. Arcane. Elemental. You're Kelly Denning. A courageous and stubborn woman. When I pulled you from the room, thinking you were dead, part of me wanted to die, as well. I wasn't thinking of what group you belong to, Kel. All I could think of was you."

Kelly's heart skipped a beat. "I've missed you, Sam," she said, her voice catching.

This man had saved her life, had risked defying his lieutenant to save innocents. He was a true hero.

If only he could be hers once more. Once he had been. Could they ever go back again? Or would they always have their loyal alliances to their own people come first?

Stroking her cheek, Shay felt like drowning in her eyes. So sweet, pretty and seemingly fragile, yet inside Kelly was a core of solid steel.

Gods, he missed her with every single breath he drew into his lungs. For so long, he'd tried to forget her and erase her from his heart.

Didn't work.

Now he told himself to concentrate on the mission.

Stepping away from her, Shay sent streams of white energy into the streets. Good, pure magick shot through the village, touching everyone inside.

He lowered his hands. "I sent an exposure shield through the town to protect the villagers. It's not as powerful as I'd like, but it should suffice. With a small bonus."

"Which is?" she challenged.

Shay rubbed the back of his neck. "Any Arcane will have an extremely visible aura to Elementals."

Kelly turned over her palms, as if trying to discern her own natural aura. "Smacks of profiling to me."

"I know," he said gently. "But it's the only way we can identify the Arcanes. We know what the potential enemy is, but not which ones."

"Sam, you painted a bull's-eye on my back. What if an Elemental decides on target practice?"

"They won't, as long as you're with me."

"So as long as I'm with you, an Elemental, I'm okay. Because they'll assume you're restraining me. Like keeping a vicious dog on a leash." Kelly bit her lip. "No matter what I do, or even how many of your people I save, I'll never be free, will I? Your kind will always despise me. Use me, but hate me."

Shay went still. Her stricken expression twisted his heart. She spoke the truth.

His gaze swept the streets, filled with the soft gold glow of Elemental auras. His people. The righteous ones, who thought themselves better than Arcanes. The thought disgusted him.

"You're right. They will never value you for who you are, Kel. I can't promise things will change. But I will promise to do everything in my power to convince my people of how wrong they are. Until then, I need you to stick close to me."

Something in his chest eased. He released a deep breath.

And what about later, when he had to turn her over to the authorities? Could he make the pigheaded council listen to reason?

Somehow, he must. Because not only Kelly's life depended on it, but that of her entire people.

They went to a small restaurant, where Kelly ordered tea. Outside, he called Dakota, relieved to finally contact his lieutenant.

Shay quickly explained what had happened.

His lieutenant's voice crackled over the phone. "Plans have changed. Get your ass on the next flight from Tegus with Kelly until we figure out what the hell is going on."

"No way, LT. Too dangerous on these roads at night. We'll leave tomorrow." Shay told him about the village filled with Elemental Mages.

"And you're a target. Stay out of sight. Need a safe house?" Dakota asked.

Shay closed his eyes, leaning his forehead against the lamppost. He remembered one place no one would ever look for them. "Got it. Need a car, though. Have one waiting for me at the Atlanta airport."

"We're finishing up here, cutting this training op short." Dakota hesitated. "Take good care of her, Shay. Kelly is our only link to this, and if something happens to her, we're screwed. No one else can see the Death Mask."

He hung up and then made a reservation on his cell. Then he returned to Kelly and tossed some lemps on the table. "Dakota officially ordered me to take good care of you."

"Forget me. We have to find those kids, and they're back in the States."

"We'll find them. We'll get a room for tonight and head out tomorrow. I booked us on the afternoon flight from Tegus to Miami and then Miami to Atlanta."

As she started to protest he put a finger against her lips. "It's getting late and I'm not risking driving in the dark and running into another Arcane itching to kill you."

A morass of politics muddied everything. Soon as they returned to the States, Shay knew the council would be riding his ass to hand Kelly over to its custody.

Chapter 16

Sam clearly had no intentions of leaving her alone. Placing a proprietary hand on the small of her back, he scanned the crowd as they walked the cracked sidewalk paralleling the main street. Seeing his scowl, and the pistol he now carried openly, Elementals gave them a wide berth.

He booked them into a single room in a small hotel in a private cul-de-sac. Frying peppers and onions from the little restaurant downstairs scented the air as they climbed the narrow staircase. Inside the room, he set down their packs. Kelly gazed at the sapphire-and-emerald-embroidered quilt on the wide bed.

"Planning to sleep on the floor again, Sam?"

"We'll see," he said softly.

Downstairs, he found the corner table by the wall gave a wide view of the restaurant as he sat facing the front. Other Elementals nodded respectfully to Sam but gave Kelly cool looks of disdain. Lust flared in the gazes of a few males. Kelly hunched her shoulders, hating the tight blouse.

Sackcloth would suffice.

"Those guys keep staring as if I'm your toy and they're next at the sandbox," she murmured, reaching for a corn chip from the bowl their waitress placed on the table.

His gaze a warning blade, Sam scowled until the interested Mages looked away. He leaned back and took a long pull of beer. "I don't share."

"And I'm not a plaything."

"But you are fun in the sandbox. I always enjoyed the times we played together." A corner of his mouth pulled upward as he winked.

Blushing, she glanced away. He was accustomed to women tumbling into his bed. Flirting came naturally to Sam, but not to her. Work came first, an effective barrier between her and a potentially hurtful world.

"You look so pretty when you blush. Your cheeks don't turn pink like other redheads. More like fire, a passionate, living flame," he murmured.

It hurt so much to hear his seductive whispers, just like those that came from the man she'd known, that Kelly put up a hand. "Stop. This is too much like old times. I can't do this."

Sam drew his brows together. "Do what?"

Pain wrenched her insides. Did he truly forget what they'd shared, the passion and the heated desire? Kelly swallowed hard. "Pretend I'm normal, and you're acting as if you want me."

"You *are* perfectly normal, and it's not an act," he said softly. He covered her hand with his, the strength in those fingers able to snap a man's neck now gentle as his thumb slowly stroked her skin.

Like an addict craving a drug, she hungered for more. Sam still held her hand, his caressing gaze turning her nipples hard as pearls. He stared at her mouth with such intensity, she had to squeeze her thighs together to stop squirming.

She knew if she surrendered, she'd end up sprawled naked

in bed, those same clenched thighs spilling open as he settled between them…

A wiry metrosexual Elemental in a lavender polo shirt stared at her. He elbowed his male friend and laughed. She couldn't hear the words but discerned their meaning. Flicking his tongue in a crude manner, the Mage formed an O with one hand, licked his other finger and then plunged it rapidly in and out.

Heat crawled up her cheeks. Shame and humiliation replaced sexual arousal. As she prepared to deliver the bastard a stinging insult, Sam glanced over. Seeing the obscene gesture, he narrowed his eyes.

It happened so quickly, she didn't see Sam move. And then he was shoving Polo Shirt against the wall hard enough to make the picture frames rattle.

He gave the young Mage's throat a powerful squeeze. "Got a problem?"

At the gasping head shake, Sam gave a dangerous smile. "Good. Because next time you insult my lady like that, I'll crush your windpipe, cut out your wagging tongue and shove it up your…"

"Sam!" Kelly hissed.

He glanced over, his gaze softening. "Okay."

As he released the Mage, the man rubbed his throat and wheezed. "Chill out, man. She's just an Arcane. Don't know why they let scum in here."

Sam gave a thoughtful look. "Right. Scum shouldn't be allowed in here."

Wincing, Kelly watched Sam drag Polo Shirt through the restaurant and toss him onto the street. "Adios! I'd leave town now. If I see you again, I'll rearrange your face."

Then he swept his hard gaze over the onlookers, suddenly absorbed in their meals except for a few women, who sighed in apparent admiration, and Polo Shirt's companion, who dropped money on the table and ran after his friend.

When he resumed his seat, Kelly shook her head. "Was that necessary?"

Sam gave a mild look. "What? Taking out the trash?"

"You didn't have to make a scene."

Rolling his muscular shoulders, Sam shrugged. "If I didn't, others would take his place. They won't bother you anymore, Kel. I always protect my own."

Barely leashing her temper, she scowled as Sam bit into a crunchy taco. "You're acting and sounding like a bad B-movie hero."

He swallowed a mouthful of taco, his expression mild. "Funny. I always thought I was more the A-list type."

"I fight my own battles. I don't need your protection. I'm not a spineless coward they can push around."

Speculation in those hazel eyes now flared with intent. "You never were a spineless coward. But you were naive and sweetly innocent in the ways of men."

He'd taken that innocence and turned it into experience in taking her to the heights of pleasure. Tension steeled her spine as she leaned forward, feeling the electricity spark between them.

"Sexually inexperienced before, but not now. I can handle guys like that."

"When you're with me, you won't have to. When I saw how that bastard was humiliating you, I had to teach him a lesson."

"Dial down the testosterone, Sam. I never enjoyed domineering males."

"Once the bedroom door was closed, you did."

His satisfied smile made her flush. Deep inside, her feminine side felt aroused at the memory of Sam, insatiable, sexually aggressive, uncontrollable. Dominating her thoroughly in the bedroom. Sam responding to the sheer desire in her eyes, fisting a hand in her hair as he bent her over the bed's edge and took her from behind like a wolf.

Sam, his ragged breath echoing in her ear as he pushed her

from one shattering climax to another, refusing to stop, making love to her until they both lay exhausted.

Sam, the sexually dominant male turning tender and endearing as he pulled her into his strong arms afterward, stroking her cheek as they shared their hopes and dreams.

That was in the past. A fantasy.

Fantasies aside, she resented him playing the shining knight. She could take care of herself. "I'm not the girl you once knew, who'd fall into your arms if you snapped your fingers."

"No, you're not," he murmured. "But can you handle what I want to give you now?"

She locked gazes like a bull touching horns. "I can take whatever you want to give. Are you willing?"

A dangerous smile touched his wide, full mouth. The kind of smile that lured women into opening their thighs. "Maybe you couldn't in the past, when you were innocent." Sam's voice deepened. "But now…you're more exciting, spirited, stronger. The kind of sensually mature woman who makes a man wonder what she'd feel like splayed naked beneath him."

Kelly choked past a sip of beer. "Try it. Not going to work."

"I enjoy a challenge."

The husky intent in his voice stroked over her shivering skin. Once he'd whispered words of passion, his big hands caressing and coaxing her until her shyness and control fractured. Daring her to reach beyond her inhibitions, coaxing her into the heights of unbridled sexuality.

Sam leaned forward, flames dancing in his darkened eyes. "Do you? Because I won't lie, Kel. I want you so badly right now, it's hard to breathe. You think that asshole turned me aggressive? No. It's being around you and the thought of that bed upstairs. Manners and politeness go to hell. I turn into a man with one thing on my mind…."

Breath caught in her throat at the dangerous glint in his eye. "Dragging you upstairs and getting you naked into that bed.

Making love to you until we're both panting and exhausted. I want to make you sweat, make you tremble, make you scream, and just when you think I'm done, I'm going to push you harder and harder until you scream again. And again."

His voice thickened. "I want to make you mine. So I'll ask you again. You up for the challenge?"

Beneath the table, Kelly pressed her thighs together, feeling the space between them grow warm and moist. So long since fire had raced through her blood, arousing her until her own clothing felt tight and restrictive and every breath constricted her lungs. If he didn't take her soon, she'd die.

Her voice dropped to the barest whisper. "Oh, yes. So get ready."

The past hadn't escaped them after all. Because it was here, vibrant and alive, in all its fervent need, Shay realized.

Not a flirt, nor experienced in seduction. So she'd said. Not true. As they ate dinner, Shay watched her with growing hunger. He saw her pulse beat wildly at the base of her slender throat. He itched to stroke his tongue over that jumping pulse, feel all warm, soft female skin as he stroked her naked flesh.

Kelly moistened her wet, red mouth with the tip of her tongue. She looked flushed, hot. Oh, man, so very hot.

Shay set down his beer, his blood surging straight to his groin. He stood, the chair toppling to the floor.

"Upstairs. Now." He hardly recognized his voice, deepened by sexual urgency. His cock hardened painfully inside his jeans.

With languid grace, she stood. Each sinuous sway of her hips sent blood surging straight to his groin. Seeing the other men watch, he turned and shot a warning glance.

Mine.

Upstairs, he pulled her into the room and slammed the door shut with a hard boot kick. Breathing jaggedly, Shay pinned her to the wall, desire cranked up to a frenzy at the flush of sexual heat on her face, the glittering arousal in her blue eyes mirroring his own.

"I want you so much," he muttered. "And I'm no gentleman, Kel. So if you know what's good for you, you'll run into that bathroom and lock the door and stay as far away as you can before I touch you."

Shay released her. "You have two minutes. Maybe less."

Breathing hard, she gave a sultry smile. "I never did like what's good for me."

They tore at each other's clothing. Shay peeled off boots, socks and shirt. Then he reached for the buckle of his belt and slid his pants down and kicked them off.

Thick penis erect, Shay held on to his control by a bare thread.

With a soft sigh many a silly man would take as surrender, she slipped off her panties and bra.

Not surrender, but a fracturing of barely leashed desire. With a rough growl, he lunged, pushing her naked body back onto the bed.

Her lips were warm and soft, as delicious as he'd remembered. He could kiss her all night, if it meant holding her this close. Shay cupped the back of her head as he devoured her mouth, licking and teasing.

He reached for her, but this time Kelly was the one touching him, her eager hands pulling the sheet off, her palms flattened against his chest. Her mouth against his skin, trailing tiny kisses over the hard line of his jaw, his throat.

A sharp intake of breath as she saw the silvery stretch of old scar tissue on his thigh. "What happened?"

Speechless, he went still. Words evaded him after the freshness of the nightmare still lingered, the piercing cries of Kelly's screams.

Her soft palm rested on his thigh. "The fire?"

A quiet statement. He nodded.

Moisture gathered in her eyes. Shay reached up and wiped a tear threatening to spill from her eyes. "Don't cry, sweetheart."

"It hurts me to see you like this," she whispered. "I wish I could have helped."

Shay held her gaze, willing her to see the truth. "You did help. My memories of you carried me through. You sustained me when I found it impossible to take the next step. You gave me a strength I never knew I possessed."

Kelly bent her head and kissed the scar tissue, her soft, warm mouth sliding over a wound that had never fully healed.

Those tender kisses chased away past pain and banished the horror of what happened. She kissed the inside of his thigh, the hunger inside him growing to the point of pain.

Kelly stopped and stroked a finger along the underside of his rigid cock.

Shay dragged in a deep breath as she encased his erection in her hand and took him into her mouth.

Closing his eyes, he let his head drop back as her sweet mouth caressed him.

Oh, gods, the exquisite pleasure of Kelly, her scent swimming in his nostrils, the softness of her lips against his aching flesh, the little humming sound she made. Like a cat with a bowl of cream, her little pink tongue delicately flicked the rounded knob of his weeping cock.

Desperate to get inside her, he pulled her away. Kelly sat back, red hair tumbling around her shoulders, pink suffusing her cheeks. His gaze dropped to the lush swell of her breasts, her dusky nipples standing to points. She looked so pretty. So sexy. Shay felt the last of his control fracture. Fisting his hands, he fought to control their shaking.

And then he reached for her again. His Kelly, his intoxicating drug he thought he'd gotten out of his system for good.

When all the time, she'd never truly left.

* * *

Oh, gods, Kelly wanted this man all over again, skin to skin, their bodies sweat-slicked and rubbing against each other.

They rolled on the bed, tangling together.

Sam touched her, big, calloused palms skimming up the small of her back, stroking the curve of her spine. "I love it when I get you all wet and ready for me," he muttered against her mouth. "It drives me crazy to hear those little sounds you make."

Then he fisted a hand in her hair, bent her head back and kissed her with such passion she could barely breathe. Kelly could think of nothing but Sam, his spicy taste in her mouth as he kissed her hard and deep, his skin slick and firm against hers, the silky hairs on his naked thighs rubbing against hers.

Kelly opened her thighs, exposing herself to him, the first man she'd ever given her body to. Sam slipped a hand between her legs and caressed her, drawing a finger through her swollen folds. Little gasps came from her mouth as she clutched him, her mouth tasting the salty slickness of the hard curve of his shoulder. Kelly nipped him lightly, earning a hiss of breath. With a thumb, he teased her clit and then sank a finger deep inside her. Every delicious stroke worked incredible magick on her, cranking the sweet tension higher until she was panting. She was so close, close…

Sam's mouth encased one hard nipple. He bit lightly.

Screaming, she shattered, her nails digging into the hard muscles of his back.

Pride and masculine possession shone in his gaze as he sat back, watching her. Sam reached into his wallet and withdrew a foil packet.

Trembling, she lay back, watching him slip on the condom.

His limbs were long and sturdy and roped with muscle. Wide shoulders gave way to the classic V of narrow waist and hips. A few scars nicked the planes of muscle dividing his back.

Then he was nudging her thighs open, settling between them. Desire ignited the green in his eyes. Sam laced his fingers between hers, his muscled weight pinning her down.

The position was sweetly intimate. Sam's body atop hers, his hard chest pressed against her soft breasts, his sleekly muscled flanks entwined with her slender legs, his heated gaze fused to hers. She was the only person in the world who mattered to him now.

Sam lowered his mouth and dropped a singularly sweet kiss on her lips.

The hard knob of his cock slid against her soaked folds. The slow, teasing move made her grit her teeth. An impish grin, so typically Sam, warned he knew exactly how the motion drove her crazy. Kelly rolled her hips upward.

He thrust hard into her, pushing past the resistance of her tiny internal muscles, sealing them hip and hip. Kelly flinched a little. It had been a long time since she'd had sex.

A long time since she'd opened herself up to a man, let him into the most private part of her body…her heart.

"Ah, gods, you feel so damn good," he muttered. Concern flared in his gaze. "You okay, Kel?"

She drew a long, trembling sigh. "Now I am."

Pleasure rippled through her as he began to move. Slowly out and then back inside her, building the heat between them. All the while his gaze was warm and soft on her, the look on his face telling her this was more than sex.

More than making love.

It was reigniting the flame they both thought had died, had wanted to die.

It consumed them, sending them spiraling together into erotic bliss as his hips drove harder and faster. She pushed upward, meeting his frantic moves. Kelly tightened her hands around his as the crisp hair on his chest rubbed against her sensitive nipples. She squeezed hard around him, feeling the incredible pressure build until she cried out and climaxed again, gasping for air, feeling as if she were flying.

And would never descend.

Sam closed his eyes and threw his head back, the corded muscles on his neck straining as he gave one last thrust. His cock twitched inside her as Sam shouted her name. He bucked and shuddered against her.

Wrapping her arms around him, she held him close as he collapsed atop her, his muscled weight pressing her against the soft mattress. Sam's ragged breathing bellowed into her ear as he pillowed his head next to hers.

Finally he pushed himself off, sat on the bed's side and disposed of the condom. Kelly felt a sudden chill at his business-like actions. Was this only sex? Or something more?

But then he joined her again, pulling her into his arms and sweetly kissing her forehead. For a long few minutes, they lay together, Kelly stroking the sweat-dampened hairs on his muscled chest.

"Incredible."

He playfully touched her nose. "Yes, you are."

Sex lowered the barriers between them. She kissed the curve of his shoulder. "I wish we had never known each other before. Then everything would have been fresh and new to us, instead of these dark secrets between us."

Sam lifted his head, his brows knitting. "What?"

"Real lovers don't share the past we have. They don't hide their hurts from each other."

"I don't want secrets between us," he stated quietly.

"Then tell me. Why did your duplicate push your buttons like that? What was he talking about?"

Jaw tensing, he looked away.

"Please, tell me, Sam. I must know. If it's my fault…" she whispered.

Expelling a breath, he shook his head. "It's not you. Not

your fault. It's Christmas. I haven't spent a single Christmas with anyone, except my family."

Sickening realization hit her. "You visit them…"

"At their graves." A husky whisper, pain haunting those dreamy hazel eyes. "It's all I have left, so I go there every year instead of friends' homes."

Pressure built behind Kelly's eyes as she saw the real Sam. The cocky, charming Sam. The cool, efficient SEAL. What a falsehood, when the real man was alone, hiding behind barricades of duty, honor and obligation.

"Go on."

"That bastard Arcane was right. I'm a sentimental fool. I couldn't save him, so I try to make up for it. Petie loved Christmas, loved seeing the gifts under the tree. Most of all, he adored hanging the tinsel on the trees. Silver. He said it looked like stars sparkling beneath the lights. He always asked me to sing carols…."

His voice cracked. "Every year, I buy silver tinsel and a little tree and place it by his gravestone. Keep thinking he'd see it from wherever he was and it'd make him smile. And then I sing his favorite carols. Stupid. As if he'd know."

Stupid? It was the sweetest thing she'd ever heard. A horrid ache settled in her chest as she envisioned him sitting on the ground by his little brother's grave, cold wind whispering through the cheerful silver tinsel as Sam sang Christmas carols.

So alone, haunted by sorrow…

"Why do you put yourself through it every year?"

He stared at the ceiling. "I don't want grief and anger to turn into blind hatred. The ritual keeps me normal when I feel like I'm turning cold and empty inside. It connects me to Pete and his ability to love everyone unconditionally."

Kelly had the odd feeling she finally had seen straight through to his heart. He wasn't a cold, efficient warrior, but a grieving man determined to keep hatred and bitterness at bay. The navy had molded him into a disciplined, purposeful soldier, someone she thought she'd never connect with again. Truth was, they had plenty in common. Just like her, Sam was lost and alone, but not broken.

Never broken, she thought vehemently.

Raising herself up on her elbows, she dropped a tender kiss on his jaw. "Pete knows. I'm certain of it. You have a generous, loving heart."

Emotions shadowed his gaze. And then he rolled her beneath him and loved her once more, this time longer, sweeter, slower, until she wanted to never leave.

Recapturing what she'd once thought was lost forever.

Kelly lay asleep on the pillow, long, inky lashes feathered against her pink cheeks. Guarding her rest, Shay studied his lover.

Hell would come with the morning light, and the consequences, but for now, he wanted to banish the future. Banish the past. Live in the present moment.

A smile touched his mouth as he protectively tucked her closer. For a wild moment, he imagined it could be like this always.

He could make love to her through the years and never grow tired. Sam felt plugged into her, electrified when he took her, as alive as he'd never felt before.

The smile faded. In the rosy afterglow of hot sex, he'd made a huge mistake by lowering his defenses and baring his most shameful secret. With others, he'd kept his private life private, too proud to admit he still deeply grieved. Strict boundaries were enforced to keep everyone, especially women, at a distance. Men were tough. SEALs were tougher. And he was impenetrable.

Except to Kelly.

Now Kelly had penetrated the wall, leaving him exposed

and vulnerable, just as his father had once predicted. Shay couldn't afford vulnerability, or losing his heart to her again.

You're going to have to let her go.

The disturbing thought chased away sleep long into the night.

Chapter 17

A shaft of leaden daylight spilled through the partly opened drapes. Shay woke up to the sight of Kelly draped over his body. Long, dark lashes feathered over her cheeks as she slept as innocently as a child, red hair spilling over the white pillow. Just as he'd dreamed about all these years. He eased out of bed.

Stalking over to the balcony, he lifted the blue drapes with the back of one hand. He saw a hard pewter sky streaked with a rose-gold sun that was breaking the horizon. The street was deserted except for one elderly couple sitting across the street on their front stoop.

That could be you and Kel, years from now. Rocking on the porch, watching the grandkids play in the yard. Holding hands...

A family of his own. The dream shimmered within reach.

Hearing a rustling of sheets behind him, Shay turned.

"I feel so alive this morning. Free." She gave a languid stretch, which did amazing things to her breasts. Shay steeled against the driving urge to tumble her backward and love her until he'd coaxed another sweet cry of pleasure from her mouth.

He turned back to the window as she climbed out of bed.

Wrapping her arms around his waist, she snuggled against him. He closed his eyes, desperately wanting to never let go of her but knowing he must.

Shay pulled away and picked up her jeans. "We need to move out, get on the road. Go shower. I'll go downstairs and get us breakfast."

No censure in those eggshell-blue eyes, only confusion.

He softened his tone. "I have to secure a vehicle before we get to Tegus, and it'll take time."

"Sam, we have time. The flight doesn't leave until this afternoon. What's going on?"

Uncomfortable with the scrutiny, he gestured to the bathroom. "I'll shower after you."

Best to keep her at arm's length. But deep inside, he yearned for the connection shared last night, a bond he must shatter like a hammer before it was too late.

The red car looked held together with string and wire clothes hangers. Kelly rubbed a rust spot as Sam checked under the hood.

He'd paid an overjoyed villager cash for this clunker. It was hideous, with fuzzy dice hanging from the rearview mirror. Sam told her they were headed back to the States, to a safe house where she'd go unnoticed.

Not that he noticed her now.

Kelly hit a tire with the toe of her sandal. "*El Milagro.* This thing looks like it'll take a miracle to run."

No answer.

"Maybe I should throw some magick on it. There's an ancient Arcane spell to go faster, but it's for a donkey. The 'move your ass' spell."

Still no answer from under the hood.

Sam, talk to me, she thought, clenching her fists. *Stop being so damn distant.*

Finishing, he slammed the hood down and wiped his hands with a clean rag. "Engine's in good shape. Let's roll."

Efficient as ever. Transportation secured? Check. Engine operational? Check. Hotel bill paid? Check.

Last night's lover hustled out the door? Check.

The tender Sam who'd made love had vanished, leaving behind a stranger. He'd barely spoken at breakfast. Every bite of the delicious huevos with *queso* stuck in her throat as he sipped coffee and scrolled through email on his cell.

Would the real Sam ever return, the chivalrous man who'd defend her to the death? The Mage who whispered passionate words and tenderly loved her as if she were his entire world?

On impulse, she caught his hand, feeling the rough calluses and tensile strength. Those hands had roved over her naked body, culling an exquisite pleasure.

Sam closed his fingers around her wrist and gently removed her hand. The physical act hurt worse than a verbal rejection. But she refused to ignore what happened between them. "Last night was pretty special. Like old times, and I'm not talking about the sex."

Tension knotted his broad shoulders. "What do you mean?"

"I feel like I've found the real Sam, the one I lost, the man who set aside carousing for an honest, real relationship."

"I don't have time for relationships. I'm a SEAL, always gone on a mission."

"Other SEALs have relationships."

"Not me."

Kelly's heart dropped. "Talk to me, Sam."

A questionable look, the guarded expression hiding his thoughts.

Taking a leap of faith, she plunged ahead. "I can't tell what you're thinking, how you feel. You're a phantom, a ghost who isn't really here with me. I want Sam back in my life, the solid flesh-and-blood man who kissed me last night as if he meant it."

Sam tossed down the rag. "We can't all have what we want, can we?"

"Don't do this to me." He wanted to fight, use anger as a defense. She refused to be baited.

Kelly drew in a calming breath and slowly released it. "It was fine at the café, when you were the big, bad navy SEAL protecting the poor, threatened Arcane. You know how to play that role. But the minute you opened up and shared yourself last night, you regretted it and shut down."

Sam's jaw turned rigid as stone. Honesty was needed, but it was so difficult to confess how she felt. Never had she felt more vulnerable.

"I know what it's like to feel alone and grieving, surrounded by people oblivious to how badly you're bleeding inside. So you hide behind your work. You can trust me. It's okay to share your feelings. You've kept me safe and protected, and I'll do the same."

She touched his cheek, feeling the muscle twitch violently as if he were a machine gun ready to fire. "Please. I feel like we reconnected with each other. I don't want to lose that."

A glacial remoteness entered his eyes, as if all warmth and life inside him turned to ice.

"It was just sex, Kelly. A good fuck. We fucked each other and got what we wanted."

The words stung. Crushed, she stared at him, her rising hopes shattered as if he'd shot a bullet into them.

She dared voice her worst fear. "You wouldn't say that to an Elemental woman, even if it were true. Remember? Back at the mansion, before we became lovers? When they shared your bed, you walked them to their Porches and Jaguars the next morning, politely opened the door. And afterward, sent flowers and chocolates. The ones like me were snuck out of the house like a shameful secret."

"I never treated you like that, Kelly."

"But you are now."

Sam's jaw ground hard as he stared into the distance.

Silence confirmed it. So, that was it. Gods, it felt as if she'd extended her hand in trust and he'd sliced it off with his combat knife. It hurt badly, but more so, she hurt for him. The Sam she'd known was gone for good, replaced by this efficient, chilling…

Elemental.

Kelly removed the pendant and unfolded his palm, placing the silver triskele inside. "Here. You need this more than I do."

He pushed it back. "You're an Arcane and don't have enough power to protect yourself. It's to keep you safe."

Too late, she thought dully. They were back to Arcane and Elemental, and she was just another score. "You have the bigger disadvantage. You're dying inside, Sam. You just don't realize it."

Kelly turned for the village square.

"Where the hell are you going?" he demanded.

"I need to be alone. Besides, you should take another shower. Rinse off the Arcane stink left from last night."

Sam called after her, but she ignored him, jamming her hands into her jeans pockets. As she walked, people sidestepped as if she were something to scrape off their shoes. *You're welcome,* Kelly silently told the Mages. *It was a pleasure using Arcane magick to free you from the spell, hmm, a spell you fell under despite your almighty powers.*

Feeling even more alienated, she hunched her shoulders and kept her gaze down.

In the town square, elephant's ear trees stretched out their shady branches, providing relief from the constant heat. Violet-, crimson- and pumpkin-colored flowers bloomed among thatches of grass. A mother sat on a stone bench, watching a young boy kick a soccer ball on the walkway. She glanced at Kelly and gave a small smile.

This makes it all worth it. They have their lives back.

It was the reason why she'd started Sight Finders. She wanted to reunite families who'd been torn apart.

Because you couldn't reunite Sam's, a voice mocked in her head. *All these years, you've tried to atone for your father's actions. He's alive, while Sam's family is cold in their graves.*

Emotion clogged her throat as she watched the little boy chase the ball. He was about Pete's age. Sam adored his little brother. Promised to always take care of him.

I'm a reminder of everything he's lost, she realized. *Everyone he loved.*

Turning her back, she walked away from the little boy. Straight toward…

The Elemental college student who'd called her a bitch. Was anyplace safe from these damn Mages? The girl spotted her, grimaced and whispered to her companion.

Enough. Better to take Sam's cruel coldness than a stranger's insults.

A flicker of movement from the bushes caught her eye. The slither of a forked tongue testing the air. Kelly's heart went still as she glimpsed fangs bigger than steak knives. The searing stench of blood and death tangled in her nostrils.

Sam's warding hadn't killed all the monsters.

"Oh, dear gods." Panic rose in her throat as the girl and her friend drew closer, seemingly oblivious of the danger.

Kelly murmured a quiet chant and sent power streaming into the bushes.

The snake opened its mouth and swallowed the streaming current like a tasty morsel.

She settled for a verbal warning. "Get out of here, move it!"

The girl scoffed and continued advancing. The snake slithered out of the bushes, aiming for the Elemental's ankle. As the reptile rose up to attack, Kelly launched herself and grabbed the snake, yanking it away.

Hissing, it turned and bit Kelly's shoulder. Fiery pain

licked down her arm, but she grabbed the snake around the neck, struggling to contain it. Screams and gasps from onlookers. Magick words escaped her, spells lost in a red haze of pain. She needed powerful magick, Elemental magick… she laughed, a sob of white-hot agony as she remembered the triskele in Sam's hand.

You picked a lousy time to make a statement.

White electromagnetic energy crackled. As precise as a bolt of lightning, the energy struck the snake and killed it.

She looked up at the girl, who held out her glowing palms.

"Good shot," she rasped. "Thanks."

Respect shone in the girl's face. "Thank you, for saving my life."

Gritting her teeth, she managed to pull into a sitting position, the agony in her shoulder feeling like muscle pulled off bone.

She heard the screech of car tires. Sam jumped out and left the door to *El Milagro* open, the engine running. He crouched down, took a knife from his boot and tore open her shirt.

The wound had turned an ugly grayish mass. Blood seeped from two puncture holes.

"Ilthus," she managed to say. "Don't know how it evaded your magick."

Sam glared at the crowd. "Goddammit, get back, give her air. This isn't a damn sideshow."

The crowd quickly dispersed, except for the girl she'd saved and her male friend.

"I'm Nancy," the girl said, kneeling down beside Sam. "How can I help?"

"Got hand sanitizer?" At her nod, Sam handed her his knife. "Sterilize this."

When she'd handed it back, he turned to Kelly. "Hang on. This isn't going to be fun. I'll try to go easy."

"Don't," she grated out. "Just take care of the poison."

Sunlight flashed on the blade he raised to her skin. Burning pain laced her shoulder, the agony making her stomach clench as warm blood flowed down her arm. Oh, gods, that hurt.

"I've lanced the wound, but the venom already invaded your central nervous system." He sounded calm and cool. "I'm going to have to send my powers streaming into your body."

"Ah." Kelly bit her lip so hard she drew blood. The pain made it hard to see, to breathe. She inched away from him, shaking her head. "You're going to fry my insides."

"No, I'll hold back. Trust me."

Shuddering in agony, she drew away. The hurtful words he'd flung at her still stung. After he'd shattered her fragile hopes, how could she believe him?

"Not when the trust isn't mutually exclusive."

He sighed. "I know I acted like an asshole. I'm sorry I said those things. But please, let me help you."

Hand on her chin, Sam tilted her face upward to meet the regret in his gaze. "Please, Kel? I fucked up royally and insulted you badly. But don't let that stand in the way of me doing my job."

Now the pain felt as if she'd thrust her arm into a roaring furnace. Tears leaked out of her eyes. "Duty and honor. Doing your job. You want to save me because you're under orders and you'll obey, good SEAL that you are."

"No," he said quietly. "Screw the order. I want to heal you because I care about you and if I lose you, part of me will die, as well."

At this glimpse of the real Sam, the tightness in her chest eased. Kelly nodded. "Okay. Fry my organs, but have someone serve them with fava beans and a nice Chianti. Very yummy. Or so says the good Dr. Lecter."

He gave a soft smile. "That's my girl."

Sam stretched out his hands, warming them in the sun. Power pulsed through him, wreathing his muscular body. His expression intense, like a predator's, the green in his eyes a blaze of emerald, he went very still.

Cold knots twisted her stomach. He was going to throw that current at her, inside her, and she'd seen living things vaporize beneath the force of that violent power.

"Stay as still as possible."

Kelly closed her eyes. She felt Sam's hands on her shoulder, strong and yet gentle. Warmth spilled into her body, shooting down from the wound into her shoulder. She felt it snaking through her core, chasing away the hot agony with cooling relief. Strength returned to her weakened muscles.

"Oh, wow, sweet," Nancy murmured. "I've never seen that before."

"Curing through energy manipulation," her companion stated in a smug voice. "Basic electromagnetic light therapy, commonly used in healing ceremonies. Although I've never seen it demonstrated on an Arcane, because that kind of power is wasted on them."

"Stop it, Mark," Nancy snapped. "I'm sick of your attitude. She saved my life."

The last of the venom vanished beneath the humming current of Sam's power. Kelly felt refreshed and energized.

"You okay?" he asked, searching her face.

"I could run a marathon. But I'd need a few power bars first, because I'm really hungry."

"I'll be damned," he said softly, gazing at his still-glowing hands. "I still have power."

"But you healed me."

"I held back. Didn't want to risk burning you." Sam glanced around.

"Thank you," she told him. "This is the second time you gave my life back to me."

Sam stroked a single finger down her cheek, his gaze tender. Nancy looked at her with newfound respect, while her companion snorted in derision.

"She's just another Arcane. No big loss. If you're that hot

for them, you can always find another bitch to spread her legs," Mark said.

Kelly winced. Nancy gasped, shoving her friend. "Mark, I wish you'd just shut up!"

Sam flicked his hands, sending an energy current at Mark, knocking him unconscious to the pavement. "Wish granted," he told Nancy.

Then he stood, pulling Kelly with him. Nancy glanced at her. "I never thought an Arcane would risk her life for me. I was wrong." She glanced at the unconscious Mark with disgust. "About a lot of things."

"I'm sure he has some redeeming qualities," Kelly offered.

"Like drooling on the sidewalk," Sam muttered. With a nod to Nancy, he guided Kelly to *El Milagro.* Inside the car, he draped the triskele over her neck.

"You scared me to death. Don't ever take the pendant off again." He hesitated and added, "Please."

Silence lay between them, intense and heavy, as they drove out of town. After a few miles, she turned in the seat, avoiding a spring sticking up through the cracked leather.

"Do you know what happened back there? I thought your powers healed me, but if you still had them, they didn't."

"I sent only enough energy into your body to find the venom and neutralize it, not repair the damaged muscle." Bone strained against flesh as he tightened his hands on the steering wheel. "You healed yourself."

"That's impossible. I don't have enough power and certainly not any healing abilities without the triskele." Unless they'd formed a new, unique connection. Arcane magick and Elemental.

"I don't understand it, either." He gestured to the back. "I packed a cooler with snacks and water. We have a long way to go."

Chapter 18

Enormous stands of pine, maple and hemlock ringed Sam's isolated log cabin in the remote Tennessee mountains. A vista of rolling green hillside, punctuated by a weathered barn, stretched before the back porch. Wisps of gray fog drifted up from the pine trees, smoking the chilly air as Kelly braced her hands on the porch railing.

After the flight from Miami to Atlanta, where he had a car waiting, she had no memory of the long drive or Sam carrying her inside and tucking her into the big bed downstairs. He'd taken her to the place she'd least expected—his private retreat, where they'd first made love.

The cabin felt much smaller. Or maybe it was the rugged, virile man who took up all the space.

Rain now splattered on the porch roof as she stood under it.

Sam stepped onto the porch and handed her a cup of steaming coffee.

They sipped in silence a few moments. Sam set down his cup on a side table. "I called Curt, my CO."

Kelly tensed.

"I told him I had you secured in a hidden location in the United States. He said it was a matter for Mage authorities now and insisted I give you up."

Jaw tightening, he stared at the rolling hillside. "I insisted otherwise."

Her heart skipped a beat.

Sam kept a white-knuckle grip on the railing. "Curt wasn't clear on what protection you'd have. In fact, he was very evasive. And then he launched into a rambling, confusing speech about the chain of command and how much trouble I face."

"You think he's been replaced by a duplicate?"

Anger and frustration snapped in his gaze. "Yeah. Curt never talks that much. Or wastes words."

Sam flexed his hands. "I said you were in my custody and I'll hand you over to the council myself." A grim smile touched his face. "The entire damn council. At ST 21's base, because you felt safer there."

She saw the logic. "It'll take them days to assemble. Doesn't one live in Thailand?"

"Right. And my uncle is on his annual retreat in the Azores. No phone, no communication."

"That buys time, but what if someone comes here looking for you?"

"Legally, the cabin belongs to a dummy corporation I formed long ago. No one knows I come here."

"No one else?"

Sam glanced at her. "I haven't returned since the fire. The corporation hires a cleaning crew to maintain the place. You're the only other person who's ever been here."

Unease filled her, a burning question she hadn't dared to ask all those years ago. "Sam, back then, did you bring me here so no one could see us together?"

Sam sighed. "It was easier, and more private. Kel, you have

to understand, my father put a lot of pressure on me to settle down with someone from my own class."

Kelly's stomach churned. "I get it. You were ashamed. Good for some things but not others. Like in Honduras. A good fuck."

"Stop it," he snapped. "Don't cheapen yourself like that."

"I didn't say it, Sam. I'm only repeating what was said to *me*."

Two strong arms encircled her waist, tugging her against him. Resisting, she stiffened as he sighed deeply into her ear.

"I'm sorry I left you all those years ago. And I'm sorry I said those cruel things back in Honduras. I insulted you, badly. If I could take it back, I would."

"Why did you say it?" she whispered. "I was so humiliated. You made me feel like I'm… What did your father call it? An easy lay."

"Gods, Kel, never. I was scared of what happened between us."

"Like you were scared of telling your family about me?"

Gently, he turned her around and stroked a finger down her cheek. "I was going to bring you to formally meet my father, remember? The night of the fire. I wasn't ashamed of you. Never."

She rested her palms against his broad chest, feeling the strong, steady beat of his heart. "I know. Everything came between us back then. We forgot who we were and fell back to what we were, Arcane and Elemental. And somewhere along the line, we lost faith in each other."

"I should have stayed." His warm palms cupped her chilled cheeks. "I need to tell you something. My letter said I left because it was over between us."

A tiny muscle jumped in his jaw. "I left because I couldn't bear that I'd lost my family and you. I headed west, shifted into a wolf to forget the grief. I went feral. Almost killed a rancher who shot at me when I was on a sneak-and-peek, eyeing his cattle. Called me a rangy, violent pest. I ran off, but got…crazy."

He drew a deep breath. "The shotgun was no match for a wolf who could run faster than an express train and catch a man when his back is turned."

Sam, cheerful and carefree, gentle and tender. She shivered, imagining him with sharp fangs, a vicious snarl and claws.

Darkness shadowed his gaze. Sam's mouth tightened. "I let the wolf take over until grief and rage turned me into a beast. You stopped me. I thought of you, Kel, and the human part of me returned."

Horrified, she stared at him. "Did the rancher die?"

"Was in the hospital a few weeks. The council sent authorities after me when they'd heard. They made me pay the rancher's medical bills, which I would have done anyway. The council feared I'd turn vicious again and eventually someone would find out it was no ordinary wolf. They wanted to execute me."

Shock made her heart go still a moment. His eyes closed, as if reliving the moment proved too unbearable.

"How did you convince the council you weren't dangerous?"

It must have been good, because Sam *was* dangerous.

He looked away, a flash of guilt on his expression. "My uncle argued I'd acted out of grief. Because I was Elemental, they released me, on the condition to never turn into a feral wolf again. If they caught me, they'd turn me into dust."

The difference between his people and hers. Sam went free, while she stood falsely accused and no one believed her.

Except Sam.

Silence danced in the air, broken by leaves rustling in the wind.

"Sometimes I miss them so much, I can't bear it," he said finally.

Kelly's throat squeezed tight. "Me, either," she whispered.

She ducked out of his embrace, picked up her cup and headed inside to take a shower. The downstairs shower was big enough to host a dance party. Twin jets sprayed her with soothing hot water. Kelly picked up the soap with trembling hands.

I miss them so much.

Sam was right. Rescuing abducted Mage children and reuniting them with their overjoyed families assuaged her guilt and grief.

Tears rose in her throat. Splaying her hands against the cold tile wall, she surrendered to them. She'd failed those she'd promised to keep safe. Failed saving Sam's family. So much failure, too many lives lost.

The shower door opened. Naked, Sam stepped inside. He reached for her, but she pulled away, scrubbing her cheeks. Pretending everything was normal.

With gentle persistence, he pulled her against his broad chest, his hands tunneling through her soaked hair. Saying nothing, only letting her cry, loaning his strength and support as she wept.

And then she felt him tremble, felt his broad shoulder shake beneath her cheek. Kelly looked up.

Tears ran down Sam's cheeks.

He leaned his forehead against hers, cupping her face in his hands, and kissed her. The salt of their tears mingled together, washed away by the shower. Kelly opened her mouth beneath his as his tongue slid into her mouth, stealing away her breath. His kiss was demanding and yet gentle, urgent and desperate.

Then he pulled away, reached for the bar of soap and began to wash her.

Symbolic and soothing, his actions roused her desire as he slid the soap over her arms, the slope of her neck. Droplets clung to his thick brown hair and sparkled in his long lashes. Water cascaded down his strong, muscled neck, beaded in the dark hairs of his chest and slid lower.

He looked beautiful and sexy and intent, and it took her breath away.

His heated gaze remained affixed to hers as he stroked the soap over her wet, glistening skin. Sam brushed kisses alongside her jaw, sweet and tender as when they'd first made love. His hands cupped the rounded curve of her hips, pulling her tight against him.

"Turn around," he said, his voice thick.

Kelly closed her eyes as he stood behind her, lathering her breasts, cupping them and gently teasing the hardened nipples with gentle strokes of his thumbs. Massaging gently, he molded his body against hers, his erection rubbing against her bottom. Each languid stroke aroused her senses, chasing away sorrow and regrets and replacing them with sensual awareness.

Cleansing them both, Sam washed away the past, replacing it with new and fresh feelings of heightened desire.

"Slippery when wet," he whispered. Taking the lobe of her ear between his teeth, he gently bit.

She moaned as he turned her around.

His mouth went from her ear to her throat, nuzzling down to her bare collarbone. He suckled her breasts, his tongue flicking over each crested peak, creating new, aching need inside her. Kelly sagged bonelessly against him, pushing her hot skin against his questing mouth. More. More. Sensation speared her, so fresh and tantalizing, it was as if she were a virgin once more. A girl who had never experienced passion, felt desire or the tender touch of a lover's strong, skilled hands.

Sam's hands.

Sam's hands…were sliding down her front. He slid the soap down her belly, dipping a finger into her navel, and then he skirted around her and dropped to his knees. Sam squeezed her bottom.

"Man, I love your ass. I've dreamed about doing this to you. Bend over, sweetheart," he said hoarsely.

As she did, he spread her cheeks wide and stroked the soap

between them. Sam washed her front, slicking her folds as she gasped, her passage growing wet and ready for him. Then she felt the delicious roughness of his tongue delve between her cheeks as he gently massaged her clit.

A nearly unbearable ache filled her lower belly as he kissed and licked her, all the while stroking her. Water streamed down her body, mingling with her natural moisture. Kelly splayed her hands against the tile as he grasped her hips.

"I'm going to make love to you now," he rasped. "Send you into oblivion until you can't take it anymore. Until we both come, together. And then I'm going to start all over."

She felt the insistent push of his cock nudge at her slick folds and then push slightly inside her. He entered her slowly, stretching and penetrating her deeply, and deeper still. Kelly made a little pleading cry as he sank inside her to the hilt and remained still, his fingers gripping her hips.

"Sam, please," she whispered.

"Not until I say what I must."

Sam bent over her, his body firmly lodged inside hers, the crisp hair on his chest against her back. He flung aside her wet hair as the water pattered upon them and kissed her nape.

"Back in Honduras, I couldn't say how I really felt. It was too intense, and there was too much between us. I'm telling you now, Kelly, I do care. You drive me crazy with need." His voice dropped to a husky whisper. "All I can think about is getting inside you, keeping you in my bed for good."

"I just want this moment, with you, to last forever. I wish it could," she whispered.

Slowly he withdrew and then thrust back inside. She reached back, felt his hand, felt their fingers entwine and then release. With a groan, he began to surge heavily into her, teasing her clit with his finger. Her breasts swayed as his flesh slapped against hers, nearly suffocating her with incredible erotic pleasure. It had always been good with him before, but now it was exquisite. Sam murmured praises of her body, how sweet and tight she felt, how beautiful she was. Each demanding stroke raised her higher and higher until the raw, stunning sensation shimmered, the pressure built in her loins.

"Now," he cried out as she squeezed him tight. "Come with me, Kel!"

Crying out, she surged and soared upward as the orgasm crested over her, feeling him pump deep inside her.

In sated exhaustion, she sagged against the wall as he slowly withdrew. Kelly turned around to see the husky glint of satisfaction in his gaze. Then Sam reached past her and turned the knob to shut off the shower. He glanced down.

"I'll be damned," he muttered, staring at his penis. "I didn't use a condom."

A glint ignited his gaze as he glanced up. "If you get pregnant, we'll get married."

Crazy hope fluttered inside her breast and then died. Sam wouldn't marry for love, only duty. "I won't get pregnant. I'm on the Pill."

Was that stark relief in his gaze, or mild disappointment? Hard to tell.

She wanted all of him, including his heart. But that organ still seemed locked deep inside despite the blaze of passion they'd shared.

She didn't want to think about that as he dried them both off and then carried her back to the bed.

For a long time they lay together, entangled in each other's arms. Kelly stroked his damp chest hairs and traced the hard brown circle of his nipple. She badly wanted to confess her feelings. But his previous attitude gave her caution. A soft purr came from the cell phone on the nightstand. Sam rolled over and pushed a hand through his hair.

"Yeah?"

His languid expression became intense. Instantly he sat up, a steel core shoved in his spine. Kelly fisted her hands in the sheets.

Thumbing off the cell, he tossed it on the bed with a soft curse. Sam stared out the window.

"The council found out you're back in the country," she guessed.

He nodded. "Gibson, the executive secretary. Curt told them and now he's ordered me to bring you in."

All good things must come to an end, she thought, hysteria rising in her throat. The tenderness of their lovemaking faded. Reality check.

Fading sunlight dappled his sandy-brown hair. How she'd loved holding him close, wishing never to let go.

She had to let go now. Because if Sam brought her back, the council would be there, including Senator Rogers, most likely. She was going to use all her magick to free herself.

"Screw this," he muttered. "You are not going back."

Picking up the cell, he punched in a number. Sam stood, displaying the cords of muscle on his back and across his muscled, taut ass.

Remembering how strongly he'd pumped that ass to thrust deep inside her, Kelly squirmed on the bed. As he left the bedroom, talking on the phone, her hands fisted tighter in the sheets until her knuckles whitened.

She remained like that until he returned.

"I called Curt. Told him I'm going back to base. Neglected to say I'm going alone."

He ran his thumb along her knuckles, his touch reassuring. "You'll stay here. I warded the land enough so even a tank filled with Mages can't come onto the property. I'll break the bond between us so we can separate."

He trusted her not to run for it. She had to trust that he'd fight for her.

"What will you do at the base?"

A fierce look came over him. "I'm going to find out what the hell is going on."

Chapter 19

Shay grappled with the problem during the flight to Virginia. As a SEAL, he fought with courage, conviction and the sureness of knowing he did the right thing.

Now doing the right thing was wrong in his superior's eyes. He stood to lose everything as a SEAL.

Curt's voice echoed in his mind. "You're too involved. Step back and let us handle this." Hell, it sounded like Curt, even the clipped words. Was the man a doppelgänger?

He needed to see the man for himself.

At the airport, he flagged down a cab. He'd given a vague arrival time. Didn't want to chance getting a little surprise.

But the surprise greeted him as he walked into ST 21's ready room. Curt stood by the desk. In the front chair, Senator Robert Rogers. Next to them…

The entire Council of Mages, including Allen Shaymore, his dark gaze sharp as he nodded to Shay.

"Uncle Al. No retreat this year?"

"They cut it short." Al scowled, tugging at the collar of his white starched shirt beneath the formal purple velvet robes of a Mage Elder. "Sent an air force jet to retrieve me so I could put on this damn monkey suit. What the hell's the deal, son? You in trouble again?"

An air force jet? Shay's heart dropped to his stomach. Rogers had pulled plenty of strings to make that happen. Unless the conspiracy went a lot deeper than he'd realized.

An expectant hush filled the air as the Mages looked at Lieutenant Commander Curtis.

"Where is Kelly Denning, Chief Petty Officer Shaymore?"

Curt never called him by his full title. *Guess I'm in a little trouble,* he thought humorlessly. *Or maybe this isn't Curt.*

He shrugged. "Looks like a welcoming party. If I'd known you'd go through all this trouble, I'd have brought the beer."

Al laughed, but Curt scowled. Rogers stood, his elegant frame trembling with rage. "Where the hell is Kelly Denning?"

"Chill, Senator. Don't want to burst a blood vessel." Shay kept his body loose and ready for action. If that SOB came at him, he'd get a fist smashed into his surgically altered nose.

"You're a U.S. Navy SEAL and you were ordered..."

"I know my orders," Shay fired back. "Yeah, I'm a SEAL. You call us adrenaline junkies, but we're trained professionals. And part of any op is gathering good intel before we deploy."

His gaze swept over the council. "I need information."

"You are a soldier. You follow orders. Your job is to do what you're told." Rogers's mouth thinned as he flexed his manicured hands, as if itching to wrap them around Shay's neck.

"I'm not turning Kelly over until I know why she's being charged, and what the formal charges are." Shay narrowed his gaze.

Before Rogers could retort, he pushed on. "Section five fifty-seven, Code of Honor of the Executive Council of Honored Mages. And I quote, 'If an Arcane is suspected of breaking Mage law, and bringing harm to Elemental Mages, the council will ensure due process is served and appoint a skilled attorney fluent in Code law to serve as counsel to the defendant. No Arcane shall be imprisoned without formal charges until such counsel can be found.'"

"You're an arrogant son of a bitch," the senator sputtered.

He considered. "Yeah. But we're discussing Kelly Denning, not me." He flashed a cold smile. "She deserves a lawyer. Are you trying to circumvent our sacred laws?"

"Of course not," Rogers snapped. "We will, of course, see that she gets a fair trial. If she's guilty, she'll be executed."

But the truth was carved on the faces of each Elder, except his uncle. Kelly was a dead woman.

"He's right. The girl deserves representation. I'll make sure she gets it." Allen's gaze was sly as he looked at his nephew, who grinned back.

Expecting Rogers to retort, he watched Curt signal to a waiting aide.

"We have a small surprise for you, Chief Petty Officer Shaymore. Someone who's been missing all these years, who wanted dearly to see you again. Someone who will make you see reason." Curt smiled.

Right. Not a fat chance. Shay's hand dropped to his sidearm. And he nearly dropped with cold shock as a ghost strolled into the room. A gray-haired, stately ghost with hazel eyes like his own.

"Dad," he whispered. Couldn't be. The council was playing tricks on him. Or maybe this was a doppelgänger, as well… but sweet hellfire, how could they have taken his DNA if his father had been dead for twelve years?

The room spun around like a top. Shay braced his hands on a desktop.

"Samuel." The ghost offered a thin smile. "You're here. I knew you would come."

Only his father called him by his full name. Shay swung

his gaze to his uncle, who stared at the floor and then back to the ghost. "I buried your remains…"

"You buried a servant who lost his life in the blaze. I'm here and quite alive. Samuel, my son. How I have missed you."

"You're dead."

"Quite alive. I've been in hiding all these years. Too crazed with grief, living in the shadows." His father's face contorted with emotion. "In a way, I have been a true phantom, a ghost."

The crack of a fist slamming into flesh. Shay watched in quiet satisfaction as the ghost stumbled backward.

"Don't feel like a ghost to me," he said, flexing his fist.

Colton wiped blood from his split lip. "Excuse me. I need a moment alone with my son."

Shay fought for control as they walked to a nearby storage closet. Nothing ever surprised a SEAL. They had to adapt swiftly to sudden change. But all the hard training never prepared him for this.

Closing the door, Shay leaned against it.

"I will forgive you for hitting me because I owe you an apology for not telling you sooner."

"Apology? You owe me a hell of a lot more," Shay snapped. "Sooner? Twelve years ago would have been sweet! Why didn't you tell me you were alive? Where the hell were you when the fire broke out? The day I fucking buried your body?"

Something flickered in his father's eyes. "I had gone out the back door to sneak a cigar. Your mother disapproved and I didn't want to upset her. The flames spread quickly and were too hot. I couldn't try entering the hallway to save them."

Shay had tried, and he had the scars as a result.

"Dad, how could you leave me?" Shay whispered.

Another flicker of emotion. Shame? Guilt? Hard to tell.

"I'm sorry, son. I went mad with grief over losing your mother. I ran away and by the time I regained some sense, you had gone."

"And returned a year later, goddammit. What was your excuse then?"

Silence draped between them. Colton tensed, white lines bracketing his mouth. "I was on a blood hunt to avenge their deaths."

Shay went still. "You went looking for Kelly's father."

"That bastard Arcane took my beautiful Annabelle away from me. I sought revenge against all his parasitic kind." Colton's eyes sparkled with rage. "And now I have the means. Those goddamn Arcanes, always trying to steal what is ours. No more. I met a most remarkable Elemental Phantom who convinced me to come out of hiding and put my skills to good use."

"You couldn't tell me? Enlist my help?"

"Not after I discovered you and the parasite's daughter were having an affair."

Guilt pierced Shay as his father regarded him with the look he knew well. Sheer disappointment. Even though he'd fought hand-to-hand combat with terrorists, his father still made him feel as if he was nine years old. "How did you know?"

"I found out a few days before Christmas. One of the servants saw you and Kelly go into the underground tunnels."

They'd thought themselves safe, invisible to the world. And all the time, someone had known.

"I knew you were sneaking off with someone, so I sent her to watch you."

Shay's mouth twisted. "Nice touch, Dad. Spying on your own flesh and blood."

"You worried me, Samuel. No discipline, restless and disobedient, more headstrong than ever. If you were in trouble, I needed to know." Colton rubbed a hand over his face, and suddenly Shay saw how much he'd aged.

"An Arcane. Really, son. I understand the fascination. But what in the hell were you thinking?"

"Watch it, Dad," he softly warned. "Don't you dare insult her."

"She's a slut like her father."

Shay jerked the door open. "This conversation is over."

He wanted to scream but clamped a lid on his temper as they returned to the ready room. Sickened, he watched his CO put a hand on his father's shoulder. "Colton heads a new civilian committee to assess an Arcane threat. We're going to work with him, Shay. All of the Phoenix Force."

"A committee? You mean a hate group." Shay swung his gaze over the silent council, including his uncle, who glowered at Shay's father. "You approve of this, all of you?"

"It's necessary," Rogers said tightly. "If there is a threat against our people, we need to be prepared to destroy it. Just as you and the other SEALs do."

The meaning became clear. "We fight to keep our country safe, not kill innocents."

"Self-preservation," Curt put in. "Protecting our people so they can thrive. Arcanes are like cockroaches…they breed incessantly and unless you wipe out their numbers, they will always be underfoot."

His father nodded. "Only more dangerous, ready to seize everything dear to you. You must accept the truth, Samuel. These Arcanes threaten the very fabric of our lives. Bring them Kelly Denning. She is key to uncovering their plans to destroy us."

Toss Kelly to the wolves. Shay felt off balance, his world splitting open beneath his booted feet. But one surety remained. "No way in hell. She's innocent."

But Curt spoke up. "Since you refuse to comply, Chief Petty Officer Shaymore, you are formally charged with unauthorized absence."

"Curt," he protested.

"Bring in Kelly Denning and turn her over to the Mage Council Elder or you face court-martial. Those are your orders, soldier." His CO glowered. "Shay, I warned you. You crossed one too many lines and left me without a choice."

Anguished, he felt trapped. If the navy discharged him, he'd lose everything.

But neither could he hand Kelly over to Rogers, knowing the bastard would make her quietly "disappear."

Racing over possibilities, he said, "I'll do as you ask, on one condition. Show me one scrap of evidence you have that she wants to hurt Elementals. You have nothing."

Put the brakes on all this. But Colton took a brown paper bag and tossed it to Shay.

"I'm sorry, son, but here's your proof," he told him. "This was found among Kelly Denning's belongings when authorities searched Sight Finders' offices. She must have kept it as a trophy after her father set the fire."

"Just as serial killers often keep trophies to remind them of their victims. We believe she conspired with her father to commit arson," Curt added.

Colton's jaw tensed. "Now that bitch is working with the rebel Arcanes to hurt others of our kind. She's leading the Arcane rebellion to destroy our people."

Shay opened the bag.

Shock punched the breath out of him as he fished out a partly scorched teddy bear. One eye was missing. Pete had plucked it out to use as a spare marble when he was six.

It was his little brother's favorite toy.

Sawdust puffed out from a rip in the bear as he squeezed it. Shay loosened his grip, wrestling with rage and grief. He looked at Rogers and his wife, then the waiting council. Shay couldn't bear the sorrow in his uncle's eyes. Or bear to see his father's expression.

He squared his shoulders. He was a U.S. Navy SEAL, tough as Kevlar, even when his heart shattered. With extreme care, he placed the bear in the paper sack and tucked it under his arm.

"That's evidence. You can't take it," Rogers protested.

Shay thought about telling the senator to kiss his ass. Instead he nodded at the council members.

"You'll hear from me."

For a moment, he struggled to find words for his father. But knowing he'd faked his death sent razors slicing through his heart.

"Son." Colton placed a hand on his shoulder. "Do the right thing. Bring her back here to face trial. Don't lose your head over a woman and risk your career. I'm so proud of what you've accomplished. You've grown into a fine, courageous man, everything I had hoped for."

A lump formed in Shay's throat. He could only nod. *I still love you, Dad,* he thought. *But you've changed.*

Just like me.

The door slammed behind him as he left.

When Sam returned that night, Kelly could tell that something was dreadfully wrong.

Eyes red-rimmed, expression tight and distraught, he looked like hell as he sat down on the sofa. Kelly ached for him.

"That bad?" she asked.

Instead of replying, he handed her a worn paper sack. A shocked gasp escaped as she drew out the battered, scorched teddy bear.

"This is the evidence the council has against you. They say you kept it as a trophy after your father set the fire. They're even suggesting you helped him. It was found at Sight Finders."

No emotion in his flat voice. Kelly placed the bear in his lap. She had to step carefully or risk splintering the fragile trust between them.

"That was low of them, Sam. Seeing the bear must have torn you apart."

Tension knotted his spine as he looked away. Instinct warned his hard-won control was ready to shatter like glass.

"There's nothing I can do to bring him, or your parents, back. I wish I could. I'm sorry for all the pain you've suffered."

Sam's brow furrowed. "It's not your fault. You didn't set the fire, Kel. No matter what the council or anyone else says, I know you didn't do it."

"Maybe I didn't strike the match, but I'm the one who insisted on you meeting me instead of spending time with your family. If I hadn't, you'd have been there and could have saved them." Kelly drew in a trembling breath. "All these years I've tried to save kids because it was my fault Pete died."

Anger darkened his gaze as he lightly shook her shoulder. "Stop it. It was my decision. You're not at fault. I tried to get to them in time, but the flames were too much. I should have found a way…."

"And you'd have died. There's a reason you're still here, fighting the good fight, Sam. Don't ever forget that. They'd be so proud of you if they were here."

"One of them is."

She could only stare.

"My father's still alive. I saw him."

Words escaped her. Kelly blinked hard. "Impossible," she managed.

"Very possible." Sam punched a pillow and told her what happened.

Colton Shaymore, alive. And hating her people more than ever. Resolve began building. She'd stop it, fight for justice, fight to shut that bastard up before he hurt anyone….

And then she glanced over and saw Sam's face.

Sam's jaw locked so hard, he had to be hurting. Sam needed her, just as he had after the fire. She would not forsake him for her crusade.

Kelly covered his hand with hers. "I'm sorry, Sam. I can't imagine how shocked, and disappointed, you felt."

Silence draped between them. He heaved a sigh. "One day, maybe, I can forgive him for abandoning me."

"But now he's back in your life. If you want any chance of moving forward from this, you must forgive him."

"He lied to me." Sam looked shattered. "All these years I worshipped him, idolized him as a man of strength, honor and integrity. And then mourned losing him. His life has been nothing but a lie."

"Was it? All the qualities you idolized in him, you sought those in yourself and that's why you became a SEAL, right?"

At his nod, she continued. "He made a huge mistake, but he had a huge success…you. You brought those qualities to life. His life was not all a lie."

Muscles tensed in his spine. "When I saw him, got over the shock…part of me kept hoping maybe my mother and Pete were alive, too, and all this had been a sick, fucked-up joke."

Kelly waited.

"But they're not."

His haunted look wrenched her heart. All she could offer was meager comfort.

"No, they're not. But I am. I'm not leaving you."

Kelly wrapped her arms around him. Muscles locked and tensed. Then, with a small groan, Sam pulled her tight, his head buried in the soft curve of her neck.

When he lifted his head, his gaze softened. "I have to say something to you, Kel. About what I said back in La Aurora. All my years I had it wrong. Being tight with my team, fighting as a single unit, I thought it would fill all the empty spaces inside me. A real man was a navy SEAL—strong, courageous and willing to die for his country."

Sam tucked a stray tendril of hair behind her ear. "Being a real man is much more. It's being strong enough to know I was wrong, courageous enough to admit I am afraid and willing not just to sacrifice my life, but my heart."

Kelly brushed his knuckles with a kiss. "I know what was missing in my empty places, Sam. Fill them again."

"I need you badly, Kel," he whispered. "I need to forget every lousy thing that happened today. I need you close, your arms clinging to me. I need to watch your face as I make you come."

A sharp intake of breath as she imagined Sam's face hovering above hers as they made love.

"I need you, gods, to help me forget everything I remembered when I saw my father standing before me."

Desperate hunger shimmered in his gaze, twining with rage and grief. Kelly took his hand and pressed it to her cheek. "I can't offer much, but I give you all I have, Sam."

Nodding gruffly, he led her to the bedroom downstairs. This wasn't making love as much as making each other's pain evaporate, she realized.

They tore at each other's clothes, sending them spilling to the bedroom floor. Kelly twined her arms around his neck and pressed against him, feeling the hardness of his chest muscles. Erotic need spilled through her as he kissed her, hard and deep, his tongue thrusting into her mouth as if imitating what his lower body intended. She was burning up now, the coolness of the air-conditioned room forgotten in the heat he created.

I need you inside me, Sam.

Smooth muscles flexed beneath her questing palm as she caressed his broad back. His penis was huge and hard against the softness of her belly. It twitched, as if impatient to be inside her once more. Kelly rubbed her breasts against Sam, feeling her overly sensitive nipples turn rock-hard again. Every kiss was hot and urgent, as if he wanted to devour her. Need pummeled her as she ground against him and felt his penis respond with another violent twitch. Kelly lifted a leg, curling it around one of his narrow hips. Against the wall, that would suffice. But Sam lifted her by the bottom and, still kissing her, gently tumbled her backward onto the bed.

He stood over her, breathing heavily, his gaze dark and focused utterly on her. With one powerful thigh, he nudged her legs open and then dropped to his knees and stared at her core. A faint flush ignited her cheeks. He looked at her as if she were the most beautiful sight in the world.

Sam rubbed her folds with a finger and then sank the digit into her swollen vagina. "Are you too sore for this?"

Unable to speak, she shook her head. A moan flitted from her lips as he licked her, a slow stroke of his wicked tongue across her soaked folds. He kept pleasuring her, teasing her higher and higher until her muscles contracted and her back arched. Kelly felt the climax shimmer out of reach, a distant star winking teasingly at her.

"C'mon, sweetheart," he crooned against her soaked flesh. "Come for me. Come for me."

The husky command pushed her over the edge. Fisting her hands in the tangled sheets, she climaxed hard, sobbing out his name.

Breathless, she watched him stand and backhand his mouth, his gaze filled with sharp sexual excitement. Then Sam bent over her and pushed his hard, heavy penis deep inside her.

Remaining frozen for a moment, his gaze fiercely held hers as her swollen tissues struggled to accommodate him. Kelly wriggled and he surged inside her, burying himself deeply and sealing them to the hilt. Every sensation seemed heightened, from the feel of his hard penis embedded inside her to his chest rubbing against her sensitive nipples to his face inches above hers, his fierce gaze searing her with heat.

Kelly dug her fingers into his thick shoulders, feeling sinew and muscle flex. She pumped her hips upward in a silent plea. He was hot inside her, and her body was burning.

Her fingers found his tattoo and stroked over it, over the bullet hole that had given him life. Sam's big body jerked with awareness. Closing his eyes, he took a quivering breath. Then he began to move, pounding in her, hard deep strokes that she met with eager pumps of her hips.

His expression was fierce with arousal, his mouth tight as his hips jackhammered into her wet, pliant body. This was not lovemaking but a reclaiming of what he'd lost, the possessive stamp of a man whose primal urges indelibly marked her as his own.

Kelly froze as another orgasm tightened her muscles. Heart hammering against her chest, she concentrated on the exquisite pleasure.

Sam went still as she screamed his name. And then he threw back his head and answered her cries, her name on his lips.

Lost deep inside her, wanting to forget.

Much later, they ate the sandwiches Sam had picked up at the local deli. After, he cleared the table in silence.

Sensing he needed a little space, she went into the living room and picked up the abandoned, sad teddy bear from the sofa. Sudden insight struck her.

"Sam, where did you say the bear was found?" she called out.

"Your offices at Sight Finders." He appeared at her side, drying his hands on a dish towel.

"That's impossible."

Tossing the towel on the cocktail table, Sam joined her. "My father claims you took it."

"I did take the bear. But after I found the bear, I put him in our secret hideout."

Struggling to speak past the lump in her throat, she pressed on. "I wanted to put him in a safe place. I thought if you returned, you'd see the bear and remember the good times you shared with Pete."

"I never went back inside the tunnel. I nailed the door shut when I returned to Tennessee, before I joined the navy."

Their gazes met, his filled with firm resolve.

"Whoever found this bear found it inside the bunker..." she began.

Grabbing the toy, he turned it over in his hands. "Look." He pointed to a thumb-size bandage on the bear's scorched paw. "Did you do this?"

Kelly frowned. "No. I wouldn't bandage a toy. And not this one, because it belonged to Pete. I know how special it was. Maybe Pete did?"

"No, the bandage is new." He examined the bear. "Pete did like to bandage his toys, it was something he always did as a kid..."

"And he's probably not the only one. The bandage is fresh, Sam. Which means another child did it."

Sam bolted off the couch. "That's where they're holding the missing kids. Dammit! Right under my nose. Curt must be in on it. His double, I mean."

Cutting through the hope racing through her was a chilling thought. "You couldn't tell if your CO was a doppelgänger?"

Clutching the bear, Sam paced the room. "He didn't act like Curt, but there's no way to tell. Only if we find the real Curt's body..."

"Not necessarily. Sam, you had a doppelgänger. All it takes is a touch to absorb your DNA. If an Arcane stole a Phantom's powers, he could imitate you, Curt, anyone, as long as he had your DNA."

Crazed hope flared on Sam's face.

"If the doppelgänger killed Curt, he'd have a Death Mask."

He scowled. "No way in hell am I taking you near the base. They'll toss you into prison, or worse." Sam rubbed his chin. "What about video?"

"Live stream if possible."

"You haven't seen even a fifth of what's possible to a SEAL." Sam pulled out his cell phone. "Yo, Dakota, I need a favor..."

* * *

An hour later, Sam opened his laptop and clicked on an internet link. "Live stream from ST 21's base. Courtesy of Greg."

He grinned. "Tiger boy likes toys. This one's a jacket button that's actually a small camera. It transmits through a wireless receiver hidden in the next room. Then Tiger did something guaranteed to bring him into Curt's office."

They watched a red-faced Lieutenant Commander Curtis yell at the camera.

"What did Greg do?" she asked.

"Soaked Renegade's underwear with juice." His grin widened. "I believe the juice of certain distinct jalapeño peppers."

Kelly laughed. "Wonder where he got that idea?"

Sam spread his arms wide, looking surprised. "I'm innocent."

"Poor Renegade, taking one for the team."

She concentrated on the feed, the furious commander yelling at the SEAL.

"That's not Curt. He never loses it. Let's us fight our own battles."

Her heart beat faster. "He's an impostor, but I don't see a Death Mask."

At her nod, he shut the laptop. "There's a chance Curt's still alive."

Sam dialed a number. "Admiral Keegan Byrne," he stated quietly.

He waited, tense and grim, and then his expression smoothed out. "Admiral. Sir. It's Shay."

Shay. No titles, not even his full name.

Sam flashed a boyish grin. "Yes, sir, I was on that op, three of us. Cakewalk. No thanks are necessary. Just doing our jobs."

He glanced at Kelly. "Admiral, we have a sitch here. I need to know why you gave those orders for my team to deploy to an LZ south of the base in Honduras to deliver Kelly Denning to Mage authorities."

No change in his expression.

"I see. One of us will be in touch. And, Admiral, watch your six. I can't say right now, sir, but soon as I have more intel, someone will be in touch."

He thumbed off the phone.

"The admiral didn't give that order. Which means Curt's double did."

Sam nodded, his spine tensing.

Kelly squeezed his forearm. "Your CO has to still be alive. Don't lose hope."

His steady, reassuring gaze gave her strength. "Hang tight. I'm calling Dakota."

Time to call in the troops.

Chapter 20

"I remember the tea parties your mother hosted. She loved dressing up," Kelly mused as she looked down on the grounds of Sam's estate.

With their clipped hedges and brightly colored flowers blooming in cultivated beds, the gardens were well. Visitors had come for miles in the spring to admire the blooms, which had been carefully coaxed to life by her father's loving hands. Annabelle Shaymore had held themed teas in the Chinese pagoda, enlisting Kelly's help to pour. Sam's mother had worn a crimson kimono with a bright yellow sash, the waves of her soft brown hair pinned up with sticks. Kelly had tottered around the glassed table in a plain white kimono, serving bite-size cucumber sandwiches while Mrs. Shaymore's guests had chattered.

And even though Sam's mother was kind to the motherless girl living on her estate, Kelly had been a servant. Those celebrated tea parties made it clear, for no one acknowledged her. She was invisible.

Sam now scaled the massive stone wall ringing his family's estate. Shunning the rope, Kelly found familiar footholds and then dropped down to the other side. Sam whistled.

"Impressive."

She shrugged. "Did it quite a few times. Sometimes when your mother scheduled a tea party, I'd sneak off the grounds. If she couldn't find me, she couldn't ask for my help."

Amused, he shook his head while coiling the thin rope. "Why didn't you say no?"

She stared at the sugar maples and hemlock trees. This estate had been the only home she'd ever truly known. "I kept hoping she'd invite me to the party, treat me as a…daughter, not a servant." Her voice cracked. "My mom died giving birth to me. I never had a mom. Guess I hoped your mom might fill the role. Stupid. All she did was treat me like a servant."

Sam tucked the rope around his waist and crooked a finger at her. "C'mere."

With a soft sigh, Kelly slid into his embrace.

"I'm not my mother." He kissed the top of her head and rested his cheek against her hair. "I'd never act like that."

"That's a relief. If you paraded around in a kimono and started sipping tea instead of beer, I'd really worry."

Sam laughed and then focused his attention on the barn in the distance. "You ready for this?"

Ready to watch you confront old ghosts, or ready to rescue the children? Acid churned in her stomach. She nodded. Two miles down the road in a dark van, Sam's teammates J.T. and Dallas waited for his signal to storm the castle.

Soft grass silenced their footsteps as they passed the stone pagoda with its tattered Chinese lanterns swinging from the rafters. Kelly felt like a ninja, moving as Sam had taught her, darting from tree to tree.

Whoever broke into the estate knew not only its location but also the entrance to the underground bunker.

"Curt knows all about this place," Sam said as they hunkered behind a thick magnolia trunk.

He removed a pair of binoculars from his vest and scanned the stretch of open lawn. "When he became my CO, he wormed it out of me about how I had no family. Then he asked me all these questions about the estate. He loves reading history. I told him about how the bunker used to hide slaves during the days of the Underground Railroad."

"He wasn't interested in history. Only you," Kelly guessed.

"Yeah." Sam watched the grounds. "In getting me to talk about the place's history, he made me realize how important my heritage is. The estate had fallen into disrepair. I'd let it go. After, he helped me find a contractor to fix up the burned wing, gardeners to tend the grounds."

"He sounds like a good man."

"None better. Damn good fighter and sniper. Scored twenty kills in Desert Storm." Sam lowered the glasses, voice remote and cold. "If they did kill him, he wouldn't have gone easily."

Insects hummed in the trees. The stillness in the air felt heavy and unnatural. Impatient for action, Kelly wanted to race across the lawn.

Sam closed his eyes. "Nothing's been by this way in months. No trace scents. Wish Dakota were here. His sense of smell could pick out a pebble in a stream."

"The wolf can, you mean. Any wolf."

"Not going there. We do this the old-fashioned way, on two legs, not four."

Knee-high meadow grass brushed against their legs as they headed toward the picturesque split-rail fence dividing the estate's grounds from the adjoining farm. Kelly followed Sam to the barn. Inside the air was moist and still. A slightly foul stench made her wrinkle her nose.

"Someone's been here. I smell something dark and evil."

Sam dropped to a crouch and pointed to patterns in the

dust. "Someone who didn't bother erasing prints, meaning they're either careless or arrogant."

Kelly's heart squeezed painfully as Sam lifted the round iron ring on the floor. He drew out a pistol from his backpack. "Stay here."

"They're probably being guarded. Sam, let me go with you." Panic lodged in her throat.

"If something happens to me, get word to J.T. and Dallas. You're more important, Kelly. You're the only one who can tell a real Elemental from an Arcane who killed him and stole his identity."

"I'm not going to lose you, Sam," she whispered.

She did not recognize the intense, determined look on his face. "Let me do my job."

Every cell cried out to join him, but he was right. Should he run into trouble, Sam possessed the needed skills.

"Be careful."

He vanished into the black hole that gave way to a small airless room holding rusted farm equipment. But another door, hidden and opened by only a spring mechanism, gave access to a tunnel that led to the estate's wine cellar. Kelly sat on the floor, hugging her knees as she waited.

Waiting. How did Sam and his team do it? Sometimes they remained motionless for hours as they waited for a target to move out, he'd told her.

Sam's selfless devotion to duty opened her eyes to her lover's other side. She'd thought bravery and honor as mere words.

Sam had shown her those words in action.

Muscles cramping, she stretched out. A crow flew inside and perched on the overhead rafters, scolding her. Kelly leaned down and drew a heart and initials in the dust.

K.D. loves S.S.

Smiling, she let her fingers trail over the letters.

The cellar door creaked open. Hastily, she dusted away

her impromptu drawing as Sam climbed the steps, his expression remote.

"They're not there. They were, and not long ago, but they've been moved." Ice coated his next words. "They wouldn't risk hurting the kids now until they stole the last one needed for the rite."

Disappointment stabbed her. Kelly gazed around the barn. "Do you think they're off the estate?"

"Hard to tell, but maybe somewhere around here. Moving that many kids is difficult, even if they're drugged. Curt is a whole other challenge. He's like me. Won't give up the fight, and if he goes down, takes someone with him."

His merciless tone told her exactly how challenging.

Kelly couldn't fathom the risks Sam and his team took. Every time he went on a mission, he knew he might not return home.

Sam was cool and collected, even now when their search efforts failed. His calmness gave her strength.

I can do the same.

"We need to track them." Kelly pointed to her pack. "The bear has their scent."

A guarded look dropped over Sam. "It'd be difficult to trace from here."

"Not if you shifted into a wolf."

"I'm a good operator, Kel. I've tracked targets through snow and sand as a man, not a wolf."

He stood, dusting off his hands. "Let's head downstream, follow the bank. If they moved them off the estate, the splashing water would disguise their movements."

At the stream, they walked along the bank until Sam squatted down and shook his head.

"Nothing. I doubt they came here."

Kelly hugged herself, studying the current. "You taught me how to swim here."

"I always took Pete tubing in this place. Spring rains and

runoff from the mountains would push up the creek. Made sure to stay behind so I could keep my eyes on him, just in case."

"I watched you once, from this tree." She pointed at an overhanging sugar maple.

Sam looked up. "Why didn't you join us?"

"I told you, I couldn't swim."

"I'd have taught you."

And Pete, in his cherubic innocence, would run home and tell his parents. It'd been safer to watch in silence.

"Sam, there's only one way to find them. You have to shift into a wolf."

His gaze grew haunted. "I don't want to risk turning feral and hurting you."

She took his face between her hands. "You'd never hurt me, Sam. All this time, you've endangered yourself to keep me safe. The wolf will do the same."

Kelly kissed his mouth, feeling the strong line of his lips, the responding warmth. "Do it for Curt. He'd trust you to find him, and use any means at your disposal."

"No, he'd trust me to do anything I could to find the kids. He'd die trying to keep them safe. Maybe he already has." Sam stood, stretching out his hands. "We can't talk when I shift, so listen."

He went over a series of signals used to communicate. "And if I nudge you to follow me, and you balk, I'll give you a nip."

Demonstrating, he took her hand and closed his teeth gently around her wrist, the pressure light. "Like this. Not hard enough to break the skin, but to get your attention."

She nodded, her pulse beating hard.

"Stand back, Kel. And don't get too close."

The look in his eyes warned her.

Backing off a few feet, she watched as a golden glow surrounded him. Sam closed his eyes, drawing his magick from the earth, wind, sky and water.

The change came over him instantly. The broad-shouldered, handsome man vanished. A gray wolf, thick with muscle, its fur sleek, watched her in silence. The wolf seemed big as a tank. He bared his teeth in a low growl as he looked over the acres of pasture.

Shaken, she took a step back, her gaze never shifting away from those teeth. Fear oozed through her pores. The wolf lifted his muzzle, and she knew he scented it.

She drew the battered, well-loved teddy bear out of his pack and held it out.

"Find them, Sam."

Instead of sniffing the toy, the wolf loped over to Kelly and sniffed her, and then he gave her hand a gentle lick. Large brown eyes swimming with intelligence regarded her.

With a hesitant stroke, she caressed the wolf's head, rubbing between his ears. The wolf licked her hand again and then sniffed the bear. His head dropped to the ground, and then he raised his muzzle.

Then he took off, loping across the field.

Kelly sprinted, trying to keep up, lungs bellowing with each breath. Stunned, she watched him zig and zag, following the scent trail. Then the wolf bounded down a path cut through the tall grass.

A path she remembered well. Sam had cut it years ago so she could access the barn without notice. It led from their weeping willow tree, wound around the lush, jewel-toned gardens cascading down the pristine lawn…

Straight to the mansion's formal, and locked, west wing.

The wolf ducked behind a huge magnolia tree, hiding as he gazed up at the second-story windows overlooking the fields.

Kelly joined him, squatting down, her fingers curling into his thick fur as a snarl drew his lips back.

"Easy, Sam. They're still alive. I have to believe it, and you do, as well."

They moved from tree to tree, the gardens' decor and the

assorted shrubs providing cover. Then the wolf snuck away, toward the same path they'd just left.

Frustrated, she tried to hold him back, but Sam kept nudging her. When she refused to move, he gently nipped her bottom.

"Hey," she whispered, rubbing the back of her jeans.

She swore his gaze twinkled with mischief.

Keeping low, Kelly followed the wolf back down the path, until they reached the barn.

Inside, Sam shifted back. "Thanks," she told him, rubbing her bottom.

"I warned you, disobey my commands and I bite."

"You said a nip on the wrist."

He grinned. "Your ass is so pretty, I changed the target zone."

Then he shifted his attention to the trapdoor. "This is why I turned back. The passageway leads to the house, and I can access the west wing without being seen."

"I'm coming with you."

Sam drew out his pistol from his pack. "No, you're not."

"Don't leave me behind like this. You need my help."

"I need you safe."

"And I'll be fine. We're together in this, Sam. They're my people, remember?"

Sam went still, muscles tensed, body coiled for action. He blew out a deep breath, nodded and gave her his cell phone. "Follow me and if there's trouble, run. Call Dallas. He'll pick you up."

The yawning blackness of the passageway stretched before them. Unease rippled through Kelly as they traversed the tunnel, aided by the thin pencil beam of Sam's flashlight.

A few hundred feet ahead, the tunnel forked. Sam flipped a switch, turning on a meager bulb that barely cut the darkness. Sam flicked his light downward and spotted a small footprint.

Hope sprang to life. He moved faster.

Sensing a disturbance in the air, Kelly crept backward toward the fork and turned around.

An arm hooked around her neck, jerking her back as a palm slapped over her mouth. She struggled against the powerful grip, feeling hot breath at her ear.

"Don't scream."

Okay. Instead, she bit his hand. She heard a hiss of pain, and then the fingers around her throat tightened, cutting off air.

"They wanted me to kill you, but you are one of us," the whisper came. "We are your people. Join us, Kelly Denning. Your father embraced the darkness. It is in your blood."

Shocked grief filled her. She drew in a breath and gasped with relief as the pressure against her throat eased. "My father was not. I have no darkness inside me."

"Liar," the voice whispered. "You feel it growing. You hate the Elementals as we do. Kill Sam Shaymore and become one of us."

She struggled. "Where are the children?"

Hands around her throat squeezed tighter against her windpipe. "Join us or die."

Elbowing him hard, she dropped, rolled out of reach and reacted. Summoning her magick, she flung out her hands, directing currents of white-hot energy at her attacker. He threw his hands to block the blow and screamed. Flesh sizzled and sparks crackled, lighting the tunnel.

In the glow, she saw the man lying on the ground, skin shriveled by the heat.

I killed him, she thought, stunned. Without a chant, with Elemental powers.

Was he right? Had the darkness been inside her all along? How else could she have eliminated the Arcane with magick not her own?

Bringing her hands up before her, she staggered backward, stricken with horror.

Maybe she was the enemy, not those she hunted.

The unmistakable sound of a wolf growling echoed through the tunnel.

Sam had shifted. And he'd gone feral.

Chapter 21

The dull glow of the single bulb cast the wolf's face into shadow.

Then he stepped into the light, directly in front of Kelly. Glowing eyes filled with rage stared. The wolf advanced, lips pulled back into a snarl.

"It's me, Sam. It's me. Kelly. I know you're in there. You won't hurt me. You'd never hurt me."

Crouching down to his level, Kelly spoke quietly. "Sam, I'm okay. The bad guy's dead. He's down. Come back to me, Sam. Come back."

The wolf swung its massive head toward the corpse.

He attacked. Kelly shrank back against the terrible sounds of tearing flesh.

"Sam, please, come back to me."

Her voice dropped to a painful whisper. "I'm scared. And I need you."

The wolf lifted his head and loped over to her. Blood dripped down his muzzle, staining the sleek fur.

Kelly held out a hand in absolute trust. "You're Samuel J. Shaymore, Mage and navy SEAL. And I know you won't hurt me."

"You won't hurt me."

The words cut through the red fury hazing Shay's mind. Rage roared through his blood, the urge to rip and shred and tear overriding all else. Muscles and tendons shuddered with the effort to check that rage, to keep from springing forward with animal instinct.

An avalanche of emotions tumbled through him. Fear for Kelly, hatred of the one who'd dared touch her.

Feral and uncontrollable. He'd lost so much, and the rage and grief engorged him as the smell of terror cut into his wolf's brain.

Samuel J. Shaymore, U.S. Navy SEAL.

Elemental Mage, with an Arcane lover.

Sam shook his head to clear the blinding need to attack. This was his Kelly quivering before him, his lover.

The urge to protect overrode the instinct to kill. She was scared, and someone had threatened to hurt her.

"Come back to me."

Kelly. Her name sang through the wolf's mind, a calm and soothing chant. She needed him.

Lifting his head, he looked at Kelly.

He looked down. Sam blinked, realizing he now stood on two legs. He'd shifted back into a man.

Voice hoarse, he reached out to pull her upright. "You're okay? He didn't hurt you?"

Sweat glistened on her forehead and trickled down her too-pale face. "I killed him, Sam. With these."

He kissed the digits she flexed. "Too good for him."

"You didn't turn feral."

"You kept me grounded," he said quietly, brushing his mouth over her knuckles.

Shay clothed himself by magick. Kneeling by the dead body, he studied the look of frozen horror on the man's face.

"I killed him with thoughts, not chants. He wanted me to kill you, said I was one of them, filled with darkness." Horror tinged her faint voice. "Am I, Sam? How else could I summon power enough to do this?"

The terror on her face wrenched his heart. "No. I don't know how you did this, but you're not evil, Kelly. All this time, you've thought nothing for yourself, only those you want to free. Your intentions were honorable and your heart is good. Evil seeks only to seize power for itself and cares nothing for others. Evil has no compassion. It can't love."

They forged ahead. The tunnel ended at a stone wall with a heavy steel door set into it. The door opened noiselessly. Someone had entered the house through this corridor, wanting to keep their passage secret.

They stepped onto a landing and mounted the steps.

A faint scream sounded in the distance. Kelly froze. Sam squeezed her hand. "Steady."

Anything could be on the door's other side. He pulled the handle.

It opened to a cavernous room. Once it had housed a grand piano on a dais and a gleaming parquet floor. Guests had danced beneath the light of hundreds of crystals shimmering in the cut-glass chandelier.

Now it lay empty and still, the shine on the floor dulled, the chandelier dusty.

The children were here. She felt it. And beneath the sweet scent of innocence, vanilla and spring, he scented something stronger and deeper, more forceful.

Curt.

Sam drew out his weapon as they cut through the ballroom. The gilded double doors were open to the hallway. He sneaked a peek.

Empty.

They made their way down the hall, past portraits of his ancestors scowling at them from the yellow walls.

Behind two stately double doors was the library where once he'd carved her initials into shelving containing love poetry. "Because we write our own love story," he'd told her.

Sam told her once he hated that room. Lost count of the times he'd waited for his father to lean forward in the rigid leather chair, place his palms on the English walnut desktop and begin lecturing him again.

Kicking the door open, they burst inside.

Huddled in a corner, near the polished bookshelves, were nine frightened children. Relief turned her legs to jelly, until she realized a pulsing glow surrounded them. Force field, she thought.

"Can you break it?" she asked Sam.

With a determined look, he lifted his arms. Current snapped and sizzled. Sam chanted a long spell, ancient words to vanquish and banish darkness and evil.

Somewhere in the house, several high-pitched screams sounded and then cut off. The shield holding the children vanished. Kelly rushed forward, the children embracing her, chicks around a mother hen. As she soothed them, Sam squatted down.

A little girl in a plaid jumper gave him a wary look. "Are the bad men going to take you away, too? Like they did to the other tall man who came to rescue us?"

Sam exchanged glances with Kelly. "What's your name, honey?" Sam asked gently.

"I'm Molly."

"That's a pretty name, Molly. Can you tell me what happened to the tall man?"

She shook her head, fear clouding her gaze. "I don't want to remember."

"I know it's scary, Molly, but I need you to be a brave girl.

Pretend it's story time and you're telling a made-up story. Do your parents ever read you stories at night?"

"Mommy does."

"Well, now it's your turn. But you can share it with me. We'll be story buddies, okay?"

A lump clogged Kelly's throat at his gentle, kind patience. Molly nodded. "Okay."

"What were the bad men like?"

"They were short, and smelled nasty. And then they brought in this tall man," the girl lisped. "He had dark hair with white sides. He smelled nice, like pinecones."

Curt's hair was dark brown, touched by silver at his temples.

"The tall man started glowing, like my daddy does when he's using his magick. But one of the bad men grabbed Joshua and put his hands around his neck, and said if he didn't stop, he'd hurt Joshua." Molly began to cry. Kelly hugged her, murmuring assurances.

Concern punctuated Sam's expression. "Joshua?"

A boy about eight nodded solemnly.

"You okay, son?"

At his nod, Sam looked relieved. "He's okay, Molly. See? Nothing happened to him. Go on, honey. Finish the story."

"The bad men and the tall man talked. The tall man got this funny look. Then he smiled at us and told us everything would be okay. We'd be with our parents soon. Then the bad men left with the tall man."

"Molly, do you know where the tall man went?"

"We heard sounds down there."

The girl pointed to the floor. Kelly exchanged glances with Sam. "The basement," he said tightly. "When the guys get here, we'll head down."

He called his teammates. "Get up here. Upstairs library, south end. Nine to evacuate."

Kelly removed her pack and plucked a worn copy of *Green*

Eggs and Ham off the shelf. She settled on the floor to read to the children. Finally, a vehicle tore down the gravel driveway and skidded to a stop. Relief spilled over Sam's face as he lifted the lace curtain with the back of a hand.

"J.T. and Dallas are here."

Minutes later, the two SEALs stormed into the room, weapons drawn, greasepaint smearing their faces. The children screamed.

"Dial it down. I only need to you evacuate," Sam said.

Dallas scowled. "You said exterminate. Damn, Shay, get a new phone."

The two SEALs studied the cringing children. "They okay?" Dallas asked.

"Can you take them someplace where they'll be safe until we can locate their parents?" Kelly asked.

J.T. considered. "My sister's got room. Ever since she became an empty nester, she complains it's too quiet."

He looked down at their new charges. "You look like a fierce bunch of tangos. Guess I'll have to surrender."

"Navy SEALs never surrender," a boy cried out.

"Never. Except to aliens with death ray guns." Dallas winked at Kelly and pointed a finger at J.T., who dramatically clasped his chest.

"Not…the death ray gun! Kids, help me! Quick, let's head for the starship." JT staggered back.

"Parked conveniently out front," Dallas added.

The children gathered around, fear turning to fascination. Leaving the SEALs to take charge, Sam and Kelly hurried downstairs.

At the basement door, Kelly shivered. She'd always hated coming down here to do laundry. Despite the bright lights Sam insisted his father install, shadows still darkened the corners.

Sam opened the door and flipped the light switch. Nothing.

He fished the penlight out of his cargo pants and then palmed his pistol. "Watch your step."

The wood stairs creaked with age as they descended into darkness. Anything could lurk down here. But no sound except for an ominous, steady drip met them.

When they reached the landing, Sam flashed the light around the cavernous space. In a corner, a shadow moved. Kelly's heart raced.

"Over there," she whispered.

Sam flicked the penlight as she pointed. The shadow darted away. The stench of sulfur filled the air, mixed with a sharp smell of wine turning to vinegar. "Who's there? Are you injured?" he called out.

No answer. He handed her the flashlight. "I'm fixing the lights."

Hand shaking badly, she swept the beam into the corner. Not a demon. A girl, tears streaking her pale face, huddled in the corner. Inky-black hair spilled over her naked, trembling body. Shaking uncontrollably, she rocked back and forth.

Though she looked no older than eighteen, bleakness shadowed her face, as if she had lived many, many more years. The girl buried her face into her arms.

"What's your name?" Kelly asked gently.

"Keira."

"Are you hurt?"

The pencil-thin light showed her head shake. "You're safe now, Keira. We're here to help."

"Finally. Got it."

Shay snapped a switch and light blazed in the room. He uttered a low curse.

Kelly turned around.

Oh, gods, oh, gods, oh, gods. Bile rose in her throat. Wearing only the shredded remains of dark trousers, Curt lay prone on a raised wooden platform, arms and legs stretched tight. Manacles encircled his bruised, bleeding wrists, and his ankles were attached to thick steel chains secured to each corner.

Blood seeped from deep gouges on his muscled torso, chest

and arms, trickling off the platform to form viscous pools. So much blood she barely could see skin. Only his taut, handsome face remained unmarked.

"Son of a bitch." Sam leaned over his commander, checking his pulse. "Still alive."

He dumped his backpack and tore into a small first-aid kit. Sam ripped open a package of fresh gauze. "Put pressure on the wounds bleeding the most. He's losing too much blood and needs an evac. Have to go upstairs, signal's too low."

Cell in hand, he darted up the stairs. Kelly stared helplessly at the commander. So much blood, it was hard to tell which injuries were worst. She pressed gauze against a long furrow on his chest.

It resembled a claw mark.

Sam returned, grabbing pieces of gauze. "They're at least twenty minutes out. Locals keep a chopper stationed nearby at the new fire station."

Somehow she knew. "The new fire station you funded, along with the trauma copter."

A rough nod from Sam.

Lieutenant Commander Curtis stirred, blinking his eyes. Jaw tensing, Sam leaned over his CO. "Curt, it's Shay. Kel's with me. Hang on, buddy. Trauma copter's coming."

Curt moaned.

At the painful sound, the girl cried out. Kelly turned. Overhead light reflected an eerie glow in her green eyes as Keira stared at Curt like a wounded animal.

When he raised his head, she shrieked and pushed back against the wall. "He's awake, oh, no. Don't," she whimpered. "Don't make me hurt him again. Please. Not again, not again."

"Kelly!" Sam's voice was sharp. "Never mind her. Get these chains off him. I've got to pack his wounds."

Using her powers, Kelly broke the chains. They fell to the floor with a heavy thud.

Face squeezed tight, the commander slowly moved, hissing

through clenched teeth. "Easy now," Shay soothed. "Muscles are stretched tight. Who the hell did this?"

"Centurion demons," the girl whispered from the corner. "Condemned to wander the earth for deserting their legion, they search for a brave warrior for me to torture and so they can claim his strength to free themselves."

Curt seized Kelly's wrist with surprising strength. "Go," he whispered through cracked lips. "Take the girl…find the children, get out…before they return."

"They won't." Kelly gently squeezed his hand. "Shay reclaimed the house with a protective spell. Nothing evil can penetrate."

Agony flickered in Curt's gaze. "The children…Demons told me when I died, they'd start on them. Couldn't…let that happen."

So he'd held out, enduring the pain, refusing to die. A lump clogged Kelly's throat as she squeezed his hand again. "Your courage saved them. They're unharmed. J.T. and Dallas are bringing them to a safe place."

"Base not secure…"

"J.T's sister's house, until their parents can be found." Sam applied pressure to a nasty gash directly over Curt's heart. "Don't talk. Save your strength."

"Sons of bitches got the jump." Curt's eyes opened, anger blazing there, fueling his strength. "Rogers texted. Missing kids were here. Sending private jet to base. Walked out to meet the pilot, next thing I remember, I was in the library with ten bastards. Smelled like a Roman orgy. Showed me the children, said if I didn't cooperate, they'd suffer. Then they dragged me down here, in chains… Ahhh!"

The commander screamed as Sam pressed against his torso, trying to stanch the blood flow. Sam jerked his hand away.

"This wound's been stitched. Kel, hand me the scissors and tweezers from the kit."

With extreme care, he snipped open the threads. He used

the tweezers to probe and then remove a pointed metal object from Curt's body. Kelly's stomach roiled as he held it up.

Two interlaced crescent moons the size of a silver dollar.

"What is it?" she asked.

"Some kind of magick amulet. I've never seen it before."

Whoever had done this had torn open his skin and inserted the pendant. Then he'd sewn the skin back up, sealing the pointed symbol inside to cause excruciating pain.

"They packed it into the wound to torture him," Sam said tightly.

"No!"

They turned around. In the corner, Keira shook her head. "Not hurt. I did it to protect him from bite of the wolf."

His entire body trembling in rage, Sam shook the amulet. "You did this to him?"

A shaky nod confirmed his suspicions. Keira lowered her head into her arms and sobbed. With a snort of disgust, Sam tossed down the amulet.

"The demons forced me to hurt him," Keira said, crying. "I could not let my wolf kill him."

The sounds of weeping tore at Kelly's heart. She hesitated. Whatever the girl had done, she hadn't done willingly.

With her help, Sam managed to bandage the worst injuries. His worried gaze met hers. "That damn chopper better get here quick. He needs a hospital, or he's going to die."

A low growl from the corner iced Kelly's blood. Chills ran up her spine as she dared to turn around.

Keira was gone, replaced by a black wolf bigger than a Shetland pony. This wolf made Shay's animal look like a toy poodle. Stunned, Kelly backed away. The beast raked its enormous claws over the concrete floor, leaving gouge marks matching the ones on Curt. Then the wolf raised its head, a silent plea in those green eyes. A moment of fierce connection flared between them.

Like her, this wolf had been a victim.

Shay moved forward, blocking Kelly in a protective manner. The wolf growled. Clenching his fists, Shay growled back. Sparks shimmered around him. Amber flashed in his gaze. He was going to shift.

Kelly placed a calming hand on his arm, feeling fur ripple along the skin. She drew him aside.

"Don't, Sam. She doesn't mean us harm. She's scared."

"Right. And she didn't mean to turn Curt into shredded beef. Let me at her."

"So you can turn feral, forget me, forget him?" Kelly stroked a single finger down his cheek. "Your commander needs you, soldier. So do I."

Gritting his teeth, Sam closed his eyes. She could see the enormous effort it took to leash the spiraling fury. Finally he dragged in a huge breath and opened his eyes.

They were a normal hazel, shaded with green.

"Thank you," she said quietly. "For Curt, and for her."

He looked around, puzzled. "Where did she go?"

Kelly glanced down at the floor. The pendant had vanished, along with the wolf.

Chapter 22

No more surprises today. Please. Demons and wolves are enough, Kelly pleaded as she and Sam headed into the house to retrieve her pack.

They'd waited outside for fifteen agonizing minutes, having secured Curt to a makeshift stretcher, before the rescue chopper arrived. The shocking extent of his injuries proved the Mage's fierce will to live. After the chopper lifted off, Sam excused himself to call his lieutenant.

She couldn't figure it out. The Arcane imitating Sam's CO hadn't killed him and siphoned his magick, so how could he duplicate Curt?

Sam opened the library door.

Kelly's jaw dropped. Gasping, she took a step backward.

A ghost sat in the antique leather chair. Although Sam had warned her, seeing him in the flesh sent shock waves through her.

"Samuel." The ghost offered a thin smile. "Welcome back home, son."

"Goddammit, Dad. What the hell are you doing here?"

"It's my home. I came here to talk with you." Colton Shaymore's gaze turned icy as he glanced at Kelly. "But not in front of her. Get out."

Sam gave her an apologetic glance. All the old feelings rushed back. "I'll wait outside," she told Sam.

But as she hovered in the hallway, he left the door ajar. Enough for her to eavesdrop.

"Samuel, I came here to talk some sense into you."

"I didn't see a car out front."

"Do you think you're the only one who ever used the underground tunnels?" Colton chuckled. "I was sneaking in and out of the house long before you lost your virginity."

A reluctant laugh from Sam. Forced. "How did you know I'd be here?"

"Your lieutenant, Matthew Parker, asked me to dinner. I wanted to meet your friends and colleagues. He told me you suspected the missing children were held here. So I followed you. Good job, son. I knew I could count on you to fight for our people."

"Fight for our people? Kelly and I freed the children. And now my CO's ripped to shreds. He could die."

"You know every war has collateral damage. It's why we must eradicate the Arcanes before another brave Elemental is injured. Eliminate the threat and cleanse our populace."

Acid churned in her stomach. Kelly bit a knuckle. Eradicate. Colton talked as if her people were roaches.

"Jesus, Dad…I came here to stop the slaughter, not participate."

"It's your duty to protect Elementals, Samuel. Your heritage to your people and your birthright. Do you wish to throw it away for a manure-dwelling whore?"

"Don't insult her." Sam's voice deepened to a dangerous tone.

"Kelly Denning is Arcane." The chair creaked, as if Colton

sat up. "Who suggested the children were here? Who was found with Billy Rogers? Everything points to her. She's leading the uprising against us."

"It's not an uprising, just a few…"

"A few who will turn into a mob and take away everything we love." Colton sounded anguished. "Is this how you chose to honor the memories of your mother and brother, by associating with the Arcane bitch whose father took them away from us?"

Kelly peeked through the door. Anguish twisted Sam's face. Her heart ached for him.

"The committee's leader wants her dead. He said if you kill Kelly Denning, make it look…like an accident, it will prove your loyalty to your people."

"And you, Dad? Is that what you want most? Blood on my hands, the blood of an innocent woman?"

Silence for a moment. When he spoke, Colton sounded torn. "I have no wish to harm innocents."

"But Kelly is one."

"Let the committee be the judge of that. I am only relaying their wishes."

The chair pushed back. Kelly ducked behind the door.

"I must head for a meeting tomorrow. The committee needs followers. Since the council refuses to take action, we must protect ourselves. By any means possible."

Colton paused. "I'm proud of you, son. You've turned into a fine soldier, the man I knew you could be. If you respect my wishes, you'll join us."

Kelly ducked into the shadows as the door opened, watching Colton walk down the hall. When he headed down the stairs, she ran into the library. Sam stood at the window, hands jammed into his pockets. Deep grief lined his face.

"Sam…" Lost for words, she stared at him. "You let him go," she finally said.

"I know where he's headed. Dakota tagged him with the

same GPS security chip installed in you and gave me the transponder to follow him, just in case. He's...lost all sense."

Sam scrubbed his face with a hand. "And he's not the only one. There are more who agree with him. Tiger and Stephen pinned down the location of this meeting. Farm in West Virginia at four o'clock tomorrow. They're planning to start rounding up Arcanes."

Her throat went dry. "Can't your team stop this?"

"Dakota tried, but Admiral Byrne's hands are tied because of council politics. It's not a military matter. Until the slaughter begins, he's powerless to stop it." Sam looked bleak. "My whole life, I've looked up to that man. I damn near worshipped the ground he walked on. And now...knowing he's aiding in the slaughter of thousands?"

Silently, she slipped into his arms. As Sam embraced her, she whispered, "What are we doing to do?"

He tilted up her chin, his eyes fierce. "You're going to J.T.'s sister's house. I've made up my mind."

His cell chirped. Sam fished it out and walked out of the room. When he returned, his expression was tight. "I've been ordered back to base by Admiral Byrne. SOP for a security leak. We've taken care of the problem of the fake Curt."

"How..."

"He's dead."

Seeing his expression, she didn't ask how. Someone had avenged Curt. But something else shaded his expression.

"What's wrong, Sam?"

Tensing, he shook his head. "Curt's doppelgänger was a Phantom Elemental."

Kelly's jaw dropped. "That's impossible! Why would an Elemental imitate him?"

"I don't know and it bugs the hell out of me that our hands are tied, ordered to base while something's going down. But yeah, he was Elemental." Sam clenched his fists. "Dallas recognized him when the bastard died and shifted back into his true form. Good friend of Curt's from Desert Storm."

A chill shuddered down her spine. Betrayed by a friend and then tortured by demons. "Do you think it was personal and had nothing to do with the Arcanes' plans to create a Dark Lord?"

"Maybe. Dallas said the guy had issues, never advanced in rank like Curt. But if it was personal, why did his doppelgänger give the kill order on us and set up the ambush?"

"Sam, I'm worried." Kelly hugged herself. "If other Phantoms are involved, their powers makes this even more dangerous. Can you imagine an all-out war, brother against sister, no one knowing who is who, whom to trust?"

They both fell silent.

Sam rubbed his neck. "Tomorrow, I'm heading back, after I drop you off at J.T.'s sister's house."

"But your father…"

"I'll figure it out later, after I'm back at base." He stroked a finger down her cheek. "If I don't, they'll report me as AWOL, Kel. I have to do this. Got no choice."

They stayed in a guest room that night. As Sam slept, Kelly slipped out of bed. Taking the flashlight, she went into his parents' bedroom.

Sam had started to renovate the room, but stopped. The walls sported new Sheetrock, but the flooring was only partly finished. Only the brick fireplace looked the same. Emotion tightened her throat. All these years she wondered if her father was truly innocent.

Did he set the fire?

Kelly tried to envision the room as it was, the elegant furniture, cheerful fire crackling on the brick hearth…

She went to the fireplace and bent down. Workers had dumped plaster and trash into the hearth, probably in their haste to leave. No one had bothered to clean it. Kelly crouched down and sorted through the trash, looking for any small clue from the past.

After a few minutes, she started to give up when she saw something glint.

She swept the circle of light over the object.

Plaster dusted her trembling fingers as she picked up the twisted, partly melted find that she'd almost missed amid the trash. Gripping the fireplace for support, she stared in disbelief. And then everything became clear.

Colton hated her father for killing his wife and son. But the hate was misdirected. Now she understood what truly happened here. Kelly hung her head and sobbed.

Her father was dead.

Finally, she clenched the object and stood, her mind racing.

If she told Sam, it would crush him. He'd go after Colton himself, risking his career.

And maybe, if she confronted Colton before his meeting, it might snap him free of blind hatred. Sam's father hated her, but she could protect herself.

Back in the guest bedroom, Kelly dressed in silence. She went into Sam's pack and removed the GPS transponder.

For a moment she stood over him, watching him sleep, thrashing about on the bed. *I love you,* she thought in agony. *I wish I had the courage to tell you.*

Silently she stole out of the house.

With luck, she could catch a flight to West Virginia and be there by morning.

Kelly was gone. So was the GPS transponder.

Shay jammed a hand into his hair, glancing at the clock and cursing himself for sleeping past dawn.

In five hours, he'd be officially AWOL. But Kelly was missing.

He needed the location of that meeting, now. Standing by

the desk in the library, Shay dialed Dakota. When he was done speaking, the Draicon werewolf sighed.

“Get your ass back here, Shay. The admiral has Stephen spying on that group.”

And the vampire wouldn’t be at full strength until sundown She might be dead by then. His fingers tightened around the phone. “Screw it. I’m going after Kelly.”

“You’re throwing away your career.”

So be it. Shay leaned his forehead against the wall, seeing everything he’d accomplished slip away like dust. Logic dictated returning to base and following orders.

But logic didn’t account for a fiery redhead with a strong will, a woman who’d claimed his heart.

All his life, he’d lived according to everyone else’s standards. His father’s. And now the navy’s. Those standards had given him control in a crazy world filled with grief and pain

No longer did he want to live by standards imposed on him by others. *I make my own choices now.*

Life wasn’t about control. It was about doing the right thing Such as following your heart to West Virginia to protect the woman you loved.

“Sorry, Dakota. Got to do this. Give me the location of where my father headed. I’m going after Kelly.”

He scribbled it on a piece of paper. Then Shay gave a wry smile. “Thanks, man. After they kick me out of the navy maybe we can share a beer sometime.”

Shay thumbed off the phone and headed for the door.

Chapter 23

Nestled amid the rugged Allegheny Mountains, the Sweet Valley farm had a rolling vista of meadow and sunflowers. It was a lovely spot to toss down a blanket, enjoy a picnic.

Or hold a gathering of Mages intent on eradicating an entire race.

Kelly parked her rental car out of sight on the roadway and walked along the long gravel drive. Disguised as Sam. She had his DNA, after all.

The white farmhouse had a wide porch filled with rocking chairs. Kelly mounted the steps and didn't bother knocking.

She opened the screen door and stepped into a living room with plaid furniture, a basket of wildflowers in the fireplace hearth and Colton Shaymore sitting on a chair.

His face lit up with an enthusiastic smile as he stood. Kelly felt ill, knowing the reason.

"Samuel. You decided to join us."

Kelly shifted back into her true form. "Not exactly…Dad."

Shock twisted Colton's face. And fear. Of all the emotions,

she'd come prepared for hatred, prepared for him to attack and kill her.

Not this.

A dawning suspicion pushed aside her dread. He was afraid of her. The knowledge fed her strength. No longer would she remain silent, a cowering ghost in his household.

Disgusted, she advanced, watching his wary look. "I came here to settle old scores, Colton."

Finally, after all these years, she'd dared to speak his first name.

"I found something of yours in your old bedroom, something you probably never wanted back."

Kelly opened her palm. In it lay the twisted, partly melted remains of Colton Shaymore's most precious possession.

His wedding ring.

"Your wife used to brag at her tea parties about how you loved her so much you never removed your wedding ring. I found this in the master bedroom, where the fire originated. If you loved your wife that much, you'd leave your wedding ring on after her death. My father never removed his wedding ring after my mother died. But you took yours off.

"You threw it in the fireplace, didn't you? You lied to Sam. You hadn't been outside, after all. You were in the bedroom when the fire started."

Blood drained from his face. Colton stepped back as if she waved a sword. "Stop it," he said hoarsely.

"What happened that night? Did you see Dad in your bedroom with your wife? Thought they were having an affair, not realizing he was there to clean up the oil he'd spilled on the carpeting?"

Anguish twisted his face. "That bastard stole my wife!"

"And you stole his life, goddammit. Your hatred blinded you to the truth. You're a Phantom. You can imitate anyone." Words bubbled up like lava, the pressure on her chest increasing.

"Did you duplicate my father and run out of the house, knowing he'd be blamed?" she screamed.

Silence hung in the air.

"Yes," he whispered.

Staggering backward, he collapsed into a chair. Colton buried his head in his hands. "Annabelle," he moaned.

Hatred boiled inside her. She wanted to shake Sam's father, kick and scream at him for what he'd done. Ruining her life. Ruining Sam's.

The man, unlike his son, was a coward.

Kelly took a deep breath. Hatred solved nothing, only brought more grief. Something eased deep inside her.

"I should hate you, but I don't. I'm only sorry you're Sam's father. He's a good person who deserves much better than you."

It felt oddly freeing to state those words, as if they'd been locked away for a long time. Now she finally believed them.

A noise sounded in the doorway.

Dressed in camouflage, pistol in hand, Sam stood in the room. Shock slackened his jaw.

"You killed Mom and Pete?" he asked in a broken voice. "Dad?"

"Yes." Tears glistened in Colton Shaymore's hazel eyes, so much like his son's. "They're dead and it's all my fault."

Shay couldn't think. Breathe. He stared helplessly at his father, and the world stopped spinning on its axis.

He must be dead and this was hell, the claws of his father's words reaching into his heart and shredding it. Blood rushed to his fingers as they loosened from the death grip he kept on his Sig.

Shay holstered the weapon. He'd come here expecting to save Kelly, the headstrong, brave woman who thought she could stop a genocide.

Instead, he walked into a nightmare.

Colton wiped his eyes. "Annabelle, my beautiful Annabelle…I found out she never went to her bridge club. She was with Cedric, that bastard. Christmas Eve I saw them in our bedroom, whispering. They looked guilty as they jumped apart. I tore off my wedding ring and threw it into the fireplace. Picked up the poker, came swinging, shouting he would never take away my wife. Annabelle tried to stop me, but I kept hitting until he dropped. And then I turned and saw Annabelle…lying on the floor, so much blood…"

Shay's chest squeezed tight. His mother, always the peacemaker.

"It was an accident. I never meant to hurt her."

"Where is my father?" Kelly whispered.

"Burned. I incinerated his body to erase evidence. And then the fire got out of control. I ran to grab an extinguisher down the hallway and I heard Pete screaming. I tried to go back, but the flames were too much."

Shay staggered to the sofa and collapsed. *I know my heart's beating because I can feel it pounding against my chest.*

Ever since becoming a SEAL, he'd sought to live with honor, fight with honor, hoped to die with honor in combat. Just doing his job, like the other operators on the team.

He followed his father's example of discipline, courage and control.

His father, whose uncontrollable jealous rage caused the deaths of Shay's family and Kelly's father.

For the first time, nothing was worth fighting for. Then he felt the softness of a warm hand sliding into his, the gentle reassuring pressure squeezing his palm.

Nothing worth fighting for? Kelly was. His team. His country.

The future of all Mages.

"Can you forgive me, son?" Colton asked.

Shay found his feet and went to his father, his idol.

For the second time in his life, he hit him. Colton fell down, blood streaming from his split lip.

Wiping away the blood, Colton sat up, gazing at the floor. Shay felt an eerie sense of déjà vu. So many times he'd looked like this, head hung in shame as his larger-than-life father verbally thrashed him for failing to live up to the Shaymore name.

Gods, he wanted to vomit, but he forced himself to swallow the bile burning in his throat.

"Is this why you wanted to kill Kelly's people? Because you blamed Cedric, thinking they had an affair?"

Colton remained silent.

"They weren't," Kelly put in quietly. "Annabelle was aiding my father with an underground resistance to achieve equality for Arcanes. That's why they whispered. Your wife was a gentle soul who loathed injustice but knew how much you hated my people."

Blind panic spread over Colton's face. "No, it couldn't be. The man organizing us into a coalition convinced me it was Cedric's fault because he was Arcane. In fact, he is organizing others who believe as I do, others who would eliminate the Arcane threat for good. The cleansing campaign starts tonight."

Shay stared at his father, a once honorable, good man. "You're condoning genocide."

"Of course not," Colton snapped. "I support elimination of the threat against Elementals."

"By killing my people, even those who are innocent?" Kelly cried out.

"Are they innocent?" he scoffed.

"My father was. He didn't kill your wife. And he didn't take her away from you. You drove her away, with your blind hatred and jealousy. Would you have killed your wife had you known she was aiding Arcanes?"

The man's eyes widened and he stared at her, as if the truth finally slammed full force into him. "I loved Annabelle with all my heart. I'd never hurt her."

"But you did," she said softly. "She died by your hand, not my father's."

Colton pressed fingers to his temples. "The committee chairperson said I was within my rights to destroy Cedric and administer justice. Oh, gods…what have I done?"

A horrible suspicion filled Sam. "Who is this person organizing the committee?"

"Senator Rogers, the council Elder. He should have been here by now. He wanted to meet with me early." Colton sounded uncertain for the first time in his life.

Shay stared at the man. The crunch of tires on the gravel driveway drew them to the window. Shay scanned the open room and spied a closet, shuttling Kelly inside.

"If you dare tell him we're here, you'll regret it," he told his father.

Colton looked shaken, broken, a shell of the man he'd once known. Shay didn't give a damn. He joined Kelly in the closet and cracked the door a notch.

The screen door slammed. Footsteps sounded. Not the heavy tread he'd expected.

Shocked, Shay watched a woman enter the room and look around, her nostrils flaring, the aristocratic cheekbones sharp blades against her skin.

Moira Rogers, the pampered and privileged wife of Senator Robert Rogers.

"Moira? Where's your husband?" Colton's voice was courteous but suspicious.

She gazed around the room. "Colton. Has your son killed Kelly Denning yet?"

"I thought you were more inclined to hair appointments, not politics and assassinations," Colton said, dropping the veneer of politeness.

"You fool. You have no idea of the real power behind my husband."

A flicker across his father's face. Behind him, Shay heard Kelly's muffled gasp.

"A shame your son is so disobedient. Denning's death would herald the new era of our people no longer tolerating the Arcane threat. The first wave takes place tonight, in this community. A small pocket, but enough to declare a victory against those roaches."

Colton hardened his expression.

"No. I've had a change of heart. There will be no killing of Arcanes until this entire matter is officially investigated by the council. And if you, or your husband, try to start, I'll not only have you arrested, goddammit it, I'll toss you into prison myself."

Flesh tightened against the woman's cheekbones. "You would not dare. You lack the power."

"I am an Elemental Phantom Mage. Try me."

The senator's wife raised her hands and began a series of chants Shay remembered well. Chants to call for the powers...

Hellfire! Dark energy snaked out of the sky, burned through the screen door and shot into her hands. She released the tendrils and struck Colton. He sailed backward, hitting the fireplace and sending pottery smashing to the floor.

Enraged, Shay emerged from the closet and fired, but the bullets burst into metallic dust in midair.

A soft, almost gentle laugh as Moira flicked a finger. Agony blasted through him as the burn of dark magick hit.

"You can't destroy me with bullets," she said, her tone amused.

The pain faded like a needle prick. Shay narrowed his gaze, moving around Moira, gauging the best way to take her down. Kelly crept out of the closet. "Sam, use this!"

He caught the triskele one-handed. Power hummed in his blood, a gathering force swelling like the sea, thundering through his pores. But before he could release it, Moira hurled more dark energy, sending him flying backward.

What the hell… Stunned, he realized the woman was no ordinary Mage.

From his peripheral vision, Shay saw his father move.

"No one," Colton grated out, "touches my son. You bitch."

As she turned, his father wrapped his hands around Moira's throat and squeezed. The senator's wife gasped as two thumbs pressed against her windpipe. Snarling, she tried to throw him off, but Colton persisted, even as her power seared his skin.

Talons emerged from her fingertips, and crimson stained the crisp whiteness of his father's shirt as Moira sank them into Colton's chest. A red glow suffused them, the power cooking his father from the inside out.

A wheezing gasp as his father's face paled with agony.

Shay flung back his hand, ready to send more energy bolts into Moira. Hell, he couldn't do it, not without hurting his father.

"Let her go, Dad. I can't hurt you."

Colton's pain-racked gaze met his. "I've been a fool, a pawn in their ideology of hatred. I have to make up for what I've done. Don't let hatred rule like it ruled me, son." He moaned as the claws sank deeper. "I love you."

Stricken, Shay regarded his father, his powers shimmering in his palms. "I love you, too, Dad."

Then the Shaymore patriarch spoke in the firm voice Shay remembered well from his childhood. "Do it."

Shay released his power as Colton snapped Moira's neck. Her final scream cut off as the white-hot energy surged into them both, suffusing them in an eerie glow.

Colton dropped to the floor beside the senator's wife.

Panic surged through Shay. He ran to Colton and cradled him, fingers searching for a pulse. Hazel eyes, much like his own, stared sightlessly at the ceiling.

Shay gently lowered him to the floor. Throat tight with grief, he glanced at Kelly.

"He wanted you to be proud of him, Sam."

"I am," he said quietly as he closed his father's staring eyes. "He finally did the right thing and saw how wrong he'd been."

If it had only been sooner. All these wasted years. Bitterness had killed his father long ago. But maybe in those last moments, Colton had finally felt a sense of peace.

"Sam, look at her," Kelly whispered. "She's changing."

Blinking, he studied Moira Rogers's corpse as it slowly shifted into a stranger's face, a man's slightly overweight body.

"If that wasn't Moira Rogers, then who is that? And where's the real Moira?" she asked.

Shay shook his head. "Someone must have killed her and stolen her powers."

"But I didn't see a Death Mask."

Damn. He needed Curt, but his CO was out. He needed his teammates. He was going to have to go this alone. Shay glanced at his watch. In less than an hour, the committee would assemble and then all hell would break loose in this picturesque farming community. He'd have to take them out by himself. No innocents died on his watch.

Then he heard the sound of heavy vehicles coming up the drive. Shay's heart sank as he glanced at Kelly. No time for her to escape. But her face lit up.

"Sam! Look!"

He turned to the window. The cavalry had arrived. Two Hummers parked in the drive, and out climbed seven men, dressed in battle gear, submachine guns in hand. The entire Phoenix Force. Even Tiger.

Shock loosened his jaw. The screen door banged as he ran outside.

"What the hell are you guys doing here? You're AWOL!"

Dakota looked quietly at him. "Yeah. But we couldn't sit on our asses, knowing you needed us."

"Besides, you didn't think you'd hog all the fun, while we stayed at the base, did you?" Renegade asked.

"Especially after you told Dakota where you were headed.

We gauged the timing to arrive before you did," Jammer added.

"Except we're a little late. Dakota drives like an old lady," Sully said.

Emotion at the thought of their loyalty tightened his chest. Words failed him. Instead, he slapped Renegade on the back.

Kelly stood on the porch, watching them quietly. "If Arcanes and Elementals were all SEALs, we'd never have a problem. Because we'd finally learn to work together, instead of apart."

She gave a small smile. "Even if they poured jalapeño juice into our water."

The men laughed, but Renegade shook his head. "Still owe you for that one, Shay."

"Collect it tomorrow. Here's what's going down. In less than an hour, Senator Rogers arrives. He's spearheading a committee that plans to slaughter Arcanes, starting in this community."

Silence filled the air. Dakota's expression hardened. "What's your plan?"

Shay narrowed his gaze, looking out at the sweeping meadows, the jagged mountains. "We're going to arrange our own welcoming committee."

Chapter 24

The eight navy SEALs were all trained professionals, ready to demonstrate their skills. In military fatigues, black vest, compact submachine gun in his hands, Sam looked lethal. Kelly now saw another side of him, the quiet professional who got the job done.

"What's the plan, Shay?"

Though he was the lead officer, Dakota deferred to Sam. They were a team.

"Wait inside and get the drop on them from in here. On my word."

With smooth efficiency, the men set out on their assignments, moving the vehicles to conceal them, arming with extra clips. Kelly's throat tightened as J.T. and Dallas lifted Colton's body with extreme care and placed him in the back room.

They were much less careful with the other body.

Then, as the SEALs went into the farmhouse to wait, Kelly looked at Sam.

"I'm not leaving. I'm here with you, all the way."

Tension turned his jaw to granite. "Wait inside, Kel. I'm not risking your life. You're the one they want dead."

She reached up and kissed his cheek. "I love you," she whispered. "I don't care if your team knows, or if anyone else knows. You stay alive for me, Sam Shaymore."

Leaving him standing alone on the porch, like a brave sentinel, Kelly went inside into a corner bedroom facing the porch and cracked the window so she could hear.

Time crawled to a stop. Kelly shifted restlessly but heard nothing from the other SEALs. They were so quiet. Patient.

Finally a car pulled into the driveway. Senator Robert Rogers got out and saw Sam on the porch in full battle gear.

"I see you're dressed to kill Arcanes."

"Not Arcanes. You, you son of a bitch, are under arrest."

Rogers laughed. "And exactly who are you arresting? Me or…"

The handsome features blurred, shifted, changed.

"Or my wife."

In an elegant black suit and black heels, Moira Rogers faced Sam. "Excuse the boring dress. I'm in mourning for my husband."

Sam's stony expression never changed. "Who are you? Are you the real Moira Rogers, or did you kill her, as well?"

"There's only one of me. I'm an original. Poor Robert, he didn't stand a chance. I killed him the day before you and your men rescued Billy from the island. And then I assumed his powers and took his place."

"Then who took yours?"

Moira's smile was sly. "A Phantom friend imitated me. He made an excellent duplicate and did not mind playing the role of a woman. He respected women, unlike Robert. My husband was a vain man. He never believed a woman could hold power. Not like your commanding officer, a true gentleman. So courageous. I knew he'd bring a tidy profit."

Moira laughed. "One does need financing to start a war. I couldn't risk withdrawing that much cash."

"You sold Curt to those…things?"

"Centurion demons will pay for the right victim. They needed a courageous man for their wolf bitch to torture. They gave me one million for his delivery. All it took was a lure of children in trouble and Curtis came running."

"The Elemental children we rescued were never endangered, were they? It was all a ruse to cast suspicion on Arcanes and trap Curt." Sam narrowed his eyes. "And you're the one who sent the email to Sight Finders, to stir up fear about a genocide."

"There is a genocide planned, only of Arcanes, not Elementals. I prefer to call it an extermination of cockroaches."

"Then why did you try to drown me in Honduras?"

"Because of who you are, Samuel Shaymore." Moira flicked a hand. "I needed you dead, and if I could use you as a sacrifice, all the better. But it was more important to eliminate you any way possible. If you died, Allen would resign. His sole motivation is protecting you from trouble. There'd be gridlock on the council, because those old windbags would take forever to replace him. Chaos. No authority to stop me from whispering how Arcanes should be destroyed."

"So you kidnapped your own son to get the ball rolling."

"Billy isn't my son! He's the bastard of Robert's kept Arcane whore, his secretary, Catherine. Robert wanted an heir. I couldn't have children, so we adopted Billy and Robert pretended he was mine. All these years, humiliating me. After everything I've done, raising his bastard as my own child, helping Robert navigate the political waters in Washington, Robert started getting soft on the Arcane problem. He said he loved her and wanted a divorce."

Jealousy had tipped Moira over the edge. Kelly stared outside at the woman, seeing a mirror image.

Kelly was an Arcane resenting privileged Elementals.

Moira was a privileged Elemental resenting Arcanes.

The senator's wife allowed insecurity about the younger, prettier Catherine to overshadow everything. Moira's power, wealth and status meant nothing. Hatred had blinded her to the tremendous good fortune of simply being born into status.

Oh, gods, it can't be too late for me. Sam, I promise you if we get out of this, I'll let you go. I love you, and I want you to be happy, be it with an Arcane, an Elemental, it doesn't matter.

"But you can't complete the transformation to a Dark Lord. I saw the spell book. You didn't have the children or the Mage for the sacrifice." Sam spoke in a calm voice but gave hand signals to his teammates to start moving in.

Kelly saw a shadow slip outside.

Moira laughed, the sound like fingernails against a mirror. "My transformation is complete."

He scoffed. "Elemental Mages can't be Dark Lords. We don't carry the sickness within us. It was written in the ancient book of spells for Arcanes."

"You misread the book. It's a book for Mages, not exclusive to Arcanes. The council decided long ago the book was too dangerous and had copies destroyed. But the Arcanes had hidden a copy in a small village in Honduras, right beneath Elemental noses. I gathered together a few Arcanes imprisoned for sedition, paid them well and promised power if they joined me and led me to the book of dark spells. And then I killed them. All the while I had my real supporters, Phantom Elementals who feel as I do and would do anything to exterminate the Arcane species. One pretended to be your commanding officer. And the others lowered themselves to pretend to be the hated Arcanes in order to carry out my plans and fool the council into thinking there was an Arcane threat to kill all Elementals."

Her voice dropped to a thin whisper. "The ancient texts called for the blood of a courageous Mage. Gender isn't exclusive. So I killed the bitch. And Catherine had plenty of Arcane nieces and nephews to complete the sacrifice. She proved her courage when she tried to stop my Elemental Phantom supporters from killing them. It was almost too easy, pretending to be Robert and luring the children into attending a party for Catherine."

Horror pulsed through Kelly.

"There are good and honorable Elementals who will stop you and force others to listen to reason," Sam said quietly, his gaze never leaving the woman.

"But they cannot. Far more powerful is an Elemental who chooses the path of darkness."

The woman's features began to change, darkening, her mouth turning into a red, wet slash. Beginning the transformation into a Dark Lord.

Standing on the porch, confronting the power-crazed woman, Shay saw the last piece of the mosaic fall into place.

He'd had a hard time killing the Mage in Honduras where they'd been ambushed because the bastard was a shapeshifting Phantom Elemental with powers equal to Shay's. Only these Elementals had unleashed spells from the forbidden book of spells and learned to call the darkness, trebling their powers.

Two clicks on his radio. Everyone was in place.

He readied his weapon as the woman shimmered, a sinister black glow pulsing off her body like a dark force field. She was no longer anything remotely human, her eyes yellowed and bulging, a skeleton stretched over flesh, the Death Mask now visible even to Shay.

Talons emerged from her fingertips,

"Now," Shay yelled, aiming his assault rifle.

Bursting out of their cover, the SEALs opened fire. Moira flung streaks of black energy at the rounds, turning the bullets into dust.

"Juice it up," he yelled to the others, the code they used to resort to their powers.

Tossing aside his weapon, Shay began flinging energy bolts in a steady stream. But Moira opened her arms wide and the white light shriveled, turning into darkness as it made contact with her skin. She was absorbing his powers, siphoning them like a vacuum.

Now he understood with terrible clarity why his people were terrified of Dark Lords. They didn't fear the darkness inside Arcanes, but the darkness inside themselves turning them into a creature that could not be destroyed.

Enraged, he lifted his hands to the sky, calling forth the elements. Dark thunderheads swirled above. Shay culled down the lightning.

He flung a bolt directly at Moira, who staggered backward.

Sully teleported across the grounds and tackled her. There was a sickening crack as Moira's body dropped like a flour sack.

"Target down," Sully said into his mic.

But even as he spoke, Moira stood, her neck at an impossible angle. She straightened her head, turned and hit Sully with a power burst, sending him flying backward into a tree. His teammate's skull hit hard, and Sully dropped down, unconscious.

Darkness gathered in the air, a foulness that made it difficult to breathe.

"Fall back, everyone but Shay," Dakota yelled into the radio. "Shay, everything you've got at her!"

Shay pulled every ounce of power from the thunderclouds, feeling the sizzle and crack of electricity invade his body. He forced the power to his hands and directed light streams into the Dark Lord. Blood streamed from Moira's lips.

Screaming, she flung currents of dark magick, but her aim was erratic. One hit the house and shattered a wall. Another exploded a maple tree. Powerless to move under the constant barrage of white light, the Dark Lord kept firing her powers outward.

Shay kept up the constant pounding of his powers into the woman, feeding his magick. He felt his energy drain. He couldn't keep it up.

They would all die here. As Moira staggered backward, temporarily incapacitated, he retreated to cover inside, trying to regroup his powers.

Kelly ran to his side. "You need me, Sam. You need us."

He wanted to shout at her to get back, but the answer to the Dark Lord's destruction came in a clear flash of memory.

Teamwork. She held up his pendant. "Merge your powers with mine through the triskele. Alone, we're strong enough, but together…"

"We're practically invincible," he finished.

Like the SEALs, working as one unit. He and Kelly were their own unique team. They could fight this. Sam laced his fingers between hers and squeezed.

"You with me on this, Denning?"

She smiled. "All the way, Shaymore."

Still, they needed more. They needed…everyone.

"Jammer, J.T., Dakota, Dallas, Renegade," he shouted into his mic. "Use your powers and let's destroy this bitch for good!"

They rushed outside. Jammer directed water from a nearby cistern, sending it spiraling at Moira's mouth with the power of a fire hose. As she fought this new threat, J.T. used his telekinesis to hurl nearby rocks the size of bowling balls at her head. Stunned, Shay watched the Dark Lord's skull collapse and then regenerate.

"More," he yelled. "Keep it coming!"

The dark streams of magick were weaker now. J.T. sent a boulder the size of a Ford pickup truck into Moira. She collapsed but then rolled the boulder off her torso. The three Draicon wolves shifted and rushed the Dark Lord, snarling and tearing into her. A vicious black liquid oozed from several jagged wounds. Shay looked at Kelly.

"Let's fry her."

In unison, they fired a bolt of white energy, searing the screaming Dark Lord. She began to morph into a shapeless mass. And then Moira flung out one last stream of dark power. The energy sailed into Kelly's chest, searing her flesh, sending her screaming backward.

Shay kept firing, knowing Kelly needed him but also knowing he must finish this. Then the Dark Lord finally burst apart, black blood splattering the nearby trees.

Only her head remained intact, white bone against black dusty ground.

Shay ran to Kelly. She lay gasping for breath. Her rib cage rose and fell too rapidly.

She was dying.

Over by the tree, Renegade administered to the injured Sully, helping him to his feet. The big SEAL rubbed his head as if he had a helluva headache.

Dakota propped up Kelly's feet to keep the blood flow to her head.

Shay ripped apart Kelly's shirt and stared at the blood pumping out of the chest wound. Using her shirt, he tried to stanch the flow.

"What's her blood type?" Dallas asked, kneeling beside Kelly. Dallas was the team's medical corpsman. He fished a packet out of his vest and ripped it open.

"O positive." He stared helplessly at Kelly. "I know, because I took her to the hospital years ago when she got hurt."

"Jammer, get your ass over here. I need a donor, now!"

He quickly swabbed Jammer's arm and slid the needle into it. His teammate lay on the ground, his head turned toward Kelly. "Hey there, little Arcane. You start perking up now, hear?"

Blood flowed from Jammer into Kelly. But her face remained pale and still, her eyes closed. After a few minutes, Dallas pulled out the makeshift IV.

"No use draining him anymore," he said quietly.

"I can take it," Jammer protested. "Dallas, get that needle back in me."

But Dallas shook his head, dark eyes filled with regret.

Hearing a screech of tires, Shay glanced up as Admiral Keegan Byrne, dressed in civilian attire, slid out of a black limo. Dark shades covering his eyes, Stephen, their vampire friend and military asset, assumed the classic military position by the car.

"Damn. It's all over." The admiral scowled at Stephen. "I told you to drive faster when we found Rogers had left D.C."

Stephen gave a laconic shrug. "I warned you to let me stop at the drive-through for a quick snack. I can't move fast when I'm low on reserves. That blonde looked quite delish."

"Sir?" Dakota's gulp was audible. "We, uh… How…"

For the first time, the Draicon werewolf was at a loss for words.

Byrne smiled. "You pigheaded adrenaline junkies didn't think I expected you to obey an order to hide when this was going down, did you? Pity. I never took you for thumb-sucking sissies who quiver behind their momma's skirts."

The SEALs glanced at each other.

"Hooyah, sir, my momma wears leather pants," Sully put in.

"Glad to know you've got our six, Admiral," Dallas added. "But why the order?"

Byrne's gaze hardened. "Mage against Mage, this damn business of Elemental and Arcane. Once we all were the same, working together. Like SEALs. When that dies, everything else is shot to hell. Might as well pack it in."

"You tested us, to see if we'd forsake Shay to save our own careers," Dakota realized.

"Worked, too. Unless you don't give a damn and just wanted a joyride."

"Not with Dakota driving, sir. He makes Stephen's driving look like NASCAR," Renegade put in.

The Admiral grinned and then sobered as he glanced down at Kelly. "One of our people," he murmured, kneeling down and squeezing her hand. "How she's holding up?"

Shay struggled to check his emotions. "She's dying, sir."

"You have to let her go, son."

As Byrne reached for her neck, obviously to feel for a pulse, Shay snarled and cradled her tight against his chest.

"Don't touch her."

"Let her go, son," Byrne said gently. "I know you care. I'd never try to presume I know what you're going through. But if you love her, you have to release her spirit."

Rage clawed to the surface. "No. I'm not letting it go, not letting her go, and if you think I'm going to step back and let this happen…"

He drew in a trembling breath. "Go to hell. I'm not leaving her. Not like last time. Maybe if I had stuck around long enough to listen to her, all this never would have happened."

Maybe if he had, Kelly would be walking and talking and laughing, instead of lying so deadly still, her face pale gray, fighting for every exhale and inhale.

He stroked her damp hair. "Fight, sweetheart. Keep fighting. Don't you dare give up. You have to keep going."

The other SEALs shuffled around, looking stricken. Renegade dug a boot heel into the dirt. Shay leaned down, brushing away a damp tendril of hair from her ashen cheek. "Kelly Denning, listen to me. You sacrificed a personal life to save hundreds of Mage children. If you want to save more, you're going to hold on and fight, because I won't be accountable for what'll happen to me."

He leaned close, loaning her strength from his rage and his grief. "Fight, dammit. You're not a quitter. You never give up, never surrender. So don't give up now."

Her breathing grew so shallow Shay could barely hear it.

As he laid her back down, Shay felt the powerful vibrancy of her life fade. He glanced at Byrne, an ancient, powerful Mage, with secret depths of knowledge.

"Help me, but dammit, don't tell me to let her die."

Compassion flared in the admiral's eyes. "She needs your strength, Shay. Your powers."

Fear snaked through him. His powers? He'd been drained and depleted. How the hell could he give anything?

"I have nothing left. Both of us gave all to destroy the Dark Lord."

An inscrutable look crossed the Mage's face. "You have more than you know. Your magick, your essence as a Mage, may heal her. If you surrender all your powers to her through a White Light ritual, she's got a fighting chance."

Shay stared at Kelly. "Tell me what to do."

If he drained his powers, he'd become as helpless as a human. Lose everything.

"Being a SEAL means everything to you, Shay." Renegade looked stricken.

"Not everything." He laid a hand on her pale forehead. Kelly had given him his life back. He'd been dead for years without her.

"Let's do it," he said roughly.

Byrne gave an approving nod. "Take the triskele and put it around your neck. Then place your hands on her temples and focus all your magick."

It seemed to take too long, as blood oozed out of Kelly, her breathing growing more and more shallow. A faint white light glowed from the silver triskele.

Shay closed his eyes, listening to the words Byrne instructed him to use. He began the ancient chant, raising his face to the sun's warm caress.

"Spirit of Air, transform me. Spirit of Fire, fill me with your energy. Spirit of Water, flow through me. Spirit of Earth, ground me with your knowledge. I call you forth to drain my essence of Mage. Pour your healing spirit into this woman I share my breath with, my body with, my life with. Take all from me, for I am yours and I willingly surrender myself so that she may live."

Strength leeched from his limbs. Shay felt his heart slow, felt something reach inside him and yank. A great whoosh fled his body, a burst of golden air spiraling out of the triskele, spinning into the air and then slamming into Kelly's body.

Exhausted, he sank back on his haunches. Pink returned to Kelly's cheeks, flushing her body with a rosy glow.

Shay flexed his hands. Nothing. Not even a weak flicker. Then he saw that Kelly's chest rose and fell with life. He pressed his cold lips against her warm mouth, feeling her breath escape. She turned her head, those wide blue eyes opening.

"Hey," she said weakly.

Emotion clogged his throat. Too overcome to speak, he kissed her.

"Trying CPR again, Shaymore? Or just needing an excuse to kiss me?"

"I never need an excuse to kiss you," he whispered.

Overwhelmed with gratitude, he sat back. As he struggled to his feet, his legs gave way. Shay collapsed. Hellfire, he was so weak. Deeply ashamed, he shook off Dakota's offer of help.

Byrne watched him. "Is it worth it, son?"

Shay nodded roughly.

The admiral's expression shifted. He laid a hand on Kelly's forearm as she closed her eyes with a sigh. "Kiss her again."

Shay stared. "Now?"

"Need a reason? You're a Mage, like me."

The old fox actually grinned. Something was fishy. But Shay bent down, touched his lips to Kelly's…felt electricity stirring in the air…

POW!

Energy snapped, crackled and shot from Kelly into him.

Hellfire, it felt like lightning zinging through his veins. Shay's lips locked to Kelly's as the energy flowed through them, in them, around them. Finally, the white light faded.

Dizziness overcame him as Shay sat back, guts on fire as if someone poured a fifth of good Kentucky bourbon down his throat.

"Easy son. Takes a minute," the admiral told him.

Slowly, Kelly sat up, her hair standing comically on end. "What, ah, was that?"

"Standard bonding ritual. Sharing of powers. Shay gave you all his powers to heal, so I siphoned them back from you into him. You're equal now. And if you don't invite me to the wedding, I'll be mighty pissed off. More than if you don't name your firstborn son after me."

They exchanged glances, color tinting Kelly's healthy cheeks.

"Of course you do need a secondary channeling source, such as a pendant, or an old geezer Mage who's been around longer than dirt."

Byrne winked at the stunned SEALs. "Haven't done that in years. Gives the ticker a good thrill, and other parts, too. Remind me to get a bottle of champagne for the wife tonight. Hell, it's not even a Saturday."

"Admiral," Shay said, too choked with emotion to speak.

"You're a good operator, Chief Petty Officer Shaymore. Too good to lose. I'm not giving up one of my SEALs just because a nasty-ass bitch went on a power trip. Your CO agrees. I promised I'd look after his team while he's healing."

"How is Curt?" Shay was almost afraid to ask.

The admiral sobered. "Physically, Dale's progressing. But this scarred more than his body. SOB is too tough to admit it. I'm mandating two months of medical leave."

He glanced at Dakota. "As his executive officer, you're in charge, Lieutenant, until your CO returns to active duty. Or I can replace Dale, if all of you wish."

A rousing chorus of "hell no" from Shay and his teammates. Byrne grinned.

"Thought so."

Shay flexed his hand, feeling new strength and energy. Kelly laced her fingers through his. "This is the third time you gave my life back to me, Sam."

"Guess that means I'm committed and I'd better marry you, like the old geezer says."

Shay winked at the admiral as the other SEALs laughed.

Byrne nodded. "You'll both be fine. Don't forget, Shaymore." His green gaze grew distant, as if peering into an ancient past. "Giving of power willingly to save another means an emotional bond that cannot be broken. Only death can sever it."

Cupping her face, Shay kissed Kelly, a long, lingering kiss, feeling her breath return with each delicious exhale.

It was the most wonderful feeling in the world.

Epilogue

Sam snapped out the thick blanket, placing it beneath the weeping willow tree. An impish smile touched his mouth as he stretched out and patted the space beside him.

"Come here. I'm hungry for a taste of you," he teased.

Kelly leaned against the tree. "Trying to compromise me, sailor?"

"In every way I can," he whispered in a husky voice. "I have three weeks' leave, and I intend to spend every moment making love with you."

She considered. "My husband might object."

Sam grinned. "Not at all."

Lifting his left hand, he flashed the wide gold band around his finger, proclaiming him as exclusively hers. Six weeks after the fight at the farmhouse, they married. Their wedding had been a riot of flowers and festivity, attended by dignitaries and working-class Mages, both Arcane and Elemental. Curt, still healing but dignified, walked Kelly down the aisle.

Shay's CO had volunteered to give away the bride, an offer Kelly immediately accepted. Curt had smiled gently.

"An honor, for two people who mean a great deal to me. You both give me hope for the future," he'd said.

Shortly after the meltdown at the Sweet Valley farm, Admiral Byrne had worked behind the scenes to ensure the veil guarding the paranormal world remained firmly in place. Senator and Mrs. Robert Rogers had a big funeral, with many attendees mourning their deaths in a plane crash. And the Council of Mages had worked to unite Arcanes and Elementals. Now that the truth was out about the Mage book of spells, old fears and tensions had eased. Carl and the rest of the staff at Sight Finders had come out of hiding after the Council of Mages had lauded Kelly and her organization for their dedicated service in saving children.

Billy went to live with his biological mother's parents. His presence was helping to ease the grandparent's pain of the terrible loss of their daughter, Catherine, and their other grandchildren.

Now Kelly knelt on the plaid blanket, tickling Sam's chin with a stalk of meadow grass. They'd moved into the mansion with his uncle, who was overseeing a blizzard of contractors renovating the west wing into offices for Sight Finders and Kelly's new charity. The widowed Hilda, Kelly's dear friend, was now president of the foundation that gave interest-free business loans to the poor of Honduras. Sam suggested the first grant go to Rosa, the Honduran woman who'd helped them. Rosa had already hired two local women for her new sewing business.

"What's for supper?" Kelly asked.

He gestured to the picnic basket. "Fried chicken, potato salad, fresh corn and green bean salad. All at the house, prepared especially by Uncle Al. We have one hour before supper starts."

"And what's in the picnic basket?"

"A month's supply of condoms."

"Not courtesy of Uncle Al," she murmured. "I'm surprised you don't have a cache in the tree. Did you ever hide anything in there?"

He shook his head as he fished in the picnic basket. "Mom loved this tree. She used to sit here while Pete played with his trucks. Sometimes she read."

A strange expression crossed his face as he pulled out a red leather book. "What the hell? I didn't put this in here."

She took the book and opened it. A note fell out. "Sam, your uncle did pack the picnic basket after all. This letter is from him."

He scanned the paper. "He says this is my mother's secret diary. She gave it to him for safekeeping because my father was getting suspicious about her activities and if he found the journal, he'd burn it. She knew you and I were in love and wanted me to know the truth about who you are, Kelly."

Now that you two are finally married, the time is right, Al had written.

Sam flipped through the book until reaching the last few entries.

"Does she say why she teamed with my father to bring justice to my people?"

Shock darkened his gaze as Sam glanced up. "Not your people. Our people. You're Elemental, Kelly. And Arcane."

He handed her the red leather book.

Kelly scanned the entry. Her father wasn't Arcane, but an Elemental who disguised himself to marry an Arcane he dearly loved. Cedric raised their only child as an Arcane to teach about the injustices suffered by her mother's people, a deathbed promise made to his wife. When Annabelle had learned of his true identity, and how he sacrificed a life of riches to empower Arcanes, she'd agreed to help.

Sam was right. The triskele only amplified her true powers. She was Elemental, and Arcane.

Kelly shut the book, her mind whirling with this revelation.

"It makes sense. Arcanes have red auras. Yours is crimson, shot with the gold of an Elemental. You heal in sunlight, a rare Elemental ability."

Sam cupped her face, soothing her with his calming touch. "You're a true hybrid, the first in many generations, I suspect. That explains how you can call the elements."

Wonder filled her as she leaned into his caressing touch. For a few moments, they said nothing, just held each other.

Kelly pulled away. "It's really over, isn't it?"

He nodded and set the diary down carefully.

Tightness filled her chest. "Except for one thing. Back when this first began, you said my memories would be erased. No one's supposed to know ST 21 is a SEAL team with paranormal powers."

"Yes." Sam stroked a thumb over her leaping pulse. "No one except immediate family, such as a wife."

Her heart skipped a beat as he gave that seductive smile she knew so well. "Love me, wife."

He kissed her, long and deep, gently brushing away her tears with the edges of his thumbs. Then he sat back and gazed deep into her eyes.

"I told you earlier, life with the team filled all the empty places inside me." His voice went husky. "Except one."

Sam placed his hand over his heart. "I didn't realize how empty it was until you came back into my life."

"You never left my heart, Sam," she whispered. "I just tucked you away into a safe corner, where I could try to forget you. But I never did."

Those dreamy hazel eyes softened with love.

"I don't have enough days to spend all the time I want to spend with you. I could live to be a thousand years old, and it would still be a passing moment. Because that's how I really feel about you, Kelly. I love you. I want to keep you in my arms forever."

He placed a possessive hand over her flat abdomen, causing her to flush. "Make babies with you and then sit on a rocking chair when we're old and gray, and watch our grandkids play at our feet."

Kelly slid her arms around his neck. "What about your job? What if I lose you, Sam?"

Resolve shimmered in his hot gaze. "I love you, Kelly. And being a SEAL means everything to me. I can't promise that I'll be there as often as you'd like, but when I'm home I'll never leave your side. And I promise I'll try my damnedest to always come home to you."

"It's good enough." She pressed a finger against his lips. "I think we both need to stop talking."

He captured her mouth in a swift, demanding kiss that claimed and conquered. Then he rested her palm against his rapidly beating heart. "I was dead inside, Kel. Until you walked back into my life. I'm never letting you go, no matter who frowns at us because we're different classes of Mage. I'm not giving up another chance to be happy and to make you happy for the rest of your life."

They fell back to the blanket, kissing and entwining together like snakes. Sam caressed her bare breasts with a tenderness that equaled his ardent passion. He nuzzled and kissed his way over her body, igniting her arousal to a fever pitch. Then he sheathed himself with a condom and lay back, his penis rising thick and full from his groin.

Hand securely on her hips, Sam guided her atop his shaft. Inch after delicious inch she sank onto him. Fierce need blazed in his eyes.

Slowly she rode him, rising and falling as he fondled her breasts, the gentle wind caressing their naked bodies. Trembling violently, her core clutching him tight, Kelly placed her hands on his chest and let the wild sensuality take over. For a moment she fully understood what drove him to become a feral wolf. She felt abandoned and joyful, wildly free as they joined together.

They shattered together, their cries piercing the valley.

Afterward, Kelly lay naked in his arms. With quiet bliss she watched the clouds lazily chase each other.

Sometime later, they dressed. As Sam packed away the blanket and carefully placed his mother's diary inside the picnic basket, Kelly went to the weeping willow. A breeze ruffled leaves as swallows chased each other in the dusky gray shadows.

Time had faded the initials carved on the tree's shaggy bark but could not erase them.

P.S. Was Here.

She felt the breeze lift and caress her hair, like a mother's loving hand. Tears burned the back of her throat as she remembered Annabelle watching her youngest son gleefully dig into the bark, a memorial to childhood. So much deception and loss.

She and Sam had much to overcome. The past mustn't be forgotten, but it could be forgiven.

Feeling someone tenderly touch her head, Kelly turned. No one there. But a soft breeze touched the bells on the nearby Chinese pagoda.

Smiling through her tears, Kelly touched the willow tree.

Time to leave her own mark. Rust had dulled the knife left in the small hollow. Kelly struggled to dent the bark and succeeded only in chiseling out small chips of wood.

"Let me try."

Sam stood beside her. With his help, Kelly began to carve below Pete's lopsided scratches.

K.D. + S.S.

No longer would her feelings remain in silence and secrecy. The declaration stood against the tree in stark relief.

Sam smiled. "Pete would like us sharing his tree."

Then he set the knife in the hollow and took her hand.

"C'mon. Uncle Al has supper waiting."

As they walked away from the tree, Kelly could swear she heard the distant sound of boyish laughter floating across the meadow grass.

* * * * *

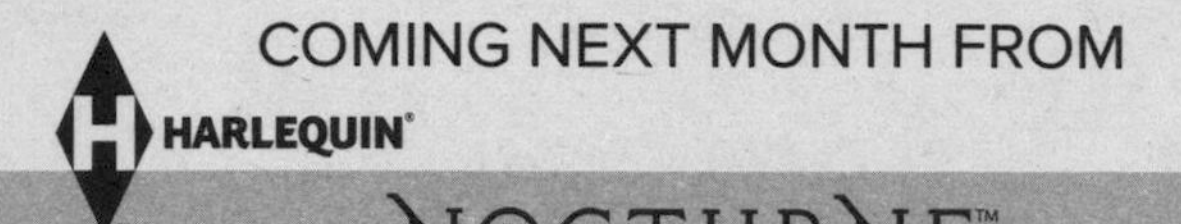

Available July 1, 2013

#163 KEEPER OF THE DAWN

The Keepers: L.A.

by Heather Graham

In this last book of The Keepers: L.A. series, Allesande Salisbrooke returns to Los Angeles when she receives a cryptic message from a friend who had been researching illusionists. But once she arrives, she is shocked to find that her friend has been gruesomely murdered, and by the looks of it, at the hand of a vampire. Now there's only one person who can help—Mark Valiente. The sexy vampire cop will help Allesande investigate the murder...and the chemistry growing between them.

#164 BEAUTIFUL DANGER

by Michele Hauf

The Order of the Stake, an ancient order of slayers, gave Lark a reason to live after her husband's death—and a reason for revenge. Her mission: to track down vampire Domingos LaRoque and kill him. Determined to achieve her goal, Lark is blindsided by the deep attraction Domingos elicits from her at first sight. Now Lark is faced with a tortured choice: let her guard down and surrender to their building desire or obey her one order as slayer.

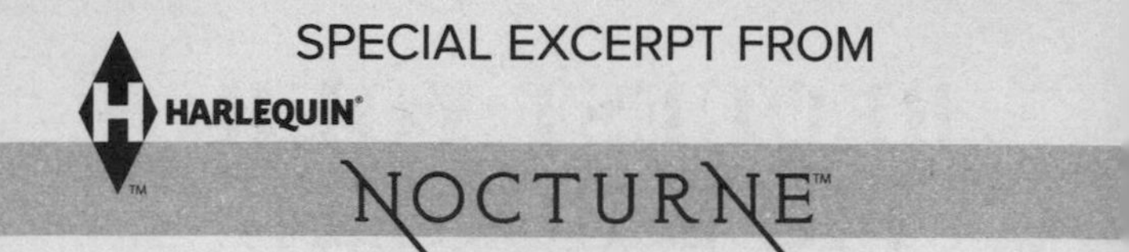

Alessande Salisbrooke has been warned about the legend of the old Hildegard Tomb. But when she narrowly escapes becoming a sacrifice herself and the bodies continue piling up, working with vampire cop Mark Valiente may be her only hope for finding answers. But can she trust her feelings for her new partner?

Enjoy a sneak peek of

KEEPER OF THE DAWN

by *New York Times* bestselling author Heather Graham, book #4 in THE KEEPERS: L.A. miniseries.

As Mark approached the iron-gated entry to the grand mausoleum, he could hear chanting. Night had fallen, but peering inside, he saw that the people who stood around the tomb of Sebastian Hildegard carried firelit torches. A caped figure stepped forward carrying a burden—a woman who was dressed like Fay Wray in the old *King Kong* movie; she wore a white halter dress with her long flowing hair falling around her. She was either dead or unconscious.

And then he saw her fingers twitch. She wasn't dead, Mark thought. At least not yet.

There was still no sign of his partner, Brodie, but the chanting in the tomb was growing louder. Friends in the L.A. Underworld had warned them that they'd been hearing tales about a growing belief that blood sacrifices on the tomb would bring the old magician back to life, and bring stardom, power and glory to those who worshipped at his feet.

Fearing they were almost out of time to save the "sacrifice," he forced his way past the locked gate and shouted, "LAPD! Stop where you are!"

The tomb erupted in chaos as mist filled the room. Mark could hear Brodie catching up with those who tried to escape.

When the mist finally began to clear, he could see that five people lay cuffed on the ground. The others had seemingly vanished into thin air. Whoever was at the head of this wasn't one of these humans. The head of this particular operation was a shape-shifter. And they had missed him.

Or her.

"The woman… She can't be dead…they needed her alive," he said. But when he reached the woman and saw her face, he nearly froze.

Even though he'd never seen her before tonight, she had been the bride in the daydream he'd had just prior to entering the tomb—a wedding that had ended in bloodshed.

HNEXPQBK4

Love the Harlequin book you just read?

Your opinion matters.

Review this book on your favorite book site, review site, blog or your own social media properties and share your opinion with other readers!

Be sure to connect with us at:
Harlequin.com/Newsletters
Facebook.com/HarlequinBooks
Twitter.com/HarlequinBooks

HARLEQUIN®
TM
A Romance FOR EVERY MOOD™